FLAME OF REVENGE

by

JOSEPHINE SCOTT

CHIMERA

Flame of Revenge/Twin Pleasures
First published in 1997 by
Chimera Publishing Ltd
PO Box 152
Waterlooville
Hants
PO8 9FS

Printed and bound in Great Britain

New authors welcome

FLAME OF REVENGE

Josephine Scott

This novel is fiction - in real life, practice safe sex

For TC, whose story this really is.

Part 1.1.

So let it begin.

It begins with a stroke, a heavy stroke, one which sends her forward and the command is 'be still!'.

Be still, hard when holding on to the rexine covered couch which gives and sways and threatens to tip forward into the wall. It's a hard unyielding wall - if the flesh and blood and bone met its unyielding solidness, the flesh and blood and bone would lose, blood would flow from the flesh and the bone would hurt.

Inconsequential thoughts, chasing like hamsters in a wheel round the circles of the mind as stroke follows stroke, as pain overlays pain, as glow turns to hurt and hurt to screaming agony, and the will to be still dissipates faster than September mist.

Leather on skin. Pain over pain underlaid with burning desire. Want it to stop/don't want it to stop. Need the pain/don't need the pain. Longing for it to be over, to nurse and cradle and soothe but wanting it to go on, to reach the limits and over, when it all goes into the next level, the one which gives nothing but pure lustful satisfaction.

"You're taking it well." The voice intrudes, the hamster-like thoughts stop chasing the contours of the mind, the concentration returns. It is hard to concentrate when tears stream freely, sobs wrack the body, screams tear the throat and the quim shudders. The mind shouts 'give me more!' in its writhing protest at the body being abused.

Finally giving up, collapsing, head down, bottom high, on the edge now - and it stops. Mercifully it stops.

"Get up," and the body slowly gets off the couch where the knees have dug holes large enough to bury a whole ego. The body aches, the cheeks quiver and shriek, the tears still flow, the hurt yet to abate.

"Kneel down. Take it." Sliding to knees, resting head against pillar hard legs, taking the erect cock into mouth, feeling its hardness, its softness, its salt/sex tang touching taste buds, sending more quivers to the aching quim.

Only when he was done, when he was satisfied, could the large plastic dildo be thrust deep into the ache, only then did he take the end of it and manipulate it and grant the longed for escape into ecstasy.

Then came his orders.

2. The File.

Name:	Saunders, Melanie Jennifer.
Address:	14 Forest View Road, Mellingham.
Occupation:	Housewife.
Date of Birth:	5.7.1958.
Place of Birth:	Epping, Essex.
Education:	Primary - Comprehensive, left with GCSE's in standard subjects.
Married:	Paul Richard Griffiths.
Children:	Gareth Bryan, born 1982.
	Benjamin Edward, born 1985.
	Joy Anne, born 1986.
	Ariadne Angela, born 1989.

3.

Candle flame. Never still. Smoke rising, meeting barrier of chaos, dispersing, winding, coalescing, changing, even as the candle itself changes, melts, alters its molecular structure and dissipates into wax drips which slide slowly, oh so slowly like the pre-passion tear-drop from the glans which excites, sliding slowly, slowly, slowly.

Candle flame.

Stare deep into golden depths, stare deep and even deeper and then whisper the words which will change, will alter, will stop the smoke of reality dead in its tracks as it meets the barrier of chaos and becomes -

Somewhere else.

Then and only then, whisper the name.

Melanie Saunders.

Melanie Griffiths.

Melanie Melanie Melanie ...

4.

"Listen, honey, I have to go."

Languid voice from golden languid body draped elegantly across an inelegant double bed, quilted headboard and squeaky castors.

Melanie brushed a hand across the limp inelegant member, not proud now, not demanding any more. Dried juices made it sticky. Dried feelings fuelled her impatience with a man who had promised so much but had supplied so little. Her quim still ached with unsatisfied lust. When he finally went, when his golden presence faded like sunlight through net curtains at the end of a long sultry day, it would be time to resort to dildos, vibrators, even the ribbed handle of her hairbrush if necessary.

"Of course. It's time." A vision of manliness straight from the pages of a sex magazine rippled past her, moving toward the bathroom.

Melanie lay on the tormented sheets and sighed.

Something was missing. A clichè if ever there was one, but in this case it was true. If a golden-haired golden-bodied man of 22 could not satisfy her - he with a penis the size of a cucumber, the inventiveness of a Forum reader, and the staying power of a rhinoceros on heat - then what could?

Empty. It all seemed empty, as empty as the clothes lying tumbled on the floor in a colourful rainbow of creases and folds where they had fallen in the mad passionate moments of unadulterated lust which made them want skin to skin and juices to juices. Empty as the head of the man now pulling on the creased and folded clothes, somehow miraculously filling them again with muscles and golden soft skin, the creases disappearing, the folds disappearing, the body disappearing under layers of man-made fabric. Memories of the afternoon were disappearing under layers of Melanie's disappointment. The dull throb of aching loneliness filled her quim; she shivered and reached out to turn up the heating.

"Same time next week?" Golden Boy looked at her, smiled the smile of a satisfied man who thinks he's done a good job.

The loneliness turned cold, sent shivers down her spine and into her stomach, where it curdled into a sorbet of fear. Would she ever know what it was like to be truly fulfilled?

"Sure, same time. I'll be waiting."

"If you're as waiting and willing as you were today, Mellie darling, it will be a session to remember! Can't recall the last time I had so much!"

She watched his buns jiggle as he went down the stairs, remembering the firm feel of them under her fingers, her grinding snatching fingers as she pulled and pulled so he would go deeper and deeper, and still nothing happened. Watching the shoulders swing as the hand, the hand which had touched and caressed and scratched and tormented and brought her to the edge but never tipped her over, reached out for the bannister rail, as hard and as lasting as he had been.

The lips opened, spoke words of endearment, promises of everlasting love and desire, eyes dull now as lust faded into memory, as hands grasped the money and fingers thrust it deep into pockets, as deep as they had been inside her. Both orifices, and still unsatisfied. She forced a smile from deep inside, pasted it across unwilling lips, pushed the corners up by will-power alone and opened the door to the snarling wind, shivering despite the comfort of the towelling robe.

"Shut the door, you'll be cold." Fatherly advice from a man young enough to be her son.

"See you next week." Mundane words uttered as the mundane door closed, and the mundane housewife with the very un-mundane, if ever there could be such a word coined in the English language, went back to her tangled bed, found a vibrator and thrust it deep into her quim, switching it on with eager fingers, sighing as the pulsing power ripped through her. Why could a plastic thing do what living flesh could not?

Then the telephone rang.

5.

Of all the rules handed down by parents, relatives, teachers and preachers, Melanie did not recall hearing one that said:

'Do not answer a ringing telephone.'

In a wind cold enough to cut, to dull the senses, to carry sounds, the telephone rang: clear and urgent, summoning, calling, demanding attention.

Commuters hurried past, collars up, heads down, indistinguishable from the hordes which daily travelled the trains which served no function but to load and unload a heavy burden of human flesh at the start and end of a day, and a smaller burden of human flesh during the remainder of the day. Commuters who hurried deafly by, ignoring the summons.

Melanie stood on the cold pavement, being cut by the cold wind as well as buffeted by the commuters, who saw no obstacle standing by the train timetable. A briefcase caught her shin, another her elbow. A woman glared angrily at her.

"Excuse me." Said with emphasis on the personal, the emphasis reminding the world that 'I' am the important, the One True Person in all this ant-like world - Not true.

There are many who scurry to the station, who hurry to the light from the darkness of the underground, from the dimness of office buildings, from the deep depths of the City, with its fluorescent lights, computer terminals, instant communications and lack of observation, who also think they are The One.

Melanie's red wool coat was long, calf length, large buttoned, big collared, sleeves which had room for a thick sweater, a well cut coat making room for a kilt, warmth, space for her to move. For all that, she remained cold.

The telephone rang on.

Melanie was undecided. She had been told to be here, to answer the phone, but -

Answering or not answering the ringing telephone was not part of the rules by which she played her life, rules brought to her attention with smarting slaps, with harsh words, with faces which leered into hers and which frightened by their intensity and violent emotions.

'Don't you talk to her!'

Would it be 'her' on the end of the telephone?

How would Melanie know without picking up the cold plastic and holding it to a cold ear to hear -

Cold words?

She moved a step closer.

A man muttered a curse and detoured from his chosen path. Did she make him step on a crack and break his mother's back? Was he indulging in that old superstition? Don't do this and that won't happen - don't step on the cracks in the pavement, don't speak, don't run upstairs, don't speak -

To strangers.

At last! Spiralling thoughts had brought her round to the rule she would disobey by picking up the coldness and receiving a word via a phone line.

Don't speak to strangers.

The telephone rang.

Talk to strangers. I do that every day. I speak to office workers, assistants in cafés and fast food restaurants; I speak to a paper man to ask for my evening paper, a ticket man to ask for a ticket, to the attendant when I buy petrol -

All strangers. Every one of them.

Don't talk to strangers.

How could we go through life if we didn't?

The phone rang on.

10

Disgruntled commuters glanced at it, ignored it, intent on home, warmth, family and relaxation, casting off the cares of the day, casting off the persona they donned every morning along with the sharp power suits, shoulder padded and lined, a persona picked up along with the monogrammed briefcase, who dared carry a bland blank one with no name attached? How would you know it was yours?

With her fingers cold inside kid gloves, her neck cold despite cashmere scarf, Melanie asked herself.

"Why am I standing here?"

A girl, uncaring, unwearing, unconcerned, moved to the booth, picked up the coldness, received a message. Melanie stood frozen to the pavement, unable to move, to speak, to twitch an eyelid. The girl held out the receiver.

"It's for you."

Melanie walked forward, hesitated, then stopped. This was the moment, she had to go with it or never know who or why or what and when.

She took the ice cold receiver from the girl, who immediately melted into the crowd.

"Hello?"

"Listen. I will only say this once."

"All right."

"Damn it, I said LISTEN! Go to the end of the road. A car will be waiting. Get into it."

Dead line.

Dead as a cable run into a grave, where the only sound would be the sighing of the dead and the chomp of worms as they ate through silk and wood, and were poisoned by formaldehyde or whatever it is they pump into corpses in place of blood -

Which end of the road?

Left?

Right?

How would she recognise the car in a thousand cars on their way home, lemmings moving toward the sea of television and quiet sedate undercurrented family life?

11

Melanie stood holding the dead receiver, aware she was being stared at. Who are you? Why do you stare? What is it to you if I stand here holding a dead, bone dead, cold dead, frozen dead receiver in my hand while I decide decide decide DECIDE, damn it! Are you going or not?

No.

Yes.

No.

Melanie replaced the receiver, cold on cold, and walked out of the station, coat swirling around her legs. Paper swirled around her feet, thoughts swirled around her mind.

Newspaper headlines shrieked at her:

WILL THE GOVERNMENT DECIDE?

Adding to the indecision. If a Government couldn't decide, how could she?

Turn left - Walk sharp.

Pretend you have somewhere to go.

Personal alarm clutched in her hand, loop around her wrist, one pull and an earsplitting 107 decibels of sound would cut the night air. It was a comfort, a companion, a safeguard.

IF she found the car, and who was to say she would find the car by turning left?

IF she found the car she could sit with her alarm, knowing people would hear it. Walk past car after car: black cab, mini cab, black cab, Granada, Sierra, what was it with these Spanish names? We had a Cortina once, did no one realise it meant curtain? It would be curtains if she didn't find the car -

"Here." Jaguar, door opened, blocking her path; a man looked at her, smooth faced, blank expressioned, cold as the evening air, blank as a dead leaf.

Melanie reached for the back door of the car, opened it and climbed in, filling her senses with smells of cigarette smoke and rich upholstery.

Who shut the car door? Was it an unconscious act on her part? What decision had she made to walk this way, to enter the car, to obey?

Obey - Always obey.

Get through school as only you know how: head down work steadily, never get high marks, never be outstanding. Not since the early days.

Early years.

Never again.

Purring engine humming to itself, powerful horses under large bonnet, powerful hands on the wheel, hands with hair creeping toward the fingers, a pinky ring of solid gold and signet ring set with an onyx, powerful rings for powerful hands, for a powerful man? Or was he like her, obeying orders?

"Where are we going?"

"Don't you ever do as you're told?" the man looked in the rear view mirror, dirty ice coloured eyes and no smile. "You were told to listen, right? Doesn't that mean don't speak?"

Melanie nodded, losing her voice; it threw itself down her throat and lodged somewhere around her diaphragm where it sat, uncomfortable companion with the fear consuming her.

"You'll get a good spanking for disobeying."

A spanking. What rubbish. What infantile rubbish.

Fear crept in a little further, consumed a little more. Girls get murdered like this. They get into strange cars; they go off with strange men to strange destinations and are never seen or heard of again. The alarm would be no help at 30 mph through London streets. Look, there's the Houses of Parliament, floodlit and elegant, and she was afraid: where was she going, where?

Across the Westway: streetlights, headlights, tail lights, brake lights, interior lights, pub lights, house lights, torchlights -

Into darkness: all consuming, all devouring, all enveloping, all concealing. Any moment now he would pull over, open the door, drag her out and -

A spanking.

A thrill, secret as tomorrow's daydream, ran through her, starting somewhere around her stomach and ending somewhere around her thighs: a trickle of cold, a finger of feeling, a twitching of muscles.

Motorway signs flashed past, far off places she had never visited or wanted to visit, or could have visited.

Until now.

Until the cold man with the cold hands and the powerful aura and the sense of power had summonsed her into his car and driven her off into the darkness to see these places.

Or at least as much as you could see flying by on a motorway; glimpses of homes and cars, of shops and offices, petrol stations and take away restaurants.

Oxford.

Flats, shops, universities, ancient stone, students everywhere. Oxford: dreaming spires of learning, of history. Morse country. Her favourite tv series, her favourite tv detective, and here she was, being driven through the streets Morse drove, in a Jaguar much like the one Morse owned.

The car was slowing down; she was able to see the stonework, read the university names, see the places where people lived, walked, and learned.

What will I learn here? she wondered.

"You will learn to obey."

Had she spoken aloud? Why else had the cold faced man answered her question?

The car stopped outside a house. Terraced, bay windowed, plain door, no number, no name. A solid looking brown door set in ancient stone, the surrounding wall covered with ivy: clinging, holding, disguising. A light shone through thin curtains, shadows moved and then were still.

Melanie opened the car door, slid out on to the cold pavement, stood looking around her. A quiet street, lined with parked cars, bay windows warm-lit against the darkness, shaded with drapes, flickering with blue light of television sets.

"Come." An order. Melanie followed the man along the flagged path to the doorway and into a hall. A moment to take in flocked wallpaper, cheap prints, cheap telephone table and old fashioned black telephone before he prodded her.

"In there." A door pushed open, men sitting around a low

14

glass topped coffee table on which were cups, brown rimmed with coffee. A glass winked an amber eye as someone moved it, whisky coating the sides. The men turned, looked, smiled. A small dark haired man with designer stubble. A taller foppish looking man, elegant and limp-wristed, who gave her a sideways look which told her nothing. Another brutal looking man, no neck, block shaped head, hard jaw, iced eyes, surely the brother of the man who had driven her there.

"I brought her." The driver, displaying her with pride.

"We can see that." Mr Limp Wrists gestured to Melanie. "Sit down, my dear, sit down; you've had a long journey."

Designer Stubble leaned forward and touched her knee as she sat in a moquette armchair.

"Would you like some coffee or a drink, something to eat?"

"No, thank you."

"A little nervous I should think, Gordon." A name for a face. Gordon for Designer Stubble.

"Probably. Well, Julian, what do you think of our find?"

Limp Wrists is Julian.

"I'm impressed. You never know who you're going to get when you ring a public telephone."

But you told me to be there! Her mind shrieked with silent protest, the words locked behind the fear which froze the sound in her mouth.

But did they? asked another voice. A woman told you to come. A woman whose voice held a hint of recognition but one which escaped when plastic met plastic and you put the phone down. She felt herself go cold inside, from the pit of her stomach to the top of her spine, shards of ice spiking into her head. She could see icicles behind her eyes, feel frostbite in her fingers and toes. It was all she could do to stop her knees trembling with cold.

Ice Eyes moved round to touch her hair and ran a finger down the side of her face, making her shudder.

"Nice girl."

"Ease off there, Harry."

15

Ice Eyes is a better name for him than Harry.

Melanie picked up her bag and held it on her lap, gripping the handle, fingers finding her personal alarm, wondering if it would do any good.

Why was she here?

"Why am I here?"

"Oh?" Julian raised an elegant eyebrow and leaned forward with a sinuous movement which made her think of snakes, a creature she detested and feared. "You do speak?"

"I told her not to." The driver smiled but his eyes remained hard. "I said to her, I said, weren't you supposed to listen? I said, doesn't that mean not speaking? I said to her, I said you'll get a spanking for disobeying, I said. Won't she, boss?"

Julian laughed, a trilling false sound which was out of place in this ordinary suburban room, with its glass shaded lamps and wall to wall carpet, its showroom ordinary furniture and matching drapes, prints on the walls, no original art, probably not an original thought in the whole house.

"Oh Brucie, you're so diplomatic! But you're right, a good spanking for a naughty little girl. Do you want to do it?"

"Let me, let me!" Ice Eyes pushing forward, hands clenched. Melanie strained back against her chair, eyes startled, thoughts wild. They did mean it after all.

"Later, Harry, calm yourself. Bruce did all the work, he collected her and drove here, it's down to Bruce, isn't it?"

"Oh, let Harry do it, I don't mind; there'll be other chances." Julian waved a hand, uncaring. "Then go right ahead, Harry."

A block of sheer nerves, unable to scream to fight or protest, Melanie let her bag fall to the ground, let herself be pulled up out of the chair, let herself be pulled face down over Harry's knees, hard legs, bone hard, thick slabs of muscle, thick rough trousers. She waited, staring at the wall to wall carpet, wondering where it came from, which chain store outlet, wondering why she wasn't fighting or protesting, realising her fear had locked her voice in her throat again, just as it had earlier.

Cold hands, cold air. Exposed to the men who drew in their

collective breath.

Was she good to look at?

A hand hard as wood bringing a stinging pain to one cheek, then the other, to one then the other, on top of the earlier ones. Hard, hurting, stinging, burning -

"OW!"

"Reaction at last, dear Harry, you're doing something right." Julian's lazy languid drawl, underneath a touch of excitement. Melanie was sure they were all leaning forward, looking, delighting as she fought against the ever falling hand, the ever increasing pain, the solid sound of hard hand on soft skin.

Harry spanked hard, and even through her pain and inexperience Melanie recognised an expert. It never varied in its rhythm or intensity: an expert hand, an expert spanking. She moaned, cried, begged for mercy, but on it went. Feeling suddenly very foolish, with her whole body rebelling, she shouted:

"Let me go!"

As if it were a code or command, Harry let her go immediately. Melanie fell heavily on the floor and lay there, shocked and wordless, clutching her cheeks, aware of being exposed. She got up and tugged her clothes back into position.

"Who are you?" she demanded of the men who were breathing fast, eyes bright, fingers clenched. "What do you want?"

"Amusement, dear girl. Amusement and a little excitement." Julian was back to normal, breathing under control. He raised a glass of whisky in her direction. "Thank you for that." Harry started a slow handclap which the others followed, all grinning at her. She blushed even harder, embarrassment making her feel almost physically sick.

As suddenly as it started, the clapping stopped. A hum of conversation began to build again, Harry moving over to talk to his twin-in-looks, Bruce, Julian leaning forward to talk to Gordon. No one took any notice of Melanie whatsoever. She pulled her briefs back up and sat down again, feeling the heat of her spanked cheeks flare through her, wondering what on earth they had planned and how she was going to get out of

Oxford and back to London. Thoughts fought each other to escape, words tiptoed to her tongue tip, poised ready for flight, only to take fright at the last moment and pull back. She coughed but no one looked round. 'I must do something!', she thought frantically. 'I can't sit here all night!'.

"My name is -" she began, but got no further than that.

"Your name is whatever we choose to call you." Julian's eyes flared at her; for a moment she felt the shock and intensity of his gaze. Then they reverted to normal common or garden eyes, but she still felt afraid. "Your name is - Angelica Williamson. That'll do, it's a nice name; it suits you."

"But it isn't my name!" She was on the verge of tears, it felt ridiculous, it sounded ridiculous, almost childish to say it like that, but she couldn't help herself.

"Oh do shut up!"

Then the tears did begin but no one took any notice. Melanie squirmed on the chair, bottom on fire, eyes overflowing, fingers and lips trembling, but no one spoke to her. She was nothing; a brief diversion, a small entertainment. Now she was ignored ...

... A memory crept into her mind, a memory she would rather have ignored ... Julian.

Not that Julian, not the one sitting there, not the one with the elegant ways in the house in Oxford ... Another Julian.

The flood swept over her, nasty memories of an unpleasant attempt at date rape.

Bernard set it up. Bernard Rapson. Over 6', dark haired, very good looking. Melanie had fancied him like crazy.

Darbyshire & Co. Insurance Brokers. As a temp, between real jobs as she thought of it, working in a poky office on the top floor, which meant she had to pass Bernard Rapson's door. It was always open and he always stopped work to stare at her.

One night he appeared in her doorway, smooth and inviting. Melanie had felt the crush grow stronger, felt warmth spread through her as he smiled his slow smile.

"Are you doing anything tonight, Melanie?"

"No, why?" Hoping against hope he would ask her out, oh yes, please ask me out!

"I've a friend who'd like to meet you." Heart sinking, she hoped she managed not to look disappointed. "Really he would. I told him all about you. Go on, say you will."

"Oh, all right." If he was Bernard's friend perhaps he too would be good looking, and she might transfer the crush to someone else. It would make working there a whole lot easier.

But the friend had been a man with a block shaped head and no neck ... Julian.

Misnamed, for most Julians were elegant people. He had taken her for a drink, pawed at her knee while they sat close together in crowded pub. He'd bathed in and then smothered himself in some kind of cologne, both potent and unpleasant.

"I have to make an urgent phone call," he told her on the way back to his car. "Would you mind if we - ?"

"No," being polite, not really wanting to go anywhere with this man she disliked so much. "I'm sure it won't take long."

"Oh, it won't."

They had driven to a small grubby flat, typically male, smelling of the same after-shave and cologne, floor and furniture covered in newspapers and take-away dishes. He had rushed around gathering up rubbish, pushing it behind the settee.

"Sit down, sit down, I'll make coffee."

"What about your phone call?"

"Oh that, it can wait. Come to that, so can the coffee."

Before Melanie had time to get suspicious, to think it through, he was sitting next to her on the settee, an arm around her, caught hold of a breast, pushed his other hand between her thighs, and tried to kiss her. Melanie fought with strength born of dislike and managed to get free.

"Leave me alone!" said in a cold hard voice.

Julian looked at her in surprise. "What's the matter with you? Bernard said you were a right little raver! All you girls are the same, aren't you? Giving it out to everyone! What's the matter with me?"

"I don't have time to tell you!" She picked up her bag and made for the door. Julian fell back on the settee, waving at her.

"Go, get out. You're the grottiest date I ever had anyway!"

Melanie hurried for the street, face burning, feeling dirty where he had touched her, feeling - as if she were nothing. A night's entertainment. Bernard had seen her like that - Julian had seen her like that.

She found a mini-cab number in a nearby phone box, and called them, anxious to be far away from Julian, his cologne and his fumbling hands.

Memories, unpleasant hurtful memories. She had told the agency she didn't want to go back to that temporary job because of sexual harassment but she didn't want to make a fuss. They said they understood and found her another place.

Memory, the one kept in a locked dark box in the back of her mind. Someone had found the key, had broken in, had removed some of the memories and set them walking and talking - and invited her to share them.

No one could share that particular memory. To think she had been foolish enough to allow herself to get in a position where date rape was possible! So stupid! It was a closely guarded secret, and Melanie intended it to stay that way ...

... All right! Determination flooding her, Melanie stood up and walked nonchalantly to the window, pulled aside the cheap curtains and looked out. For a moment all talk ceased. For a moment a silence deeper than a mortuary at midnight froze everyone. She felt their eyes, cold hard iced eyes, boring into her, each looking at a different part, each making its own freezing indentation. Julian was staring at her cheeks, imagining the flush, no doubt. Gordon was looking at her legs, for sure. He looked like a leg man. Bruce and Harry were just looking. Icicles touched her neck, her spine, her shoulders, her arms.

'I've shaken them!' she thought with a thrill of powerful delight, only to have it shattered into a thousand pieces at the sound of Julian's voice.

"Enjoy your memories, my dear?"

She refused to turn round, refused to take the bait, to give him any satisfaction at all. When he began to speak to Gordon again she knew she had won. But the victory was small, almost petty. The question remained, how did he know?

"I'm leaving!" Announced in a firm voice with a strength she did not feel. No one spoke, no one tried to stop her. Melanie stormed across the room, snatched open the door and walked out. Faded wallpaper frowned its disapproval as she brushed past, the telephone sneered with its memory of a call never made, and the door swung open into darkness.

Back down the flagged path, out into the suburban street, flickers of tv, flickers of indifference from those who stayed at home and knew nothing of humiliation and pain, of men who knew nothing and talked of nothing, but who scorned her existence while stealing her secrets.

A car purred alongside, a light flicked on.

"Get in."

Bruce, with the voice which stood for no disobedience. Melanie got in, feeling a twinge of heat as she sat, feet neatly together, hands in her lap, bag twisted round her wrists.

"It's all right, I've been told to take you home."

As the car purred into the dark unforgiving night, Melanie broke down into cold unforgiving tears. She had realised what was missing from her sex life. And realised at that moment that Golden Boy could never fulfil it, either.

There was a long search ahead.

6.

"You did well. She is captured on film forever, freely giving herself to a spanking by strange men, and not doing anything about it but standing looking out of a window. Now, what would her husband say about that?"

"But she had a lover."

"Ah yes, and he has too, a blonde who likes to dominate, to

21

tie him up and whip him. No canes or straps for her, but whips: bullwhips and dog whips. It is the only way he can achieve satisfaction. Now she must seek it, too."

"I am glad Master is pleased."

"Delighted. Now, did you bring me a memo?"

7. Memo.

My Master is a man of considerable experience. He knows what he wants of a dom/sub relationship and is out to get it. But to do that he needs to get inside my head, to know what his slave wants, so he can fulfil her desires along with his. He asked for memos, regular communications, setting out how I see the cp rituals with which we will become involved.

The memos I sent are stored in the computer, beginning here - with the beginning.

CP rituals always begin with a spanking. Sometimes with slipper, mostly with hand, but always with a warm up. Sometimes they begin over knickers, sometimes with knickers down; but they always end with knickers down. Imperative, being smacked on the bare bum. Whether the sub is allowed to cool down after, or whether the dom goes straight on to something even more painful is up to them to decide, but that is the start. Because it slots into a 'nursery/child' punishment feeling; a touch of humiliation. Adult mature women, put across someone's knee and smacked like a child. Humiliation: a touch of it never hurts, adds spice to the session; an essential part.

Part 2.1.

The cock stands proud, so proud, so smooth, so elegant, so perfect. No blemishes mar the skin. The veins pulse with deep burning fire and rivers of pounding blood, the glans emerges from its skin covering to gleam with lust and longing. The fingers lock around it, deep pink tipped fingers, wrapping and loving and wanting. The feeling communicates itself to quim; aching longing quim, wanting it, loving it, needing it.

Mouth reaches down to enfold, to trap, to draw on its strength.

"Did you ask permission to do that?"

"No, Master."

"So - ask me first."

"May I suck your cock, Master?"

"Certainly."

Relaxed on the massage couch, reflected in the overhead mirror, what does he see? A bobbing head, a mass of flowing hair, dark against light, white against dark. But what does he feel as the lips draw softly down the skin, as the teeth gnaw oh so gently, the tiniest of mouse like touches, what does the man feel as the woman absorbs his very manhood into herself? Is he at her mercy and power at that moment? Does he surrender all to the woman's softness? Is she totally in command for a few precious moments of her life? Or does he, even at that moment, retain supreme control with orders and directives and sheer power? Does he know? Does she know?

The hardness has gone, he is sitting up, he is swinging his legs over the side and standing up.

"You're depriving me!" Words burst out without thought.

"No, you won't be deprived." He is reaching for a cane. But I didn't mean that! Crying silently, I meant, you took that cock from me. No words, for his orders are to lie across the table where he had been, skin where his was, his warmth permeating soft, soft breasts, his coldness touching exposed and waiting cheeks, on fire now from twelve strokes of each of the canes, six from a multi-thonged whip, more from a tawse, more from the whip, without restraints. No bondage at all; fighting every stroke of the way, fighting the pain, fighting the desire to stand up and walk away, fighting the need to shout "NO!" and put a stop to the agony.

"You had 54." The voice calm, the tension palpable as sobs wrack the body, 54 explained, twelve of this, six and then another six of that, to tenderise, the tawse, the pain. Explained. Absorbed through skin and through desire. Arms encircle the shaking form, tears flow without ceasing and the consolation is more than words, more than feeling, more than breath of life.

Love is everything, love keeps you down when common-sense says walk, love keeps you there when everything cries flee! Love parades the redness, the weals, and later, the bruises.

Love says it all.

2. The File.

Name:	Gordon, Yolande Gloria.
Address:	St. Justins, The Banks, Skillington.
Occupation:	Actress.
Date of birth:	1.2.1958.
Place of birth:	Waltham Cross, Herts.
Education:	Primary - Comprehensive, left with no GCSE's but with high marks in drama.
Married:	Nathaniel Sebastian Carey.
Children:	None.

3.

Candle flame. Gold as the hair of the woman. Hair as soft as embroidery silk strands, floating, drawing its way through and round and creating a picture.

And within the picture comes the woman, smooth faced, smooth thighed, elegant, beautiful, and trapped, forever.

Whisper the name, whisper it low, whisper it soft.

Yolande Gordon.

Yolande Carey.

Yolande Yolande Yolande ...

4.

The antique mirror told its own story, delicate golden wind-blown hair framing a face with down turned mouth, sad, almost haunted eyes and pale skin from too much drink and too little sunlight. Yolande stopped, caught by the image, wondering who the person was, putting a shocked hand to her mouth when she recognised herself. Embarrassed at being revealed to the world as less than perfect, she turned away, pretending indifference to the antiques on display. They could have been mine, she told herself, given the right breaks, the right parts! I have the talent! I could have made it big, had money, antiques in my home and a place to call home, not a rented place.

But the right breaks and the right parts had not come. Bit parts, plenty of those, walk-on's in sit-coms, minor roles in soaps, once seen easily forgotten, even if she did give her all to some of them, prompting the director to ask her to "tone it down, Yolande, please, this isn't the Old Vic! Just be natural." And she had - and she had been forgotten.

The flat, come on! she reproached herself, the bedsit! Was untidy, littered with theatre memorabilia, boxes of makeup, costumes not wanted any more which she had taken home and hung around the walls as reminders of WHAT she had been, and done, and been seen in. Something to look at through the bottom of the glass each night when loneliness took over and the memories walked too damn hard. Something to throw back at Nat when he sneered at her so called career.

"Call yourself an actress? You couldn't act surprised if I hit you over the head! Go and get a job, any job, supermarket check out girl, anything, just help us get out of this mess!" But work meant not being available for The Call, the one which would lead to fame and fortune. Yolande insisted on not working, on waiting, on signing on for acting and voice lessons, even singing lessons, things they could ill afford but which she insisted would be a step in the right direction.

The only steps she took these days were to the off licence.

September had turned cold, had turned vicious, previewing winter with slashing biting rain striking the windows with virulent hatred. Nat was late, again, as he had been so many times lately. There had to be someone else, she mourned into the sherry glass, there had to be! Why else had he stopped getting stiff when they went to bed? Why else did her skilful fingers fail to bring him to anything like a satisfactory conclusion? Why didn't she want him in her body any more?

"What happened to lust?" she asked the cheap lighter which flickered and went out before she could light the cigarette.

What happened to lust? That was the question. What happened to all that emotion, when a golden body met a golden body, when Nat's golden hair tangled with hers, both on their heads and everywhere else, when his cock sank deep into her pussy which seemed to be always wet, always wanting, and never seemed to consider there would be an end to the loving. After ten years, ten short years, it was "goodnight" and snoring in about five minutes, leaving a cold unresponsive back to cuddle against, a cold pillow to absorb the bitter tears of loneliness. Just how lonely can you be, lying in bed alongside a man you once loved, going over long dead lines in your head, wishing you had done the movement this way or that, made that gesture bigger and bolder, uttered those lines with more conviction, all too late, too late!

"Once loved!" Yolande smiled at the delicate glass, traced the tracery with her fingernail, felt the alcohol rushing around her body, giving her a buzz.

So what happened? In a moment of madness Yolande staggered to her feet, wondering how she had got so drunk in such a short time. There it was, among the books, books! Who opened books in this flat? The white, now soiled, photo album. And there was the white, now gone to the second-hand shop, wedding dress, all satin and bows and frills and tucks and radiance. And there she was, 26 years old, golden hair matching the golden flowers she carried, smiling with all the happiness of a new wife. And beside her, Nat, tall, youthful,

26

aspiring, ambitious, protective, even then one arm around her waist, smiling with a serious look.

The smart three bed estate home, with showroom furniture and matching drapes, wedding presents stowed in cupboards never before touched by casserole or dinner service, was a good start to a new life. Pristine carpet and pristine bathroom, they christened it all, lusting for each other's bodies, making it on the floor in the lounge, over the edge of the bath as she scoured the tiles, in the kitchen, carried by Nat to the washing machine and sat firmly on top as it went into its final spin, she screeching as loud as any tom on heat as she came and came.

The smart three bed estate house went the way of all estate properties when jobs go, back to the Building Society, and they moved to a small two bed flat, with the furniture they could retain. It wasn't the same, and the housekeeping began to slide, along with the lust. More and more money went on drink, until Nat found another job, and her own career blossomed for a little while, regular work in a travelling play, more parts on tv, talk of a film script or two, but nothing ever dropped through the door. Her agent preached patience, as always.

"It will come, Yolande, dear, it will come." So will 30, she had brooded. And 30 duly came, among a welter of barbed comments from a man two years younger than her, not yet facing up to birthdays with noughts on the end. There were flowers, and a dinner at a local restaurant, nothing too fancy, just enough to make it a bit special, and plastic to pay for it, running to the edge of the credit.

Oh but the loving had been good that night! Old or not, she had bucked and thrust, drawn the stiff cock deep inside with muscles kept taut by regular exercise, had brought him to the edge over and over and let go again until they exploded together in a riot of juices and laughter.

The job went when the drinking got serious, when the travelling play stopped travelling: the drinking got serious and the lust disappeared. Nat turned 30 and there were no more comments about old people.

God, when was the last time I had something worth while stuffed up me? she asked herself, fingering the dormant clit through the flimsy panties, wondering why she was wearing them, it was for no one's benefit, and why she didn't frig more often, wondering why she let the whole thing go.

You do it like this, she told herself, imagining a golden Nat as he was, without drink and with vigour, imagining the wonderful ways they had found to make love, in fields, behind hedges, in woods, in a bus stop one night under the long black cloak she borrowed after a performance. Faster and faster the fingers moved, stroking, touching, poking, sending sensations shuddering through her -

And the phone rang.

A cool female voice which triggered vague memories in Yolande's mind. She could almost but not quite place it.

"Ms Gordon?"

"Yes?"

"I have a proposition for you, Ms Gordon."

"Who's this?"

"No questions, please, just listen."

"All right."

"I understand you are not 'working', at the moment?"

"No I'm not, the play finished its run."

"The play folded after a week, Ms Gordon, please don't think you can fool me with such talk."

"Sorry."

"The failure of the play was not your fault, Ms Gordon, but the failure of the playwright, who managed to write in every cliche imaginable and then invented some more of his own. I know, I saw it. However, your performance was impressive enough for me to offer you a part in a video."

"Well, thank you!"

"It's an adult video..." but Yolande had stopped listening, only hearing adulation, praise from an unknown person, not a well meaning friend. And from someone who'd seen through the taffeta thin storyline and amateur writing of the playwright.

28

This person had taste, ability, and intellect, for heaven's sake.

"... meet the car at the station car park at 6 pm."

"Sorry? I missed that." Hastily putting her mind back together again.

"If you could meet the car at the station car park at 6 pm?"

"Today?"

"Tomorrow. It is already 8 pm, Ms Gordon."

And I'm drunk. All right, I hear the reproach in your voice. Defence became bluster.

"I was a little flustered then."

"Understandable." Why did it feel as if she was being patronised? "Be at the station car park at 6 pm, Ms Gordon, a driver will be waiting for you in a Jaguar. He will take you to a location where you will meet the director and the backer for the video. They will tell you more about it."

The phone line buzzed the lifeless technological sound which said 'I have gone and left you, there is no longer a voice on this line, but you insist and persist in standing there in the vague hope they will come back.'

Plastic on plastic. At least they kept the phone, while everything else went, it had to be there, for That Call.

And it had come. Video work! What sort of video? Why had she daydreamed her way through the last part of the conversation? A pop video? A promotional video? That would be good, travelling to exotic places! Perhaps it was a training video! Or perhaps a -

Porn video!

With a hand still on the warm plastic, Yolande studied the faded wallpaper, saw herself at 21, radiant, ambitious, parading around in a tiny two piece at a beauty contest and outclassing the others. Saw herself at 36, being offered a part in a video, which may or may not be pornographic, and knowing, with a deep burning despair, that she would accept the role.

No matter what.

The car was waiting. It was really there, all of its gleaming length and chrome and alloy wheels, and glittering windscreen almost but not quite concealing the solidness of a man with a task to perform, and no reason not to perform it.

Was someone pulling strings? The door opened, Yolande got in, sank into luxury, breathed in the scent of cigarettes and leather, smiled at the mirror, at the clear washed out blue eyes of the man who seemed competent and efficient, and yet had not said a word.

She saw no reason to speak either.

Whatever had been arranged, had been arranged without consultation, with the full expectation she would go with it, so she would, and she did. The car eased itself into the flow of traffic, dominating by its very presence. This was luxury, this was the lifestyle Yolande had dreamed of, only to have it taken from her with those bad parts and the breaks which never came. Now it was a rust bucket of a Sierra, damaged beyond belief by earlier owners, fit only for them to drive to the out of town supermarket and back sometimes, and to venture to a country pub another time, nothing really adventurous or even part way ambitious. This car would drive forever and not get tired.

Through London, past houses and pubs - she needed a drink - past Houses of Parliament and more pubs, offices, hotels, colours changed by sodium lighting, sodium lighting changed by ever increasing darkness. Dreary blocks, dreary streets lined with litter and dull bricked-up houses crying out for occupants, for love, for life. Now the Jaguar was one of many cars heading out, past Hillingdon, through junctions and away and gone, tyres humming over roads designed for speed, white lines flashing by, darkened blocks of trees flashing by.

The beautiful car was conveying her to -

Yolande felt no fear. It could be carrying her to her death in some far off place where none would ever find her, but it didn't matter. To be treated like this, to have a silent beautiful car waiting to take her somewhere without a word being spoken, that was a thrill in itself. After all, how many people got to die just after having a small dream fulfilled? Any dream fulfilled, come to that. And if she was to die, well, the world would not miss her anyway. Nat had someone else –

A flash of pain, like a lightning bolt, scorched through her and was gone. More a mourning for past love than recognition of a love newly lost.

It was time to switch off, to enter that nothing world of floating thoughts and random desires, to feel –

A glow down there, where glows emanate and spread and –

"Here we are." The voice matched the man, solid, chunky, determined. 'Here' was Oxford. Rain washed gentle aged stone, the wonderful theatre where she had aspired to play but lost out to someone ... be honest, she told herself firmly. You don't know where you are or who you are going to see or what is going to happen so for the first and possibly the last time, be honest with yourself! You lost out to someone younger.

There, the thought expressed if not said aloud, acknowledged and accepted with only the tiniest pang, a pin-prick of sadness, and a lot of resignation.

Sweeping down silent now rain-swept streets, curtains pulled, glowing with light and love, so unlike the dreary houses out of London. Here there was life, even if it was Suburbia, with a capital S, even if it was utter boredom and loneliness. It was still a home, still a place to shelter from the rain and cold, from the rigours of life on the outside. TV helped you escape for a while, drink helped you escape even longer – If you let it.

Quiet rained-on street, quiet rained-on cars, no sign of life, no movement behind curtains, no animal disturbed the night. The Jaguar stood outside, back in the rain tainted air. Yolande stopped, listened, hearing a train rattling its lonely way through the night, and wondered why her thoughts kept turning to loneliness. In the same instant she wondered where Nat was and what he would say when he got back and found no note, no nothing, just her shoes, bag, and coat missing.

Would he wonder, would he care?

"Come." It was said as an order, not a request. Despite her reservations, Yolande followed, clicking along a flagged path, hearing her heels, hearing the sound fracture the darkness into shards of noise, of life. I am here! it shrieked. There is someone alive in this dead city!

As if in response, a car tore down the road, way too fast for the area, cornering with screeching tyres and shock of exhaust fumes seemingly drifting back, making her choke.

Or was it her own frozen emotions?

The door opened before she could register its colour, its number, anything distinctive, and she was in a hall, with pretty wallpaper, colourful prints, and a lovely old fashioned black telephone, surely worth money at an antique dealer's.

Another door swung open, and she walked in, drawn to the light and sound of voices as surely as a moth is drawn to its death on the outer glass shell of the ever burning light.

Or, if a candle flame, to its certain death by fire.

What lies beyond the open door?

Surprise surprise, a group of men, all turning as one to survey her from head to foot as she entered, to look beyond the coat, the shoes and the tightly clutched fingers to the nervous but excited woman behind the smile.

"This is - ?" Her driver, gesturing to the men, wanting to introduce her, having no name.

A spectre at a feast, a man with elegant hands, waved at her.

"Angelica Williamson, of course."

"But I'm -"

A smaller man with an unshaven look smiled, showing dazzling white teeth. "My dear, all who come here are called Angelica Williamson, it's the name we have for the heroine of our film, so we call all the ladies by that name, to see if it fits."

Yolande sank into the chair the unshaven man pointed at, knees together, toes pointing forward, trying to relax but feeling the tension betraying her emotions all through her body.

"I -"

32

"No need to worry yourself, my dear." The spectre spoke again, a voice as smooth as ancient sherry and a look which would strip the sherry from the bottle. Yolande shivered, fearing this man. "We know what we want. Don't we, Gordon?"

Gordon was the man too lazy to shave.

"What do you want?"

"To see if you're suitable." A man had come into the room behind her, a man who seemed to be the twin of the driver, block head, washed out eyes, shoulders wide enough to carry a piano alone and hands as broad as the piano stool itself.

"And how - ?"

"Why not show us what you've got?" The driver speaking now, in a voice so similar to the twin it was hard to decide which had spoken. Yolande felt irritation that all her sentences were being chopped off, but excitement as she knew what she had to do, without being told.

First the coat, sliding her arms out before getting up, leaving it as a pool of colour in the chair. Pirouetting, the dress sliding down, revealing a lace bra, a lace trimmed half slip, sheer tights she paid a fortune for in the local shop, much to Nat's rage as the drink allowance was depleted that week.

"Oh, underclothes." The spectre's almost bored voice barbed her skin like tumble-weed, clinging and moving with her.

"You don't like underclothes?" she almost snapped the words at the pale face, wanting to see it change, to see expression come to the ancient sherry eyes, but he merely smiled a languorous smile and waved a hand at her.

"I won't want to see underclothes in the film."

So it was a porn movie.

The bra dropped snowflake silent to the floor, letting the heavy breasts follow as far as the muscles let them go, drooping invitingly, the tips rose coloured and soft, the curves cream-white, delicately veined with traces of blue. The slip argued briefly with her hips before descending to the floor, the tights gave no resistance but slipped downwards, leaving long dancer's legs to the view of the men. Yolande turned, aware of

33

her firm cheeks, shaved pubis, flat stomach, wide hips and knew she had a body to be proud of.

"Can we use it?" Gordon, reaching out to prod the flesh, to see it spring back into position, to touch and stroke and see her quiver. It had been a long time.

"Is that question for me?" she dared to ask, sensing the heightened atmosphere, the sexual tension crackling among them. "If it is, the answer's yes." Throwing all cautions away, throwing away every thought of any disease or contagious illness, knowing suddenly she desired nothing more than throbbing cocks to satisfy the dull ache which had been there for so long she had learned to ignore it.

"All four?" The spectre stood, slid a zip, let an impressive erection spring out. Yolande flushed with need and greed, dropped to her knees, nodded and almost sighed.

All four.

All four took her, one after the other, spread-eagled on the thin carpet, feeling the floorboards dig into her back, her cheeks, her thighs and loving every moment of the roughness, the feeling of fulfillment as orgasm after orgasm rocked through her, suppressed sexuality restrained by alcohol and disappointment for - how long? Hands on her breasts, mauling, pulling. Teeth at her nipples, biting hard, sucking, drawing on them, sending feelings quivering to every part, hands at her hips, touching, tracing fire, until the last one stood up, satiated, leaving her there, wet and cold and exhausted.

Somehow Yolande got to her feet, somehow she rescued her clothes from their indifference, dragged on the dress and laddered the expensive tights. It was over. The surges of excitement had died with the last orgasm, leaving her shaken, ashamed and afraid. No one spoke, no one seemed to want to include her in the conversation which featured footage, lighting, over-dubbing, whether the DAT could take the soundtrack in one go or whether it had to be split, a hundred technical points she did not understand nor wanted to understand.

She had been used.

Now she was being ignored.

Rain fell soundlessly, giving car roofs a different look, a matt finish, coating lights, cascading in the orange glow. Yolande held the curtain aside, looking out into darkness, looking at Autumn coldness, foreboding of the winter to come. Behind her the men droned on. Words came to her, words which showed dissent among the four, should they, would they, take her? Inexperienced in the role they sought, they said, unsure of her ability to take, they said. Take what? She had just taken all four of them and could have taken more! Would she measure up, they said. Why not ask me, she thought. But they didn't and she was left standing alone and apart.

All Yolande knew was that she needed the part, something to go home to Nat and boast about, lie about, exaggerate about. "Oh yes, darling, a training video!" It was a training video all right, but not in the way she intended him to believe. This was a training video for would be Masters and Mistresses, a training of slaves. Could she go with it?

The rain fell harder, looking like Roman candles on Bonfire Night. Unbidden, a memory flooded through Yolande's mind, drowning her apprehension for a moment.

Back many years. Back to cold winter nights, back to Firework Night. Back to -

Yolande shook herself. This strange location, these strange people, were pulling thoughts from her head. And all she had hoped for was a role, film or stage, it didn't matter, as long as it was - someone else. When you were being someone else you didn't have to be yourself. You could be the centre of something as wild and exotic as a firework display, colour created by spots, by sets, by costumes. You were safe, inside a wall of unreality, protected from the outside by the height of the stage, the pit if there was one, by the fact they, the audience, were out there and you, the player, were inside. That's what she missed most, being on the inside.

As if heard from a vast distance came the clicking heels of a mackintoshed man hurrying homeward with a small dog on a lead, the dog's coat glistening with moisture, the dog looking as miserable as Yolande felt.

What am I doing here? she asked herself. I'm in a house, in Oxford, with men I've never seen before in my life. I've done my bit, paraded before them, stripped, taken every last one of them, proved myself. And no one, not one single one of them, has made an effort to take me back to London now they've had their fun! And no one, not one single one of them, has made an effort to tell me whether I passed the audition.

So, what the hell do I do? Demand they take me home, or at least back to the station? Demand an entertainer's or whore's fee from them? Demand food drink and sustenance? A loo would be nice too, it's been a long time -

"What can I get you, my dear?" A female voice, a silken touch on the shoulder. Yolande spun round, wondering why the reflection had not forewarned her someone was there.

A beautiful woman, raven haired, and it was truly raven hair, glistening like the cars outside, but with the shine the rain had stolen from them. Eyes such a dark brown they appeared almost black, set in a face of perfect symmetry, arched eyebrows, aquiline nose, fine shaped lips and a jaw which spoke of strength through power.

"Who are you?" Yolande stumbled over the words, wondering why she felt and sounded so gauche, so unsophisticated, and decided the woman's elegance had overawed her.

"Meredyth." Somehow Yolande knew it was spelled with a Y and not an I. "Friend of these strange people here." She smiled and waved in the general direction of the men who were looking with interest at the two of them. "If you're anything like me, the first thing you'd like is the bathroom. Come." The word was an invitation and a command at the same time. Yolande dutifully made her way round the showroom furniture and out of the door, wondering who Meredyth might be, and why she hadn't seen her gracing the cover of Marie Clare, Elle or Options before now. Certainly the immaculately cut white jersey wool dress should have been modelled by someone like her, slender yet rounded, elegant yet sensual. Yolande felt even more awkward as she climbed the stairs, stumbling forward when misjudging the top stair, catching hold of the bannister to steady herself.

Meredyth didn't look round, for which she was grateful.

"Here." The door opened onto a cold bathroom of tiles, of shiny cold fittings and sweet relief. Or it would be, if the strange woman would only leave.

"I -"

"Want to be alone. Sure, doesn't everyone? But you're here with us, and we don't leave our guests alone." Smooth, purring, sensual voice touching parts others could not usually reach. Reddening even further with embarrassment, Yolande realised she couldn't wait any longer, pulled down the tiny panties and sat down on the coldness.

Meredyth leaned against the tiles, watching, seemingly amused. "Need before embarrassment, I see."

Yolande said nothing, just stood up, depressed the handle and tried to be dignified about the whole thing. That seemed to amuse Meredyth even more.

"Come on, my dear, we all have to piss and shit at times, don't we?"

Offended by the crude words, Yolande snapped:

"Not in front of others."

"Oh, some of us do, if our Masters require it."

"Masters?" Yolande paused in the act of lowering her skirt. Masters, the word which had been bandied about as she had stood at the window, ignored, abused, and lonely. Meredyth turned and lifted her skirt. She wore no undies; Yolande was given an unconcealed view of stark blue bruises cutting clear across both cheeks.

Shock hit Yolande so hard she thought she would pass out. NO! everything inside her screamed. NO!

"What you see is what you can expect, my dear." The skirt dropped. "Do you still want the part?"

Yolande said the word her body screamed.

37

6.

"You did even better this time. She is captured on film with four men, and how her face shows she loved it! All of them screwing her."

"She liked it."

"Indeed she did, a right little sexpot, our Yolande, when you get past the drink."

"Is it of use?"

"More than of use, excellent, it will be the centre, the very heart of the film."

"There is a film, then?"

"Oh yes, there is a film. But is there a memo?"

7. Memo.

There is something odd about the cp rituals which needs to be remembered, and that is - it invariably turns on the point of retribution/punishment/wrongdoing. At times I grow heartily sick of 'weeping girl promises never to do it again after being punished' scenario, but there it is; it's what the punters want.

The stupid thing is, while I don't really like it, and would prefer to think of and see people getting thrashed because it is what they want; I am turned on by talk of punishment. And by the word itself. It is obviously so deeply ingrained in us that it cannot be avoided.

Of course this is the basis of all the school scenarios, people setting up 'schoolrooms' for 'adult' children. I have a friend who dresses as a schoolgirl for his sessions, having gone to incredibly elaborate lengths to acquire the right straw boater, the wig, the uniform, even ladies' shoes to complete it. And then added a ribbon to the hat and everything.

What I am asking is that the question of retribution and wrongdoing doesn't enter into this - I am coming to you because I want to, because to be with you will give me pleasure and pain, which I desire in equal parts, and while I shall expect punishment if I don't obey your orders, I don't want to come with ideas of being punished for past misdeeds. Unless it is something YOU want, of course. That takes priority above all my needs and requests. Essentially I am coming because it is what I want, need, and desire. And that is very different from the way cp is normally portrayed in magazines and books.

In attempting to rebel, I have created a few problems here and there - particularly with people who do like the school scene, but I'm only being honest. I don't like it, and that's all there is to it.

Part 3.1.

And let it continue.

The promise, to beat her. The intention, to carry it out.

The case of oils sits by the side: closed, secretive, sensual, aromatic, awaiting a touch, just as her body awaited the touch to bring it alive, to bring it to its full potential. Before that happened, there was the pain.

The playroom: cream walls, black implements, is at the same time a refuge, a sanctuary, a place of pleasure-pain. The walls, the ceiling with its large mirror, the rough carpeted floor, the bondage cross, large, intimidating by its very presence; all combine to produce thrills of anticipation and quivers of fear.

"Over." The command is as curt as always, and as always the command is obeyed. Leaning over a massage table, clutching the top, feeling air on skin as the skirt is turned back, panties drawn down, and almost immediately the first stinging smacks landing on exposed cheeks. They are followed by a small cane, by something which hurt unbearably, and produced the command "lay still!" followed by tawse and more cane. Tears flowing and body screaming, clinging to table, determined not to give in, not to say 'no', not to get up.

"Get up." A break, a welcome relief from pain, a time of

relative companionship as the aromatherapy massage begins. "You have another 50 to come," is mentioned halfway through, as the cheeks ache, the tears tremble, the body waits.

Aromatherapy is soothing, the essential oils delight in their delicate aroma, hands sliding smoothly and gently; not a real massage, a sexual one, an arousing one, touching and lingering, caressing and pressing, producing the reaction needed.

"Enough!" and this time ropes are produced, wrists cuffed and tied, legs tugged roughly apart, ankles bound, facing the bondage cross. Another 60 strokes, 'ten extra because you take it so well', are laid on the abused and screaming bottom.

And then the sweet relief of the erect cock, the sense of being filled, the loving words, the hugging arms, the pride in having taken it all.

"Now get her for me."

2. The File.

Name:	Walters, Cheryl Sarah.
Address:	49 St. Leonards Avenue, Braston.
Occupation:	Financial Services Manager with a bank.
Date of birth:	19.05.1958.
Place of Birth:	Waltham Abbey, Essex.
Education:	Primary - comprehensive. No special skills.
Married:	John Anthony Williams.
Children:	Justin, aged 4.
	Glenn, aged 2.

3.

Candle flickers, moves, the aura deepens, the flame reflects, replicates itself in the pool of wax.

Wick is black, black as the hair of the woman, the red burning centre glows with the intensity of a woman's eyes in the moment of ecstasy.

Whisper the name to the flame. Whisper and capture and draw and entrap.

Cheryl Walters.

Cheryl Williams.

Cheryl Cheryl Cheryl ...

4.

The tiled subway stretched out forever, glistening here and there with moisture as clear as the tear-drop before penetration and ecstasy. Sights for the eyes - glittering, glistening, cold heartless tiles. Concrete floor glittering with quartz and other minerals trapped in its heart. Fast moving commuters, mindless and soulless, heading to their destination. Sounds for the ears - click of heels on the hard floor, swish of clothes as legs move in unison with the sound, wailing eerie echoing electronic music of a busker.

Cheryl approached. He was a young man, wild eyed and wild haired, wild clothes and smooth fingers; clean and out of character with the rest of him. They flickered above the keyboard whilst his eyes, sightless, stared at the cold heartless tiles from which came the echo to back his music; played from his heart. Cheryl fumbled for a coin, threw it into the hat.

"Thank you." The sound of coin on coin had no doubt alerted him to someone being good to him.

As she walked away from the wailing, crying, heart wrenching music Cheryl saw a beggar hold out her hands, eyes beseeching. Now in a giving mode, Cheryl stopped, turned, was on the point of foraging for another coin when she realised the hands were white and soft, the nails long and tipped with red.

"Get lost!" she snapped, turning her back on the beggar woman. "Damn cheek! Begging when you have money for nail enamel!"

Several passers-by looked at Cheryl curiously, but said nothing, just hurried past in the cold wind, seeking shelter, seeking warmth and comfort from the biting winter weather.

"You'll be sorry, Cheryl Williams!" Did the red mouth move? Did the eyes really see? Did the busker really get so close without ceasing his music?

"I gave to you," she protested, while aware the dream was slipping, slipping, slipping -

"You'll be giving more than that when you're through," and she was awake, aware, trembling, the beautiful music still echoing in her mind.

Dark overcast morning made shadows in the room, a sense of it being too early; more time should be spent sleeping, less time spent thinking about the dream, the haunting music, the wild eyed busker. The strangely attractive wild eyed busker.

"But he was blind in the dream." Cheryl spoke aloud as she allowed her hands to wander over her body; to explore, excite, arouse, while imagining the blind busker's hands exploring her smoothness, her sensuality, her very womanhood.

Frenetic fingers, pulsing the secret little spot, brought her to panting gasping orgasm. She lay still, feeling her vaginal muscles clench and open in rhythm with her breathing.

"Wow." Cheryl stared at the ceiling, at the pattern thrown by the dark morning light through the curtains and onto the white surface. "Wow." But the word seemed empty, as empty as the experience she had just had. Not even satisfying, just easing an itch, quietening a pulsing need, not satisfying it at all.

The drumming of the water in the shower echoed the music still running in her head. Dreams rarely lingered like this, it was odd, so very odd, that this one persisted.

Who had the blind busker represented? Such a wildly beautiful young man, so - intense!

Dressing was a chore, a daily choice of 'suitable' clothes for an office who gave the impression they didn't really care for women in positions of any kind, let alone financial services adviser. But it was a job, it paid a good wage, it covered the cost of the child-minders -

"Justin! Glenn! Stop that noise!" The squabble had grown to a proportion she could not tolerate so early. Hair, makeup, jewellery, all would have to wait until the boys were dressed and packed off for the day, until she returned to the state she was most comfortable with - alone. Husband John had already departed for his office, high flying job in a high flying glass tower.

At last they were gone. Gold dripped from ears, fingers, wrists and neck. Heels clicked across the concrete drive, car started first time, and she was away to town.

"The subway isn't lined with tiles, like in my dream." Cheryl sat with a steaming cup of black coffee in both hands, not really looking at her friend, just remembering. "But it's a subway all right, and there was the busker, just like in the dream. Only he wasn't blind."

"Coincidence," commented Margaret, banging her mug down in characteristic 'let's get on with things' fashion. "Dreams are weird things. You can read all sorts of things into them." The papers were pulled toward her, the coffee break definitely over.

Cheryl sighed, looked at her own cluttered desk and reached for the telephone. Whatever Margaret thought, the subway from the car park to the office was bad enough, gloomy enough, at the best of times, but to hear a busker down there, playing haunting electronic music, was enough to give her a screaming attack of the shivers. The sad thing was, the electronic music had been different, and she had lost the music from the dream, drowned under the new sounds.

She felt an odd sense of loss as she began the second round of telephone calls, coping with queries and enquiries, with slow response customers and sharp alert insurance companies.

And all the time she ached, deep down, with anticipation, apprehension and sheer pulsing excitement as she thought of the night ahead.

There were many long dark nights when Cheryl sought sleep,

kept awake by her wild frightening thoughts, wondering how to tell her husband of her deepest, most secret and urgent desires, wondering if she could tell her husband her deepest, most secret and urgent desires. How could she begin to explain her need for total domination, for pain, for ropes and gags; for everything she saw in the expensive and probably illegal bondage magazines she bought from a little shop with blacked-out windows, whose proprietor asked no questions and told no one of his customers. Magazines concealed within the pages of Marie Claire, Elle and Company, magazines designed to be innocuous to the casual glance.

That's what nosiness gets you, she told herself one dark endless night, when the duvet was too hot and the air too cold, when John snored obscenely into the small hours, when the touch of his skin fired her to heights of desperation, when fingers could not do enough to douse the fire of the mind, much more ferocious and fiery than any fire of the body.

Nosiness. A brown manilla envelope left in the Ladies, casually tossed on the chair whilst the owner used a cubicle for - what? Before peeking inside the envelope, Cheryl would have sworn a cubicle was for urinating or defecating or hiding the tears of a stress worn day. What had possessed her to look inside the envelope she never knew, but she had, and had looked and looked and put it back swiftly as the fire swept her from head to foot, as the colour burned her face powder to solid glass, as the thoughts rushed tornado-like through mind body and extremities, lighting every one up like a firework display.

Jealousy. That flooded in later, soapstone green, institution green, whatever green came to mind which was not quite jade, and not quite the colour of the emerald which sat in the pendant around her neck to offset the starkness of the office blouse. Jealousy that someone should have discovered what she had never known - that someone could possibly be acting out things she never knew she wanted to do - until that moment.

Months of brooding, months of desperation, months of secret purchases of exciting illicit magazines, and months of daydreaming fantasies, and finding out that cubicles in ladies have other uses than for urination and defecating and the occasional tears. They were pretty good for a quick fingering session and a silent head-pressed-against-the-cold-tiles orgasm which shook her to the core.

But she could not tell John, he was so staid, so rigid, so 'missionary position everything else is perversion'. This was John, who had never once laid her in the back of a car, in the soft grass, or even anywhere in their own home. What would he think of bondage, even mild silk scarf bondage, let alone the ropes, chains, shackles and straps of the women in the magazines? And the need for pain, or was it a need? Was it merely a fantasy she would reject when she found out for sure?

Tonight the dreaming could be over. Tonight the reality could intrude on the fantasy, and reveal all to her seeking, troubled mind.

Tonight was a visit to a 'client' with the promise that all would be revealed.

"This way, Cheryl!" The voice called, the voice of a friend, the voice of a stranger. Cheryl paused, hand on her heart, feeling it beat frantically against its cage, feeling it want to defy medical science and leap from her body.

This way.

Which way?

Along here, the exit from the subway which led to flagstones, to the ponds, to the inconvenient conveniences?

Or this way, back into the High Street, where crowds pushed and music blared from the music store and clothes shops?

Or this way - Or that way.

"This way, Cheryl!"

Who was calling? Who had a voice strong enough to cover the sound of the underground trains rumbling ever onward to far destinations, where underground became above ground but kept the same name, where trees nodded in sunlit suburbs and winds howled round gable ends and chimney pots in winter?

While walking blind, trying to follow the sound of the voice above the sound of pedestrians, beggars and buskers, children and underground officials, Cheryl grappled with another problem, one which refused to leave her alone -

She had seen a video. As illicit and even more expensive than the magazines, offered to her by the proprietor of the shop with the blacked-out windows, offered in a paper bag she could not refuse.

How did she know that the girl in the video enjoyed her session - afterwards? There was nothing in the video - nothing - to tell her that.

Since then, sitting in the over heated office with perspiration trickling between her breasts and running down her arms, with clammy sense of lubrication around the pubis - she knew she had to find out how she knew.

"Here, Cheryl!" The crowd parted. There he was, the blind busker from her early morning dream, standing with his keyboard, calling to her above the sound of the crowd, above the striking heels on tiles, of voices echoing back from mosaics, of children squealing with protest at being dragged along -

"I don't even know your name." How had she got here, standing in front of him, hearing coins clink as they fell into his cap, laid enticingly on the ground.

"Would you believe it's Kester?"

Cheryl smiled, resting a hand on his arm, watching the sightless eyes scan the crowd, while the delicate music soared and filled the huge expanse of nothingness of the subway.

"That sounds like something out of Precious Bane."

"I think it is." Fingers, delicate as snowflakes, pressed the keys seemingly at random, seemingly senseless, yet the sound which filled the subway was a haunting delicate melody that plucked heartstrings and pulled money from wallets and purses.

"Cheryl, you are getting nearer, you have moved from darkness into shadow, soon you will move into the light."

Light.

And she woke to fading light, twilight, and silence. The boys were still with the child-minder, John had yet another meeting, and she had -

A date with destiny, if you want to be really corny, she told herself. I did not intend to fall asleep! Berating herself for tiredness when there were things to do, places to go, people to see, things to experience ...

Rising, unrested and shadow eyed from the sleep tumbled bed. Just a small nap she had promised herself, worn out as she was from hours of fantasising, frigging and anticipating.

Hurry hurry hurry; she had to meet someone called Bruce in a subway.

"There you are!" Bruce, standing four square against the flow of people, making them divide and reform around him like a stone in a river, an island in a road, a tree in a field of corn -

"I couldn't see you." Cheryl clung to the offered arm, glad to see him once she had realised this indeed was the man she had been told to meet. Being underground always bothered her; she could just about cope with the subway and perhaps the underground train but not much else. Caves and long tunnels frankly terrified her. Picky kind of claustrophobia, choosing what scared her and what didn't.

Picky kind of sub, choosing which Master to submit to. Where did that thought come from?

Why not? It was her body and her spirit, after all!

"Julian has plans," Bruce told her, guiding her up the iron rimmed steps into the sharp biting weather above ground. Fine sleet pattered on her head, powdered her shoulders, caused her to flinch inside her thick wool coat.

"What sort of plans?"

Bruce shrugged.

"He didn't say. Something to do with your first lesson."

A sudden wetness flooding the panties, thoughts of Julian persisting in her mind, Julian she had only seen twice. Once, briefly, in the Manager's office, and later in her own office when they had discussed pension plans, with every word ap-

47

pearing to have a double meaning. Once had been enough. The dinner invitation he phoned in had been accepted without a second thought.

"Come on, let's go." A car hooted angrily as Bruce guided her across a side road, insisted she moved faster. Heels clicking, Cheryl hurried after Bruce, desperate not to lose sight of his strong shoulders.

Someone who looked like Meredyth pushed past, glared at her, and was gone. Cheryl paused, wondered who Meredyth was, wondered where the thought had come from, and hurried after Bruce again. Meredyth, what an odd name. Where had it come from? How did she know?

Meredyth - was she something to do with Julian?

Side streets, potholes and litter, rough walls and rough people, why had she ever considered herself a City dweller? Suddenly it all seemed too loud, too rough, too brash and raucous for her. She longed for the tranquillity, something like the Oxford spires and stately buildings, for the tick of cycle wheels and air of learning.

"Here we are." A shabby door, half glass, half peeling wood set in a shell canopy. Shame to let such a fine door go to ruin.

Bruce tapped twice, and the door opened. A woman stood there, smiling a dark red smile and waving dark red fingertips. The woman from the street.

"Angelica, how nice to see you again!"

"But you were -" Cheryl bit off the words, and smiled.

"Come on, Meredyth, it's fucking cold out here!" Bruce shouldered his way in and slammed the door. He pushed Cheryl toward a lounge. "I want to get warm, even if you don't!"

Cheryl allowed herself to be pushed, secretly delighting in being told what to do and when to do it.

A man sat on the settee, holding a white stick and wearing shades. A blind man, feeling the contours of the arm with delicate white fingers. He looked vaguely like the busker, but not quite. Somehow the outlines were different, the tones were different - Cheryl pulled herself up short. Stop this foolish nonsense! He's just a blind man!

"Angelica, good to see you again."

"Are you all programmed to call me that?" She said it with a smile, to take the sting from the words. "My name's actually Cheryl, as Bruce knows." She stopped again, wondering why he had said those words. How could he have known who it was, and when had he seen her?

A man wearing designer stubble suddenly appeared, arms waving, excitable words spilling from full red lips.

"There you are! Thought you'd never get here! Right, I have plans for you, Cheryl dear, or should I call you Angelica? This whole business is getting terribly confusing."

"For me too." Cheryl tried to smile, but failed. Where was the languid, beautiful Julian? Who were these strange people? The blind man sat, wearing a knowing smile, fingers tap dancing over the arm of the chair, tapping out some melody only he could hear. What could he see behind the sealed lids? Cheryl stopped, breath caught in her throat. How could she know there were sealed lids behind dark glasses? "You are - ?"

"Sorry, the name's Gordon. I make films. This one's for Julian. You know that, of course. For the purposes of the film you're Angelica Williamson. All right?"

"Sure."

As long as I get what I want, you can call me what you like. But you're rushing me, I have no time to think. Do I know what Julian has in mind?

The anticipation, the sheer excitement of being in the hands of strangers, overcame all the scruples she might have had.

"Well, to start the film, you will come in, and be confronted by Meredyth here, who will get angry and punish you - do you mind? How do you feel about being punished by a woman?"

"Pain is pain." The words were said lightly but beneath the lightness lay a grim terror. A woman? Was this really the way it had to be? Did it matter?

Meredyth walked over to Cheryl and took her hands, silk soft skin sliding over her fingers. "Julian said you want to discover your secret self, the real submissive you. He also happens to want a video made of it for his private library. Trouble is with Julian, he can't do things by halves, so he gets a film maker in to do it and a musician to hang around so he can write the music later! Hence, Gordon, No. 1 video maker, and Jez, No. 1 musician." She let go Cheryl's hands, and stood back as if to watch her reaction.

Time to lay some ground rules.

"Let me get this straight," she began speaking slowly and carefully. "You think -"

"I know." Gordon interjected, with a smile to take the sting from the words.

"You think I am of a submissive nature." Cheryl carried on over his words. "You want to film me being brought to full recognition of my own true self without script, without training, without recompense?" She wondered how she knew all that, too.

"My dear, you'll get well paid." Gordon grinned again, white teeth behind dark stubble. "And you'll benefit from understanding your true self better. After this, if it works, of course, we could go on to make all sorts of s/m films; you'll be a real star, people will flock to buy the films!"

"Look, we'll leave you to think about it for a moment." Bruce patted her shoulder in a patronising, proprietorial manner. Gordon nodded. The two men walked out of the room, discussing something in low tones.

Jez smiled. "Interesting, isn't it, how we like to explore our true selves?"

"Is that what you do?"

"Of course. Through music."

Meredyth smiled a thin model smile, and moved closer to join in the conversation. "Bit of a shock, Angelica?"

"Bit of a shock," agreed Cheryl. "Look, what is this Angelica business?"

"Something Julian likes. A continuity if you like. All the women in his video's are called Angelica, one way or another."

"Are you into all this?"

"All what?"

"Bondage and stuff."

"Yes. Gordon wanted to have me starring in a film like this, but we got to the Master/slave state too fast. You'll be better, you'll hold out longer."

"How do you know?" wondering aloud, savouring the secretly deep thrill at her secret being exposed.

"You're possibly stronger than me." Meredyth looked at her feet. "I'm too easily swayed and I rebel, knowing I'll get punished for it. Oh, don't look like that!" she went on, without even looking at Cheryl. No doubt the disapproval radiated from her in invisible radio waves. "I did it on purpose. I upset Gordon last night. I won't go into it now! but I've been forbidden to look at him today and I'm due a very severe punishment session tonight, probably with his riding crop."

"But that -"

"Hurts? Of course it does. But afterwards, Oh, Angelica, the afterwards! But it's all fantastic; when you're being dominated and made to take it, when the crop comes down again and again, cutting, hurting, lashing, and you know it's giving a hint of the pleasure you'll get later. You get your reward in bed, as it were."

"But -" the feelings were still mixed. The sensations were mixed, the dream, vision, whatever it was, still bothering her. But she knew one thing - she had a chance to make her fantasies come real, and by God she was going to do it. She took a deep breath, walked out of the room to Gordon, who was standing in the hall discussing something with Bruce.

"Let's do it. For Julian."

"I knew you would. Let me get the camera set up."

There was a lot of technical stuff going on; camera angles, light meters, light levels, direction of shot, and other stuff she didn't understand. Story-line changed, Meredyth banned from taking part, changes everywhere, baffling, confusing, worrying. What she did understand was she was wet, ready and willing for anything. All inhibitions had disappeared on a tide of adrenalin.

"Obedience. That is what's required of my women." The camera was set and everything was ready. Gordon lit one of his small cheroots, blew aromatic smoke in Cheryl's direction, and cast sidelong glances at Meredyth. "Don't I want obedience?" he threw the words at her, sharp, almost cutting in their intensity. She nodded, not looking at him.

"Obedience is sometimes hard to give," observed Cheryl.

"Obedience is never hard to give, as you'll find when we work through this film, darling. Come on, now give me the opening scene. Right?"

"Right. Just remember, I'm not an actress."

"You'll be all right. Let me tell you what I want. You walk in, take the phone, say hello, you pretend to hear the voice, then you say 'I guess so. I was told the call was for me.' That's all. Meredyth, keep out of the way until I want you."

Meredyth hastily left the room without a backward glance. The blind man slowly backed away toward a wall, out of shot.

Cheryl got up, smiled, nodded and walked over to the telephone, checking the distance. She glanced at the curtains at the window, at the circle of sagging drooping armchairs around a coffee table. An old fashioned black telephone sat on a side table, receiver lying on the coldness.

Then she left the room and waited for Gordon's call. A gentle walk in, it felt unnatural somehow, and over to the telephone and picked it up.

"Hello?"

A long pause when she thought someone might speak, then:

"I - guess so. I was told the call was for me."

Another pause, then Gordon called out:

"Ok, darling, that's fine. Oh, here's your leading man."

Bruce walked into the room, his ice coloured eyes hard as ever, but the smile he gave Cheryl was genuine.

"You all right with all this?"

"Fine," she smiled back, oddly aware of the strong leap of

her heart at seeing him. It got stranger by the moment; the man she'd never seen before - until she'd been directed to meet him - was to be her leading man, with all that might entail.

Bruce turned to Gordon. "What do you think about dressing her in leather?"

"Leather? Get her used to slave costume, you mean?"

"That's about what I had in mind."

"Well, yes. Angelica, we have a special leather outfit we'd like you to wear, but it would be better for the film if you were to put it on in front of the camera, for the viewer, as it were."

"Sure." It didn't seem to matter. Nothing seemed to matter. Not any more. She might never see these people again.

"I have to go." The blind man tapped across the room.

"Sure, thanks for coming. See you soon." Gordon shook Jez's hand as he passed.

"Leather." Gordon turned back to Cheryl, then yelled "Meredyth!" She came running. "Bruce has just given me an idea. Next time you're out, buy a leather belt, and be sure to tell the man why you want it. I want it so I can thrash you with it. All right? And be careful to wear it all the time you're around me. For now, bring me the leather outfit for Angelica here."

Meredyth brought the outfit: a tight basque laced down the back with strong long laces, high heeled boots, long elbow length gloves and another thing Cheryl could not make out. Under Bruce's watchful eye she unselfconsciously stripped naked, standing erect, her breasts full and pink, dark nipples standing up with the chill of the room.

Everything was strange; the room, the people, the outfit, the whole game she was involved in. Part of Cheryl was laughing with cynical amusement, the other part was delighting in the whole thing. Obedience. Was she not obeying everything, by stripping in front of strangers, by wearing odd clothes, by going along with Julian's wish for a new video for his collection? Just how many did he have in his collection, and how many women had he talked into this?

She struggled a little with the leather basque, it was stiff, almost unwieldy. But once Meredyth had pulled on the laces, she saw how it fitted perfectly, cupping her breasts in its hollows, outlining her slim waist, her flared hips, her rounded behind, the curve of her thighs and her long shapely legs. The boots came next. She stood easily in the 4" heels, admiring the way they thrust her forward, parading round the men with pride.

That was stopped when Bruce handed her the last item, a black full face mask with a zip for the mouth.

"Must I?" Cheryl turned to Gordon, almost pleading, but knowing better than to argue.

"Of course." He was indifferent, anxious to get back behind the camera, to give orders. Not that any were needed. All she had to do was follow her instincts, and Bruce's guiding words.

Bruce ran the camera as she had undressed, had caught every moment of her parading, and now caught her frightened look as the mask slid over her face. There was enough space to breathe, but not to see. It effectively shut out the light.

"Now." Bruce's voice was her only guide. Gordon had called for all sound to cease. "Now, come here."

She walked to where she thought the sound emanated, held out a hand, touched a jacket, a hand.

"Kneel down."

It was difficult kneeling gracefully in 4" heels, but she managed it. The sound of a zip reached her along with the rustle of clothes, and a hand reached out to undo the zip of her mouth.

"Take it." A cock was presented to her. She tasted salt, tasted warmth, as the tip pressed against her lips. She took it in both hands, running her fingers the entire length of the shaft, licking and touching, aware of small sounds of enjoyment. Its owner was already highly aroused. In a short time it jerked, spouted cream. There was a sigh of satisfaction which seemed to come from a stranger. Why did she think that?

Cheryl leaned back on her heels, waiting for another order, for a handkerchief, for something.

Nothing happened. She was left to kneel, to wait, to be still, to learn to obey, hands and mouth covered in cream. That much she understood.

It grew cold, and she grew stiff.

Then there was movement. People walked around her, a hand touched her hair, another ran a hand down her bottom, feeling the heat of her crack, touching her wet pussy. The wetness surprised her. Never before had she been aroused by such acts.

This simple act of obedience, this waiting on orders, this being unable to see, this total dependance on another being, was exciting her in a way nothing had ever done before.

I was right, she thought. I am inclined this way.

"We'll give you a new name." Bruce's voice, cold, hard, almost unrecognisable except for that firm tone that spoke of domination, of masterful being, of instant obedience to his will. "You need a new name. A name which is entirely mine to use as I will, and for no other to use."

Cheryl realised Bruce's voice had come from a distance; he was not close to her. Then who was breathing so steadily, who was touching her shoulders, her nipples through the leather, running a finger down the side of her face, tracing the length of her thighs, tousling her pussy hair, finding her wetness?

She dared not speak.

"Angelica Williamson."

Cheryl's head jerked up at the name, snatching her hair away from the man - was it a man? She wanted to cry out, to demand an explanation, but couldn't. Suddenly the name seemed alien, unacceptable, she wanted to reject it, but couldn't.

"Angelica Williamson," Bruce repeated, the voice coming nearer now. "This is for you, Angelica." Something snapped round her neck, something cold and hard, rigid and binding.

It felt like a collar.

Blind, the mask smothering her vision and her emotions, Cheryl struggled within herself. A collar meant submission - but was she not submitting by being there, by kneeling in this uncomfortable position, sucking off a man who may or may not have been Bruce?

Had she not, by becoming what was essentially a porn star,

submitted to all men everywhere? Why else would she so unselfconsciously undress before the camera, before men, before - strangers?

"Stand up." She struggled to her feet, her hands reaching blindly for support, finding a strong arm, getting up, teetering just a little, finding her balance. Then she stood tall and proud, head up, aware of the basque, aware of the fine fitting leather, sure of herself, arrogant; a strange feeling, a new emotion.

"Too proud by half." A strange voice, a different voice. "Take her down a peg or two." Hands reaching for her, more than two, pulling her forward, over a stool? Over something with leather which creaked on leather, wrists bound with swift movements, ankles bound equally fast, unable to move, staring into darkness. Scared. Where was she, what had they done to her, why was she bound?

"And before you scream or protest -" a gag was slipped round her mouth, over the mask, between the teeth of the zip, stifling a protest, stifling her instant cry.

Now what?

Lightning streak of pain clear across both cheeks; something heavy, something wide, something devastatingly painful. Head back, she tried with body language to shout a protest, but it was no good. The pain came again and then again, rapid, hurting, no chance to absorb between blows. And then it slowed, became almost sensual, one sharp crack bringing her head up, her body writhing in protest, then the pain, flaring, burning, settling, glowing.

Tears.

This is what it's all about. This is being disciplined, this is being trained, this is something I never thought I'd experience. Do I like it?

"Porn queens should experience everything."

Where did that idea come from?

"Angelica Williamson." Bruce's cold hard voice, edged in ice to match the dirty ice eyes, "You will remember to instantly obey. At no time will you stand tall before a man. At no time will you express what you consider to be your superior self. At all times you will be submissive, in body language and in voice. Your heels are there for our pleasure, not for your vanity. The leather is for our pleasure, not for your fashion state of mind."

Each statement was accompanied by a stinging stroke of the leather strap. She fought the gag, crying, wanting to protest, to say she would remember, she would submit; but the pain went on, harder and harder, overlaying pain with pain, driving the message home.

Then it was over, she was released, helped up, the gag taken off. Free to speak she had nothing to say. Free to move she did not want to move; pain flaring through her, memories stinging as much as the strap had, tears coursing lines in her makeup.

"Take the mask off." Gordon's voice. Someone untied the thick laces, someone slid the blinding mask from her face and she saw through her tears - the blind busker.

Bat blind, smooth fingered, as wild of clothes and hair as he was in her dream, he was there, all of him. She rubbed at her eyes, cleared the moisture from them and stared anew.

"No keyboard?" it sounded silly, it sounded as if she had gone through some kind of hallucination, but the busker smiled.

"Keyboard? Sure, it's here, I'll be getting it later. Gordon's asked me to do the music for the film. I'm Christopher, but people call me Kester, apparently it's the way I said it as child."

"That sounds like something out of Precious Bane."

"Out of what?"

"A novel by Mary Webb - oh never mind. And is -" she broke off. To say more would be to talk of the dream and that would never do. She turned to Gordon and Bruce. "That was a tough lesson."

"It was." Bruce came over to her, touched her face gently, almost lovingly. "You learn fast, you're a good subject. One of the best so far."

"Brilliant stuff, darling." Gordon, looking enthusiastic.

"You're going to be badly marked from that thrashing, my

57

dear. Will that cause problems?" Unaccountably Cheryl began
to shiver. Meredyth came with a thick robe, threw it around
Cheryl's shoulders and knelt down.

"Let me get those boots off for you."

"I don't want to sit." Cheryl was beginning to understand
how Meredyth felt, but still had some way to go before fully
coming to terms with being subdued in that way.

"Of course you don't, hold on to me and I'll get the boots
off."

Bruce leaned against the wall, watching.

"Would you like to go to Oxford tomorrow, Cheryl?" he
spoke suddenly, surprising her.

"Oxford? Why, yes." Calculating madly if she could get the
day off.

"Fine. I'd like you to meet my friends in Summertown. It
will be good for you to learn some more lessons too."

Cheryl tried to control the leap of interest, the flaring of
sexual excitement which almost drowned her pain. Her cheeks
ached, throbbed, burned with the strapping, yet she felt a thrill
deep inside, deep enough to perhaps not show.

Yet she had a feeling Bruce had noticed and catalogued it,
along with all the other things he had observed about her. A
frightening, worryingly perceptive man. As a Master he probably couldn't be bettered, as a friend -

"When?"

"Oh, late afternoon, I should think. London's so exciting in
the dark, and Oxford can be too."

Take a chance. "I'll - be ready by four."

"Good."

5.

The Houses of Parliament, floodlit and elegant. Across the
Westway; streetlights, headlights, tail lights, brake lights, interior lights, pub lights, house lights, torch lights -

Motorway signs flashed past, far off places she had never visited or wanted to visit or could have visited -

Until now.

The Jaguar was beautiful. A truly classic car, burnished to a high shine with hours of polishing, the walnut fascia gleaming with richness and luxury, the leather seats smelling of money and class.

"You remember your new name?" a sharp sideways look, capable hands on the wheel, hands capable of delivering -

"Angelica Williamson."

"Good. That's the name I'll use when I introduce you to my friends."

"Why are we going, Bruce?"

"Why? What sort of question is that?"

"A sensible one, I think." Cheryl huddled in the seat, watching buildings flash by; flare of headlight in the wing mirror followed by the sudden darkness as a car raced past, exceeding the speed limit even more than they were. Bruce's car purred, as if loving every moment of being driven fast.

"No, I'm not sure it is a sensible one."

"Why not? Right out of the blue you invite me to Oxford to meet your friends. I'm not your slave - yet. I'm not properly trained - yet. I don't even feel I'm your friend. So why are you taking me to Oxford?"

"I think of you as a friend, Cheryl." A quick glance of ice cold eyes. "I'm sorry you don't think of me as a friend yet. But you will. As to why; I thought it would be good for you to get out of London and meet someone else."

Cheryl slid further down the seat, as far as the seat belt would let her, and stared out into the darkness. A large supermarket flashed by, car park floodlit and packed with shoppers piling groceries into their car boots. Then a DIY place, a carpet place.

People seen for a second, instantly forgotten. People with places to go, lives to lead, happiness and depression to cope with, loneliness, accident, illness, death.

What am I thinking? she asked herself.

High Wycombe spread out, looked down upon from the superior position on the motorway, a carpet of light, a mass of people. Then it too was gone.

There was a long period of silence, no sound but the rushing of the tyres and the engine, which faded into the background, became part of the silence. A long stretch of motorway, glimpse of silhouetted homes, a rush of crash barriers, cat's-eyes, an SOS telephone; milestones in nothingness, in darkness. Trees loomed, leered, disappeared as the car rushed on. A journey that had no end.

Bruce flicked the indicator, turned off at junction 8.

"You can sit up straight now, Cheryl." Said with the edge on his voice she had noticed before. "We're coming into Oxford, I don't want people to see you slumped down like that."

Reluctantly she pulled herself upright, tugged at her coat collar and straightened the seat belt.

And then they were there.

Oxford.

Flats, shops, universities, ancient stone, students everywhere. Oxford: dreaming spires of learning, of history. Morse country. Her favourite tv series, her favourite tv detective, and here she was, being driven through the streets Morse walked, in a Jaguar much like the one Morse drove.

The car was slowing down now. She was able to see the stonework, read the university names, see the places where people lived, walked, and learned.

What will I learn here? she wondered.

"You will learn to obey."

Had she spoken aloud? Why else had the cold faced man answered her question?

The car stopped outside a house. Terraced, bay windowed, plain door, no number, no name. A solid looking brown door set in ancient stone, the surrounding wall covered with ivy; clinging, holding, disguising. A light shone through thin curtains, shadows moved and then were still.

Cheryl opened the car door, slid out on to the cold pavement, stood looking around her. A quiet street, lined with parked cars, bay windows warm lit against the darkness, shaded with drapes, flickering with blue light of television sets.

"Come." An order. Cheryl followed Bruce along the flagged path to the doorway and into a hall. A moment to take in flocked wallpaper, cheap prints, cheap telephone table and old fashioned black telephone before he prodded her.

"In there." A door pushed open, men sitting around a low glass topped coffee-table on which were cups, brown rimmed with coffee. A glass winked an amber eye as someone moved it, whisky coating the sides. The men turned, looked, smiled.

Bruce took her hand.

"Gordon doesn't need introducing, but you don't know the others. This is Harry, who looks like my brother but isn't; it's one of life's coincidences." Harry, hard looking man, no neck, block shaped head, hard jaw, iced eyes. He said nothing but nodded. "This is Joe, he works for Julian sometimes." Joe looked ordinary, the Mr Average you saw in any street.

He waved at Cheryl. "Sit down, my dear, sit down; you've had a long journey."

Gordon leaned forward and touched her knee as she sat in a moquette armchair.

"Surprised?"

"Yes!" A short sharp laugh, unlike her own. What was she doing here? Did Gordon have a camera trained on her?

Probably. It was wise to act as if he did.

"Well, what do you think of her?" Gordon asked Joe. "After yesterday I can honestly say this is my star."

"I'm impressed. I knew she had potential but I never thought I'd hear you say that, Gordon."

Cheryl flushed with pleasure, wanting to please but not really knowing why.

"Nice girl." Harry, tracing a finger down her face. How had he got so close without her seeing him move? She sat very still, determined not to move.

"Ease off there, Harry." Bruce's calm voice.

61

Ice Eyes is a better name for him than Harry.

Why was she here?

"Why am I here?"

"Oh?" Joe raised an eyebrow, leaned forward with a sinuous movement that made her think of snakes; an animal she detested and feared. "You do speak?"

"Of course."

He laughed, a trilling false sound out of place in this ordinary suburban room, with its glass shaded lamps and wall to wall carpet, its showroom ordinary furniture and matching drapes, prints on the walls, no original art, probably not an original thought in the whole house.

And he was as out of place here as a snake would have been.

"You'll find out."

He turned to Gordon, discussing film making, ignoring her.

The problem is, Cheryl told herself as she stared at Gordon and Joe, at the door slowly opening and a tray, then a woman, coming in; a woman with soft white hands and long red nails, a woman who had -

Begged from her in a subway in a dream.

The problem is, Cheryl repeated, as if dictating a lesson to herself, I know this place. I feel I've been here before.

"Maria, this is Angelica Williamson."

"Nice to meet you." A nod of the head, a cascade of straight black hair, glittering, shining with health and vitality. "Would you like a drink?"

Cheryl glanced at Bruce, caught the merest hint of a nod, and said:

"Thank you. I'd love a coffee - black, no sugar."

"Won't be a moment."

The moment lasted forever. Talk went on around the table, deep technical film making talk, moving on from points of view, depth of field and associated subjects, to grain and quality of film types. Bruce listened patiently, a small smile troubling his lips. Harry paced the room, restless, animal like.

The coffee came. Cheryl took it with a smile, not wanting to interrupt the discussion.

The longer they talked, the more she could rest, try and unwind the complexities of this situation.

I've been here before. In a fantasy or in a parallel world, somewhere, sometime. Let's think of it as a dream; it's easier.

It feels like a dream; these are people I've seen in dreams.

Cheryl shook her head. It was all too confusing; too many people coming and going, the busker look-alike, the beggar woman here in reality, serving coffee. Where did Harry and Joe fit into all this?

"Angelica, would you like a tour of Oxford?" Joe was languid, nonchalant, almost too foppish to be true. It had to be an act. No one was really like that in real life.

Is this real life?

"It's dark -" she stopped herself. If a tour was on offer, why not take it? Answers might come with the ride. "I'd love to."

"Good. Gordon, you don't mind if I remove Angelica from your presence for a while?"

"Of course not, Joe. I can get on with other scenes, the ones with Maria and Meredyth, while you're gone. I can't use Angelica yet anyway, she's badly marked from yesterday."

"Good idea - ever the film maker. Ready, my dear?"

Gordon did have a camera here, and was filming. It was a continuation of the day before. Cheryl struggled to get to her feet from the deep armchair, straightened her clothes, nodded at Bruce who smiled and said nothing.

Joe spoke to the entire room.

"We won't be long."

He took her arm, led her to the door and courteously indicated that she should go first to the car. It wasn't as luxurious as Bruce's Jaguar, but comfortable enough. Cheryl snapped the seat-belt into place, looked out of the windscreen, felt rather than saw Joe adjust the mirror before starting the engine.

"Do you like Oxford, Angelica?"

"I don't know, I've hardly seen it." Except in dreams.

"Let me show you." The car swept away through darkened

63

roads lit by pools of orange-yellow light. Cats slunk along pavements, their eyes green in the headlights. A dog paused, looked at them, and went back to scavenging.

Dark streets gave way to bright streets, to shops illuminated with spotlights, to warm inviting pub windows. Joe smiled at her in the half-light.

"St. Aldates." The darkness of huge buildings leered at her, much as the trees did on the journey there. Traffic lights winked, told them to wait, told them to go.

"High Street." Lined with shop and window-shoppers.

"Magdalen Bridge." Beneath it the darkness of inky water. The bridge, newly cleaned and restored, gleamed in the streetlights.

Round a dark roundabout with a strange building in the centre, back across the bridge, back into light and elegance.

Cheryl stared, wishing she could get out and walk, wishing she could experience the city for herself.

Wishing she knew whether it had been Julian she had seen, walking across the bridge, staring down at the dark water.

Wishing she were free to walk the bridge with him, and look down at the dark water.

Wishing the ache she felt deep inside could be assuaged with an ordinary vibrator.

6.

"Excellent. She's willing, she's a true submissive, she'll be long-ing forever to repeat that experience. Let us hope it is denied her!"

"Why - ?"

"Some questions are not to be asked, Slave!"

"Sorry, Master."

"Now, that task is done. But you have one more to do. Go and write another memo. Now!"

7. Memo.

What is the appeal of leather? Its flexibility, its toughness, its sensuality? It is all those things, but it is also the basis of a lot of my fantasies. A length of leather strap, maybe 3" wide, and maybe 2/3' long to wrap itself firmly and stingingly hard around my cheeks. My vision here is of being restrained, helpless as always; that's the key to my feelings! Being helpless and having to take what you give (is that why bondage is verging on the illegal all the time, because it's so exciting? Because believe me, the moment I bring the bondage element into the thoughts, the sweep of adrenalin triples).

So there I am, being thrashed with a leather strap. How many times is a thrashing? Six, ten, twelve, twenty - more?

Excuse me -

Went away for a quick spot of hand relief - aided by my capable vibrators.

I offered a writing magazine a 16 page booklet on writing erotica. The editor phoned, asked me what it was about. He immediately came on heavy, talking about it, saying 'God, I wish you were here now', then suddenly changed tone completely and started on about the leather strap his ex-wife used to thrash him with. And then tried to give me orders over the phone, and offered correspondence and discreet telephone calls - no way.

What is the appeal of leather, and why does the strap or tawse so thrill my very core? Skin on skin? And how often shall I experience leather at your hands, oh Master?

Part 4.1.

A game.

The playroom has changed now, from upstairs to down, from daylight to no natural light at all, from white walls to brick and dark red, from relative ambience to brooding sensuality and menace. A room designed and worked on together. Just another task, just another chore in a day. Creating a dream place for others to use, and now, to use themselves.

A game.

Ordered to the playroom to choose an implement, to stand holding it, to decide how many to take with it and to worry whether the amount was too many to take or too few to please.

Shivering with apprehension, sweating in the closed atmosphere of the airless room, standing clutching a flexible cane, counting strokes in the head, wondering whether to kneel, stand, lie down. Training overcame in the end, falling to knees, holding the cane as a supplicant would, choosing an amount in the head and staying with it, awaiting the turn of the handle, the click of the lock, the physical presence in the room.

"Well, have you chosen, slave?"

"Thirty, Master."

"Good. Very good. Any less and I would have doubled it, any more and I would have called it bravado."

And thirty were given, whipping hard and cutting fierce, burning hurting bruising damaging, causing tears and sobs, fighting to stay down to take the chosen amount.

Then it was over, somehow, and the words were said, the words which had to be said:

"Again. Get me another one."

2. The File.

Name:	Williamson, Angelica Roxanne.
Address:	17 Brewton Road, Gorling.
Occupation:	Model.
Date of birth:	21.12.1958.
Place of birth:	Waltham Cross, Herts.
Education:	Select girls' school.
Married:	William Coram Stanton.
Children:	None.

3.

Candle flame burns tall, reaching for the sky, as tall and as slim and as flighty as the passing passionate moment.

As tall and as slim as the woman the words reach out to, a woman who bends like the flickering flame when the breath of life reaches it, a woman who cares but wants to dare, a woman ripe for reaching for.

Angelica Williamson.

Angelica Stanton.

Angelica, Angelica, Angelica ...

4.

"Come on, lazy-bones! Let's up and go!"

Another day. Angelica stretched and sighed, heard music dancing in her head and dismissed it. Enough!

Was this the day, the space of daylight formulated and wrapped around in the strait-jacket of hours minutes and seconds, when she would have the nerve, the unadulterated sheer guts, to open the glass door and climb the stairs to -

What?

'What' was the thing which kept her awake at nights and tormented the empty hours of the day when she had nothing to do but watch trainee models stand and pose as the guy with a camera for a face told them to stand and pose.

He didn't really have a camera for a face, she thought, as she roused herself for the morning swim, the morning cycling, the morning routine to keep a body in pencil-slim state. It wouldn't do to be out of shape when training others who were in shape.

A body empty enough to take the whole Atlantic Ocean and still leave room for more. The filling of that space lay behind an innocent glass door.

The water slid past silk skin, much as she imagined Bill's

fine upstanding cock slid past her silk skin to touch the nerve endings and send her grasping for his shoulders, back, cheeks, anything to draw that cock deeper and deeper into herself; knowing what she really needed, unable to ask for it, unable to express it, longing and longing and never able to say why.

In the sauna, steaming, allowing her mind to wander, Angelica came back again and again to the innocent glass door.

It had been many years previously when William had come home with a catalogue; a little sheet of paper, black and white, folded over, full of titles such as she had never seen nor ever dreamed. Titles which spoke of pain, ropes, rubber, domination and secret pleasures. With a great sense of naughtiness, of illicit deals, they bought postal orders and sent off for the books. Bought the books but never ventured to try anything out, leaving it to talk and dreams to send the libido surging.

Those books still loitered in the drawer under the bed, loitered with intent to arouse, inflame, incite, and create fantastic fantasies which lingered in the mind for many a long hour, day, week and even month after the book had gone back into its secret retreat. What dark thoughts lingered in that drawer? What exciting prospect raised its head among the pages, once pure plain paper and dark dark ink coming together to produce the words to create an explosion of sexual activity?

The books led to magazines, photographs to spark desire between two people. Led to secretive looking-over-the-shoulder visits to Private Shops where magazines could be bought, where videos sat on shelves, innocently displaying a naked spine which concealed more than any clothing ever could.

Where she went wearing a headscarf, shades and ghastly pink lipstick, disguising the body with bulky clothes and shapeless coats.

Where she went in the thrill, the secret desire, that someone somewhere might recognise the long and oh so elegant nails, the shapely ankle, the smooth walk, the many things she thought shouted 'model!' to the world. That the world was uncaring and uncouth enough not to see was not a problem;

they would, given time. Had they seen her, they would have their own thoughts of what she, so innocent, so blank faced, so bloody suburban, was really like in bed. A tigress, a wild abandoned woman. Why else would she creep like a convicted shoplifter through the door? Oh, the door - the door -

The door to a new world.

Time passed. So much time, when the skin grew loose and the hair grew short and highlighted. When the make-up took a lot longer and the hemlines went up and down like a teenager's emotions. Somehow Angelica stopped modelling and started to teach modelling. Somehow the faces before the camera got younger and younger and looked like fragile flowers in a hot-house environment; one touch of real life and they shrivelled and shrank into ugliness. Somehow life slipped away and the candles on the birthday cake grew less as the years grew more.

Nor was she alone in the battle of the ages. William's hair began a retreat, the waistline fought a battle with the clothes, thought of pension came before thought of penis.

And the store of books mouldered.

Comes the big Four Oh, the turning point of a woman's life, the make or break. Every cliche in the book and a few yet to be written burst forth in her mind, in her soul, spoiling her sleep, coming between the painted face and the painted glass reflecting it back. Ever looming, stalking her through the eggs at Easter, through the daffodils and dancing catkins of Spring, dogging her heels along with the dog primroses.

Comes the time when she realised the firm who supplied the books had moved - right into her town.

Angelica stopped dead in the street, aware a baby buggy had crashed into the back of her legs, ignoring the stinging sensation of metal on skin, the trickling feeling of runs in the tights, deaf to the curses of the young mother and the postman with his large bag trying to get past.

What did they do up there? What secrets did they have up there? Did they all walk around wearing - what? Gorgeous fetish gear? Leather, spikes, rubber, PVC. Did they leave their breasts uncovered? Were they - ringed? Did they - carry whip marks? Did they give whip marks? A thousand thoughts in a single second crashed through her mind, leaving her dazed, shocked, dizzy with lust and aching desire.

Who worked up there? Came next, the secret thought, the wondering as she finally galvanised herself to move, made her feet step one and then the other, childlike, heels striking thoughts into the unwelcoming flagstones.

It is hard to concentrate on flippant, giggly girl models when your mind is in a strange building; one she could not envisage, but could build rooms in her mind ... rooms containing -

Over lunch she watched the slimmer's mayonnaise ooze seductively from between the slices of slimmer's bread, drank black tea feeling virtuous and hating it, feeling sexy and not able to do anything about it.

Then, with time on her hands, she went back to the empty studio, stark lit with floodlights and spots, with drapes and silks, cushions and luxury. Angelica sank down in a corner, leaned against the wall, gave herself up to a fantasy.

Walking along the road, heels tapping, unhesitating, pushing open the glass door, entering the tiny foyer, climbing stairs, to hear the sound of laughter, of chains clinking, of cries as leather met skin. Reaching the top of the stairs to find the girls, all young, all pretty, all busty and everything she was not, wearing nothing more than leather skirts, open weave tops, stiletto heeled boots, wrists encased in cuffs, necks encased in high stiff collars. To see one knickerless girl bent over a desk while a man, a tall, dark distinguished man, wearing leather trousers and waistcoat, white shirt and bow tie, directing a cane with fearsome expertise to lay line after quivering line on the white/red/lined cheeks presented to him, while another answered the phone and talked dirty to the customer.

Replace the knickerless girl with herself. Replace the girl on the phone with herself. Place a finger where it would do most good -

70

5.

The best of fantasies pall after a while, the most exciting of feelings need a lift. Angelica knew somehow she had to get inside that building; to find out for herself.

One hot summer day she decided. First, a discreet phone call: "Do you allow visitors?"

The throaty laugh, the virtual giggle: "Of course."

Second, the moment of truth, the day when no music was allowed in the head, but a determination to Do It; to walk in there; to see the magical goings-on for herself.

Dressing with care in a sombre suit of dark blue, light blue top, silver chain, the 'business woman at large' look. A jacket to conceal the beating heart so wildly leaping within the chest. Oh but they would be big and busty. Oh but they would be young and pretty. Oh but they would make her jealous.

But she still had to go.

Up two steps, into the tiny foyer, hand on the wood, afraid now, but going ahead with it. Climbing the stairs, hearing voices, a phone, the rattle of a typewriter. Ahead of her, a glass wall. Behind the glass someone moved.

Stopping at the doorway, looking in, seeing -

"Oh my God, Pat! Fancy meeting you here!"

"Angelica! What're you doing here?"

The pleasant 'but same age as me' face of a long time no see college friend. Disappointment like a sickness in the stomach. Ah, but the ledgers and cheque books on the desk shouted 'accounts'. No, they wouldn't have some bimbo with big tits to do the books! They resided in the other parts of the office. But it wasn't polite to rush away, to go nosing into other rooms, to search for the delights she was sure were lingering there, if only she could find them.

Small talk, ten minutes, fifteen minutes, catching up on history, face flushing as she realised this was THE office where the books came from. The woman behind the desk knew her name, knew she was a customer, knew her secrets ...

71

Pat getting up at long last. "Come and meet the others." Angelica getting up, stretching long supple limbs, pretending to be pleased to have found an old friend, and not anxious, willing, desperate to go look in the other offices.

Pat introducing her. "There's Jo on the phone and Donna, she does the post."

Jo was middle-aged, grey haired, smiling around the receiver, talking in the husky almost laughing voice Angelica had heard when she called. Donna was 17 going on 15, chewing gum and packing books into envelopes at the same time. Both were fully dressed in ordinary office clothes.

Even as she allowed her disappointment to register, a man came down the stairs, a man wearing an ordinary shirt and ordinary slacks, calling for Jo. He saw her and smiled.

"I'm Chris Donaldson. And you are - ?"

Pat introduced them. "A customer. This is Angelica, we've known each other since college!"

"Pleased to meet you, Angelica. Pretty name."

"I feel so naughty coming in here! But you're all so normal! I thought you'd be wearing fancy clothes and cracking whips!"

Chris laughed. "Disappointed you, have we? Sorry, it's a normal working office. We just publish books, you see."

"So I see."

"We do have a special room, though, come and have a look."

Climbing stairs, following the man, sensing his power, his strength, comparing him with Bill - unfavourably. This man, Chris, stop thinking of him as 'this man' she scolded herself, was big, big in height and width, big in personality and smiles. Beside him Bill would be a weakling.

A wave of a hand toward a half closed door.

"There's my partner's room, he's not here today. This is the dungeon. A dungeon upstairs, we have to be different!" He pushed open a nondescript door.

A long narrow room, white walled, hung with boots, leather, bondage photographs. At one end a huge bondage cross set in a huge frame; a room to play in, a room to dream in.

"I thought it would be bigger." But why?

"Well, there you go, we have to work with what we have."

A smell of leather, of naughtiness, of erotic dealings, hung over the room. Angelica walked and touched, smoothed a patent leather boot here, a plaited whip there, touched the cuffs and collars, shuddered deliciously at the canes and paddles, aware all the time of the man in the room; of his presence, his power, his - maleness. Suddenly becoming embarrassed at her blatant sexual interest and trying to back out with dignity.

"I'd better go, I've taken up enough of your time."

"Well, before you do ... we were thinking of renting this out. Would you and your husband like to borrow it one night?"

"Could we?" The surge of adrenalin caused an instant, tiny orgasm. She prayed he didn't notice. It was followed, like a cold shower, by fear - What would Bill say?

'Do it!' a voice whispered. 'Do it now!'

"I'll tell you what -" Was he mind-reading or something? "We'll make a gift of it. Come with me."

The office was jammed with paper, box files, books, paraphernalia of a busy man who doesn't have time to tidy. The Mystify screen saver danced to the tune the computer hummed quietly to itself. Chris dropped into the large chair behind the desk and grinned at her. He swung round and tapped the keyboard. "What's your husband's name, Angelica?"

"William. Bill."

"Which is it?" the computer stopped its dancing, showed a business-like screen, edges and outlines, figures and symbols.

"Bill when we first got together, William now he's a successful businessman."

"All - right."

Words appeared in the outline, words indicating paradise, or as close as she thought she'd ever get.

Words appeared in ink on a sheet of paper to hand to William, promising the use of the dungeon to William and Angelica whenever they chose.

She went cold and hot, then cold again. Another orgasm

staggered toward her briefs, stopping only when it met the resistance of her tightly pressed thighs.

Again, as if he was reading her thoughts, Chris said quietly:

"We're not kinky here. We're ordinary people living our lives, indulging in a bit of fantasy along the way. It's a fantasy business. We make it sound sexier than it is."

"I can see that. I was very disappointed when I came in!"

"But we have to be careful, you never know who's going to come in. We've already been raided twice. We don't want to add to our problems!"

"Of course not. I just didn't -"

"Most people don't." He held out a hand as she struggled to get up, clutch her bag, not crush her new found freedom certificate - passport? "Come and see us again, but before then, let my secretary know when you'd like the room."

"I will. Thanks! Really, I mean it, thanks!"

"The pleasure, Angelica, is all mine."

6.

In the end, though, she couldn't bring herself to give the certificate to William. Somehow, the thought of her staid husband binding her tight with ropes, lashing her body with a crop or cane, hanging clamps and weights from her nipples, just didn't sit comfortably in her mind with the man she had been married to for so many years.

But the certificate burned a hole, a large hole, in her handbag and in her mind.

If she was honest, not only the certificate, but the man who had given it to her. He would have no compunction about sticking pegs on her nipples, in bringing a blush to her cheeks - both ends, in ordering her to obey his every whim. Fantasy surged. Fantasy took over.

"You're looking different these days." William remarked over the top of the paper. Traditional stereotype and there he was,

74

an actual living example.

"Thought I'd have a change," pushing at dyed auburn hair, twisting round in the chair to show off legs encased in patterned tights leading to hips encased in a shorter tighter skirt.

"Liked you better the way you were." And there it lay between them, familiarity breeding comfort and contempt.

It took a month, a long month of sleep-torn nights. Days when only sex interested her, whether through books or Private Shop buys. Evenings when only drink dulled the edges of desire, before she had the nerve to go back to that small, oh so innocent office and pretend to visit her friend Pat again.

Somehow she knew he would come into the accounts office (he did). Somehow she knew he would invite her up to his office (he did). Somehow she knew he would ask why she hadn't taken up the chance to use the room (he did).

"I can't offer it to him," she said bluntly, watching the calculating eyes above the smile, wondering what thoughts were going through his head. He put his feet up on the desk, tilting the chair back, every inch the businessman in his own private domain. "He would never understand."

"He used to buy the books."

"He used to talk a lot, but we never did."

"You may be underestimating him, Angelica, you know that."

"I may well be, but I can't bring myself to offer it to him."

"So, where do we go from here? You're frustrated, I know that, without you telling me!"

The words tipped out in a rush, so fast she was surprised he understood them.

"I want a session, a bondage and cp session with someone; with you perhaps. I keep fantasising about it. I want it, I need it, I think I'll go crazy if I don't get it!"

Silence, deep calculating silence while Angelica quivered inside with fear and trepidation, wondering if she had gone too far, blown it forever, lost any chance of ever finding out if she really really really wanted it.

Just when the silence was ready to snap - an elastic band

under too much tension - there was a knock at the door and Donna came in with tea.

"Thought you'd like this." The cups were messily put down, the girl departing in a cloud of cheap perfume and Indian wrapround skirt.

Angelica reached for hers, glad of something to do.

Chris continued with his calculating look. Then he spoke, suddenly, startling her so the tea jumped and almost splashed the new tight skirt.

"I could arrange something, if you were interested."

"What sort of thing?" Hiding behind sipping the over-sweet and over-strong tea.

"A session, just as you asked. Bit of bondage, bit of smacking, bit of fun."

"What about - ?"

"William? He could come if he wanted. I would suggest you might be better alone, though."

"Would you be there?" Note of desperation creeping in, something to cling to, wanting but scared senseless.

"Might be, might possibly be. Have to see what's occurring. I can never be really sure."

"I would go if you were there - if you did it." Reckless, throwing it all away for an evening of - satisfaction?

"I'd have to see. I'm making no promises, but I'll try. Is that good enough?"

"If it isn't you, who would it be?"

"Friends of mine who love to tie people up, they get a real thrill out of it."

"What would it cost ...?"

"Cost? They'd pay you for the privilege!"

In that moment, it was sealed and done. Angelica was committed, knew she had to go through with it, no matter what.

"All right."

"Good." The feet came down from the desk, the eyes twinkled, the hand reached for the Rolodex. "I'll make a couple of phone calls ..."

"As long as you're there -" one last cry for certainty.

"I'll do my best."

But she longed for reassurance, that it would be this man, this comforting individual, this solid masterful male, who would do the tying, the clamping, the hurting. Again it was as if he read her thoughts as he rummaged in a crowded messy desk drawer, pulling out a set of nipple clamps.

"Want them?"

"Well -"

"Tell me the truth."

"All right."

"Take the top off."

She slowly drew it over her head as he stabbed a firm finger at the phone buttons, cursing when the ringing stopped.

"Damned answering machine. Julian, it's Chris. Give me a ring back, I might have something for you." He put the receiver down and sat looking at Angelica. "Well, how do I put nipple clamps on you like that?"

She blushed and reached for the bra clip. Her shapely breasts sprung free. Chris leaned across his desk to fondle them.

"Nice. I like women's tits, they're so soft, so cuddly. And nice to do this to." he snatched up the clamps and swiftly fitted them, along with biting snarling pain that brought tears to her eyes. "Don't take them off until you get home."

Angelica nodded, unable to speak. Pain surged through her breasts, following every nerve track, every fibre of skin.

"I'll call you about the session."

"Th - thanks," muttered, stuttered through clenched teeth, not wanting to give way, wanting to look brave in front of the man she wanted more than anything.

"I wouldn't put the bra back on, not yet. Just the top."

But the top was distorted by the strange clamps. Angelica tried to hide behind her large handbag, carrying it under her arm. It was a small disguise but one she might get away with.

"See you soon." The smile was - victorious. A Master dominating a mere woman - again. Smiling through the pain she

77

nodded and tried not to cry.

Walking hurt. She had to negotiate a corridor, a flight of stairs, Pat's office, another flight of stairs, the car, the journey home, a lifetime of pain, of misery, of blurred eyes and of a burning deep, deep inside which said yes, yes, yes!!!

Music provided no solace for a mind racing with sexual innuendos. Music: so much the food for her soul, for her life, had nothing to say. The car stereo was turned off, for every note was being played on the nerves in her nipples, on the wires which ran from the breasts to the quim, which vibrated at full tension, which brought a screaming orgasm whilst sitting at a traffic light - to the puzzlement of the pedestrians.

Wet, drained, sore, smiling, Angelica stumbled into her bathroom to painfully, slowly, lovingly, pull the clamps from the swollen distorted flesh.

7.

It took three weeks for the summons to come; three weeks during which Angelica died a thousand orgasmic deaths, gave Chris the status of a super hero, wore out three sets of batteries, and cried herself to sleep five times.

William went on his own coddled, cushioned way without realising his wife wore wet knickers and a perpetual ache, without realising his luck could have changed and he could have risked dying with a huge smile and a worn out dick. No way could Angelica tell him!

The call, when it came, was abrupt and filled her with fear more than anticipation.

"Oxford, next weekend. Make some excuses, pack a small bag. You will be collected by car from outside this office at 7 pm Friday night."

"Will you ...?"

"Might be. Might not. Can't say. My wife has Friday nights booked up, usually. Is that all right? Can I tell them yes?"

"Yes," while most of her shouted no. But silently. So silently he could not and would not have heard it.

"Good. Nice to be able to do a favour for someone, and get in the good books of someone else at the same time. They'll love you. See you soon."

And he was gone, the phone dead in her hand, as dead as William's cock, but far more rigid than he had ever been.

Reliving the phone call, Angelica pinned down the one word which turned fire into ice.

Wife.

Why had it never occurred to her the man would be -

Married.

Children? Home? Mortgage? Not free and available to her? Why should he be?

Why had it not crossed her mind that a man like that would not lack for women?

Friday. Five days away. Five days to dream up an excuse, to buy new undies, to think herself into the role of submissive woman, for that was what she was going to be.

Married.

How stupid not to think of it.

But a man like that, running a business like that, with models and slavegirls and willing secretaries - who would have thought a wife would be in the picture anywhere?!

Wife - Domesticity.

It did not sit well with the image of the sexually active and aware person who handed out pain by way of nipple clamps without giving it a second thought. While she, the poor innocent who had accepted them, hurt for two days.

With more hurt to come - Exciting hurt.

Whether or not he was there. But of course he would be there, he wouldn't miss a chance of seeing the rest of her; seeing her spanked and tied, seeing her abused and hurt, seeing her -

Come.

William bought the 'old friend asked me to go on a shopping spree and stay the night' story. Angelica fussed over a bag without him seeing, wondering what to pack, what not to pack, both as important as each other.

She was outside the office at 6.45, shaking, white faced, scared senseless and yet riding an adrenalin high before a finger had been laid on her. Spent the time scanning the street urgently, looking for the reassuring bulk of the man she fantasised about, cherished, thought she loved - did she know what love was any more? But the street remained empty; full of people going about their lives, taking money from cashpoint machines, visiting the wine store, the newsagents, the ice-cream bar. People everywhere, window-shopping, gossiping, loving each other with hugs and stolen kisses. People everywhere, but the street remained empty of the man she wanted to see.

He'll be in the car, she told herself as the time grew closer to seven and he had not appeared. He'll be in the car which is -

A huge sleek Jaguar swung round the three way junction; a classic Jaguar, almost silent, immaculate. The man behind the wheel was immaculate too; block headed, cropped hair, cold face displaying absolutely nothing. The car drew to a halt in front of Angelica, the driver leaned over and opened the back door. Angelica was being invited to get into the empty back seat.

Disappointment cut her from breast to groin, a stabbing cut which threatened to sever her body into two parts and which stopped her moving for a moment.

He was not coming.

Reason asserted itself.

He was already there.

She moved forward, got in the car, pulled the door shut, settled back, and smiled.

Of course he was already there. The whole thing had an air of mystery, of conspiracy, of secrecy, he wouldn't be up front and obvious, seen riding in a Jaguar with her!

Night was fast coming in, streetlights already on, shop lights always on, house lights filling in the gaps here and there, glowing with warmth, friendliness, welcome. Behind a window here and there a figure moved, shadowy against the fabric, a person taking off a top, another doing exercises. Angelica's mind filled in the details of the ones she couldn't see, the many ways of coupling, the many ways of tying, the many ways of pain.

How many would she experience at Chris' hands tonight?

Oh for a drink! At times the urge to drink was overwhelming, to blot out thoughts, dreams which failed, desires which faded.

How the tyres ate up the miles! Even as she watched, suburbia gave way to London sprawl, to London high rise, to offices, banks, stations, pubs. Oh the pubs, where you could buy talk along with the drink, buy companionship for the time it took to eat a packet of peanuts, walk back into the night, be forgotten in the instant it took for the door to close on darkness and trap inside the warmth, the cosiness, the bonhomie which was as ethereal as the spirits themselves once opened.

A drink. Angelica's body screamed for a drink to calm the nerves which were raw with anticipation.

Anticipation changed to fear.

What if this was the wrong car, the wrong man, going to the wrong place? What if someone other than the mysterious Julian and the reassuring Chris were waiting at the house in Oxford, for surely it was a house they were going to?

Dismiss the foolish thought. The car had stopped exactly outside the offices, the man had opened the door only after he had looked at her ... but the fear remained, a tiny worm, a small doubt, a black smudge on the sunlit disc as an eclipse began to work its way across.

Dismiss, and dream. Think of Chris, of the hands, so firm, so decisive, the fingers so delicate as they reached out and implanted pain in the form of metal clips. Think of what Chris might possibly do to the slim white body now travelling at incredible speed and with incredible smoothness toward Oxford.

That part was right, at least. The signs said Oxford, and they had not deviated from the road. Not once.

Miles were lost in dreams, time was lost in sexual fantasy, Oxford was there before she could get her senses together.

The engine died quietly, giving up without a single protest, tired perhaps, after its long journey. Still the driver did not speak, but got out and opened the door for her, indicating a flagged path, an ordinary suburban door.

"Thank you." But it felt wrong to say thank you to someone who was doing no more than carry out orders - and what made her think that?

Before she got halfway down the path, before her knees gave out under the weight of apprehension she carried like Pilgrim's burden, the door swung open and a woman stood there, shriekingly elegant in a red wool suit Angelica knew cost hundreds just from the cut and the style of it. The black hair had been expensively cut, the makeup didn't come from the corner chemist. Angelica knew so much about the business, she could recognise class from halfway down a strange path in an ordinary house in Oxford. She didn't dare stop to ask herself why someone with so much London fashion sense and expertise would be here.

The answer may not have been one she wanted to hear.

"Welcome." But the voice did not welcome, it said 'who the fuck are you?' in the nicest possible way.

Or was that paranoia creeping in, as her clothes were not as good, as expensive, as dressy as this Scarlet Female ushering her into a hall which screamed for an interior decorator to take over, to strip the wallpaper, to replace the table and the old fashioned telephone, to scrape the debris of years from the place and restore it to glory - the way she wanted but could not with her own ageing face.

A door, a blank faceless door swung open at the woman's touch.

"Angelica Williamson," she announced with all the clarity of a butler calling her name at a high class dinner.

Four men turned as one.

Not one of them was Chris.

"My dear, are you really truly Angelica Williamson?" A limpid, languid, beautiful man with beautiful hands waved at her. "We have been calling all the stars of our film Angelica Williamson, and there she is, in all her glory!"

"I was hoping ..."

A man with designer stubble and very white teeth bustled over, all efficiency and lustful gleaming eyes.

"I was hoping too, and you are everything I hoped for. Come. Sit. We have a video to show you."

Angelica found herself sinking into a cheap worn armchair, found the men's eyes to be electric drills boring into her, finding her secrets and spilling them like wood dust at her feet.

She was numb and dumb, disappointment hurting worse than the first time it had scythed through her. This time it had killed her feelings cold stone dead.

As if they knew it, the men turned as one toward the large modern TV with its stereo sound and huge screen, where a film was beginning to unfold.

"I'll get drinks," said the woman in red to no one in particular. No one answered.

On screen -

A sweeping drive, raked gravel, no weeds, clipped bushes, porticoed porch. The back of a girl; slim, long black hair reaching to her waist, walking in heels which dug deep into the gravel, yet she walked with surety and grace. No bag, just well cut clothes moving around the well formed body.

As she reached the porch the door opened. No one there. She entered; the camera following her, tracking every move, darting here and there, showing money represented by oils, wood panelling as old as time, weapons on the walls, a suit of armour at the foot of the stairs; clichèd yet looking right in this setting. A huge mirror, she looked deep into it, the face ravishing as any seen on the cover of fashion magazines. Poise, class, all marked with fine cheekbones and deep brown eyes.

Her hair glittered under the lights in the hall.

Angelica sat very still. Despite her hurt, the pain of her disappointment, she was intrigued, she was imagining herself to be the girl, walking toward a fate.

"She approaches her Master as all slaves must, with perfect punctuality and total submissiveness." The soft voice from the beautiful man was low, counterpointed by the light, almost inaudible music welling from the tv set. The girl mounted the stairs, slowly, one at a time, pausing on each, adjusting her clothing, a flicker of apprehension spoiling the calmness and serenity of the face now and then.

Up and up, slowly, taking the camera and the viewer with her to that which awaited.

Along a long corridor, pushing open a door that swung back at her touch; silent, oiled, immaculate.

A huge room, panelled like the hall. A dark oak table, the camera rushing toward it as her gaze must have rushed toward it. On the table, nothing but the implements of pain; a heavy leather strap, a cane, a riding crop.

She stood in the centre of the room, hands clasped in front of her, eyes down, waiting.

The camera waited too, lingered on her, catching every quiver of her waiting body, as if determining every quiver of her waiting mind.

A woman finally appeared, wearing black leather and floating black chiffon. She approached the girl, tipped her head back, looked at her face and nodded.

"You'll do."

As if it were a signal, a man appeared; tall, handsome, distinguished, white haired and very much in overall control.

"You're here." As with the men in the room, it was a statement rather than a question.

The woman smiled. "She's here, and has done everything we asked, Philip."

"Good." The girl obeyed his gesture, walked toward him, and stood waiting. "Then we'll begin."

84

Angelica gasped as the dress was torn from the girl, leaving her completely naked and still submissive. The fingers crept closer, she was aware he found wetness. And was aware he smiled.

On the tv screen Philip picked up the leather strap and held it so the girl could see it. She was obviously used to this, for she walked over to the small footstool and laid down, positioning herself across it so her bottom was in line with the camera and with Philip's eyes. Smooth white cheeks, rounded, softly curving down to slender thighs and long shapely calves. White, but not for long. Almost immediately Philip cracked the leather strap down, leaving a broad band of red and bringing a cry from the girl. The woman took hold of her head in both hands, kneeling before her.

"Silence!" And silent she was.

The leather strap cracked down at least ten times by Angelica's count, her body jerking in sympathy with every blow the girl silently took. The girl got up after the tenth and walked over to stand in the corner, her hands on her head, her bottom blazing pain at the camera which had followed her there. It flashed back to Philip and his woman, deeply embracing and kissing before the lens.

"And we rush forward a little." The man picked up the remote control, and fast forwarded the film.

The girl was standing patiently, the camera recording the blazing cheeks. "You don't want to see all that, it's for us dominants to savour and wonder what we would do with cheeks like that, a submissive like that."

The tape stopped, the Play button was depressed. On screen the girl turned, walked over to the stool and dutifully laid down again. This time the woman picked up the cane; flexible, whippy, it flashed through the air and missed the girl by millimetres.

Then it landed for real. A white and then deeper red cut clear across the already punished cheeks. The girl wailed, and this time no one made a move to stop her.

"Do it again!" Philip urged the woman, who needed no real urging. The cane flashed again; another line, another cry.

"God, how does she stand it?" Angelica was hardly aware she had spoken, she was so engrossed in her empathy with the girl. Her own body was almost hurting.

"She can stand it - she's well trained." The man seemed to murmur into her ear, yet he had not moved from his chair.

The girl was caned again and again, maybe twelve times, deep burning cuts which left her sobbing and shrieking, but still face down of her own free will over the stool.

Then she got up and again walked to the corner, this time noticeably slower, and with obvious pain.

The man fast forwarded the film.

"This is what I want you to see," he told her. He stopped the film and set it to Play again.

The girl stood before Philip, waiting. He took the riding crop and with deliberate cruelty brought it down across the front of her thighs. The scream almost cut the air, it was so sharp, so shrill. And yet she stood there, scarlet leaping across the white skin, hands not even beginning to search for the pain to rub it away.

"Turn round." She turned slowly and the crop came down across the back of her thighs, bringing another scream to the sound-track, and another jolt to Angelica's body. Then the crop landed across the cruelly punished cheeks and jerked the girl into action. She got down on all fours, dropped her head onto her arms and presented the burning, obviously incredibly painful, cheeks to the crop, which landed over and over until she finally collapsed on the floor in a swoon.

Then Philip and the woman walked away, arms around each other, leaving the girl where she lay.

The film stopped.

"I happen to know that after that she became a slave. She scrubbed floors, made beds, dusted the place - all without clothes, without comfort for that thrashing. At the end of her time she left, wearing nothing but an old raincoat and a smile."

"How do you know?" asked Angelica, sitting very still, on the verge of orgasm, almost ashamed of her feelings. When had that happened? When had that built inside her? Did they know?

"Since you ask, Philip and Penelope are very dear friends of mine. Well, what did you think of it?"

"I don't know. She obviously enjoyed it, afterwards, but at the time -"

"At the time she suffered, as she should. All submissives should be made to suffer deeply. If the implement used doesn't leave a mark first time and every time you're not doing it properly, the submissive isn't getting it properly, and that will never do."

The man with designer stubble spoke for the first time in what felt like ages. "You came for games, my dear, are you still interested?"

"Yes." Angelica spoke without thinking, knowing her own body would have answered for her - had answered for her by almost throwing an orgasm at someone else's expense. But then realised that was what the film was about; to give others the thrill without going through it.

"Then we'll begin immediately, with something you have not had, I understand. A spanking. I'm asking if you agree, but if you agree, in future there will be no asking."

Angelica looked down, hesitated, and then nodded.

"Good. Then we'll start right now."

She got up awkwardly, walked across the room, and laid across his lap, face flushed, staring at the floor, aware of the hair over her eyes, wondering if it mattered that she couldn't see, that she felt silly and slightly afraid.

His hand appeared soft, manicured, pampered - but it stung. The spanking seemed to go on and on, far longer than she expected. It began softly, building to a rhythm of spanks covering all her skin. It stung and burned and sent thrills she didn't expect. There was no chance to cry out now that it was enough, that she wanted no more, for she knew Julian would ignore such a cry. Instead she laid as still as she could, absorbing the spanking, absorbing the feelings, the conflicting emotions of wanting it to be over, of wanting more.

Finally he sat her up and stared at her eyes, sparkling with unshed tears, flushed with the effort of being still.

"Well done." Said with emphasis on the last word, telling her he was pleased.

"My turn," said the man who had driven her there.

And for the rest of the evening the men took it in turns to subject Angelica to the tawse, the crop, a belt; anything they could find.

She found in the tears, the sobbing, the crying, that she didn't miss Chris at all; he would have merely been one more person to add to the pain going on in an innocuous house in Oxford.

They all took her home when they were done with the abuse. Took her back in silence and in combined, raw, satiated lust, to the town where she lived, even though she said she didn't want to go. She had told her husband she was staying away for the night and look - here was the bag to prove it. They left her outside the office where she had been collected with such high hopes and such overwhelming enthusiasm a few hours earlier.

A taxi took her home. She crawled into the back seat of her car in the driveway and sobbed the night away. Broken dreams, broken fantasies, she knew she could not handle it, that the pain had been too much and not for her after all.

In the morning she went back to the station, took a train to a nearby town, walked and shopped and forced coffee down her throat until it was a reasonable time to go home.

William hardly looked at her as she walked in, bruised, sore, battered, shattered in mind and body.

"Nice time, dear?"

"Yes, thank you."

"Good."

Somehow the weekend dragged itself by as only empty lonely weekends do. Somehow Monday arrived.

Angelica dressed in her very best undies and slip-on dress

and made her way to the offices.

He was there, smiling, cheerful, dominant. In a moment her decision to leave the whole thing behind was pushed aside. She saw nothing but the man, the one she desired so much.

In his office with the latch dropped, he asked how she got on, and she showed him her bruises.

"Sorry I missed it," he said, leaning back and looking not at all sorry, "but I was filming all that evening. 21 year old, look at this!" Flicking a remote control. Yet another video unrolled before her. 21 year old, body of an angel.

Telling her, without saying it, she was too old and too suburban for his photos and his life.

Told her, without saying it, that the dream had finally, totally, completely, irrevocably died.

8.

"It gets better all the time - filmed being beaten, while others look on. A true exhibitionist even if she's not a true, or even a pretend, submissive. It is enough. What would that staid husband of hers make of that?"

"She lost her dream."

"We all do. It's part of growing up. Perhaps now she will grow up. Did you not see that not once did she ask what they meant about Angelica Williamsons for the film? She is not Angelica Williamson, she is a Stanton. Has been for years. She was too busy being obsessed with her own feelings."

"You did well. It's not normal for a Master to praise a slave, but this time I will. You did well."

"I am glad Master is pleased."

"Fine - enough of that. Is there a memo?"

9. Memo.

Possibly for every sub and every slave, the cane is one of the supreme punishment implements. Whips and thongs, martinets and crops have their place, but there is something in particular about the sight of a crook-handled rattan cane, waiting. It looks spiteful, it looks savage. I can't describe what it is.

Caning takes place over a stool, over the arm of a chair, over the end of a bed, face down on a bed with pillows under stomach for height, or bent over touching toes. And usually the person being caned knows what they are to get. Six, twelve, eighteen, twenty-four; multiples of six. The sound of a cane, the weals produced by a cane, the sting, the thrill of a cane, is equal to nothing else. It is an essential if not totally vital ingredient of cp rituals.

So tell me, what would you give? And how hard?

Part 5.1.

A casual interlude, nothing big, nothing serious.

The massage done, he rolls over, sits up, allows her to wipe surplus oil from his body, raising his arms, his legs, to accommodate the questing fingers, the gentle roughness of the towel, the attention.

"Stay there." Curt words which carry a multitude of overtones. He goes to the box, pulls out a cane, a tawse, and the multi-thonged whip.

"Bend over. I know you have a chain on, I know they're sore, but I want the tits down on the table."

And she obeys, as she must.

"You've been itching for this for weeks." But whose fault is it if a slave is deprived of discipline and has gotten soft? Equally, if a Master is not inclined to discipline a slave and allows her to get soft, should she not be grateful for the non-bruised non-abused time?

No.

A slave does not remember pain, only that she experienced it. The actuality always escapes. The detail, the memory, is blunted and softened and left to become as limp as yesterday's celery left out of the water. She longs for the pain, the control, the tears, the whole sexual sensual exciting ambience and activity of the playroom. She longs, but dare not ask. Oh, her Master accuses her of whinging and whining, of asking without asking, but appears to secretly delight in her need, and openly delight in denying her the answer to her need.

Control. Denial. Abstinence from that which she craves; good for the soul of the slave.

But now it is to come, the pain she has longed for.

And it hurts more than she remembered. She pulls away, sobbing, longing for it to be over.

"You're out of practice." And indeed she is.

"Sorry, Master."

"You'll do. Go get her for me."

2. The File.

Name:	Summers, Gemma Therese.
Address:	The Sterlings, Furze Drive, Rivington.
Occupation:	Systems analyst.
Date of birth:	28.02.1957.
Place of birth:	Ongar, Essex.
Education:	St. Revers School for Girls.
Married:	Charles Nigel Monkston.
Children:	None.

3.

Candle stands tall and firm on its base, determined to shine but staying where it is, no drooping, no leaning to one side or the other. Firm, straight, determined.

Deep in the heart of the candle is its strength, its power, its means to an end.

Look at the candle, see its stance, see that it is determined even as the woman is ... the woman whose name is whispered into the ritual, the woman she has to draw in, ever inward, ever closer, moth-like to the flame -

Gemma Summers

Gemma Monkston

Gemma Gemma Gemma ...

4.

Clothes maketh the man, clothes maketh the woman too; power dressing gives strength, determination, backbone, call it what you will. It was enough to help drive Gemma from the junior level of the black glass tower, phallic-like in its height above all the others, to the executive suite where she could look down, literally and figuratively, on all those who tried to stop her rise.

The train huffed its way into the station, brakes screeching a protest as the buffers loomed before its blind face; buffers designed to stop it tearing a huge gaping hole in the platform.

Even as I tore a hole in the upper echelons of the firm, Gemma thought as she stepped down from the carriage, dutifully minding the gap and watching where her heel was placed, while smoothing down the creases in her power suit, all shoulder pads and haute couture styling. Every buffer they put in my way was out-buffered by me. I steamed my way through the lot of them.

Steam.

Once there were steam trains, once the station was full of dust, dirt, grit and the sweet-heavy miasma of coal fired steam which puffed and panted and hung over everything.

As power does in the glass tower.

Power almost palpable, almost tangible enough to cut with knives - the ones used to stab backs - almost solid enough to be carved up with the sharp words which cross the boardroom table at times, and handed around in chunks to those who desire.

There are power plays in every organisation, thought Gemma, watching an inspector pounce on an unsuspecting traveller and begin to harangue him over dropping a cigarette packet.

And consider this: the Inspector has the power because he wears a British Rail uniform, a suit, a covering which grants him authority he would not have in sports jacket and casual slacks.

I have power because the clothes I wear mark me out as a career woman, a high flyer, an executive, a woman who has arrived.

And she had, at Fenchurch Street Station, crowded with commuters as equally expensively dressed, all heading for their own high rise carrying their high rising wishes in briefcases of black, maroon, burgundy and darkest brown, all with shining metal clips and combination locks, carrying enough paper to carpet Fenchurch Street from end to end; platforms, concourse, rails and all.

Paper to do what? To open doors, open files, open negotiations, open eyes, open thighs ...

Where did THAT thought come from? Dismiss it instantly from the heart which knew no passion except that for figures and charts, knew no desire except to rise higher and higher in the hierarchy.

Rather like American cities, the City of London had no place to go but up. And it went up, in tower blocks old and new, in glass and steel, concrete and brick, creating canyons for the click of heels, rustle of suits and money, and the overwhelming cries of pure power.

The glass doors opened as Gemma climbed the granite speckled stone steps, opened for her and the flock of suited rooks who followed. I'm the macaw, she thought, I wear the colours.

They try, oh they try with their flamboyant ties, but the shirts remain prim and starched and the suits remain dark and sober. Only macaws can fly with colourful wings and macaws have large beaks and a nasty bite.

The elevator swept them up, up, up into the reaches of the elite, dropping rooks along the way to scurry to nests of partitioned open space offices; rooks with clipped wings, who would labour long and hard over PC's and modems, flashing figures and E-mail, and not one would take the regulatory ten minutes out from the screen every hour, for fear of incurring the wrath of the management.

Of me.

Gemma smiled secretly, silently, and malevolently. Oh such power ...

"Morning, Mrs Monkston." Gemma swept an all knowing glance from head to foot of the secretary she shared with two other executives, noting the Marks and Spencer suit, the chain store shoes, the careful hair and make-up, and smiled her approval.

"Morning, Jessie."

Jessie would do - for now. Later, when Gemma moved up another floor, the receptionist would be more expensively dressed and groomed, would treat her with deference but not subservience, would not be running scared for her job in a City where secretaries were twelve to the penny rather than two.

Gemma punched in her keycode and paused in the doorway to look at the room before entering; paused to savour what she had.

Her office mirrored her personality - stark, cold, hard. Stainless steel furniture, abstract stainless steel sculptures, hard edged stark abstract paintings adorning the walls. Desk swept clean of papers, notes, pens, or any other clutter. All she needed to attend to was in a leather folder squared neatly on the blotter, or stored in the memory of the PC which patiently sat awaiting her touch, her password, her active participation in its life.

Charles was so proud of his high-flyer wife. It would have been easy, so very easy, to have gone into the family business, to have been the bookkeeper, the accounts clerk. Oh, Charles had made a stunning success of his small engineering firm, turning it into a large engineering firm employing hundreds of people. Gemma was just very glad she was not a part of it, that she could be introduced as 'my wife, a systems analysis expert in the City, you know', rather than 'my wife, who helps run the business'. It just didn't have the same ring to it somehow.

What she had instead was a large expanse of carpet, a large expanse of desk, leather suite and marble coffee table, and a large expanse of wall in a place where space was money and money bought space. Hard bought, with nervous energy and tremendous determination. Hard won, but glorious in the owning of the acquisition.

With her usual swift energetic style of movement, Gemma moved around behind her desk, sat down, put her handbag safely away in the bottom drawer, switched on the computer and opened the folder.

And stopped dead.

WHEN WAS
THE LAST TIME
YOU HAD AN ORGASM?

The note was as crude as its message, scrawled with thick black felt-tip pen on torn, ragged paper. Everything about it enraged her; the shoddy writing, the awful paper, the words, oh the words, which struck so deep they brought out not blood but her actual life force.

Who could have been responsible for this awful practical joke? For surely it was a practical joke. Miss Marks-and-Spencer Jessie out there? No - she didn't even have the keycode for the security lock.

Ralph, the ever laughing joker of the firm, he could have found his way in.

The words were finding their way in.

When was the last time she had an orgasm?

Put it another way, what did one feel like?

The intercom buzzed urgently, three beeps, Jessie's code for 'answer-me-instantly-if-you-can-this-is-important'. Gemma closed the folder and pressed the button with a long, manicured, pale pink fingernail.

"Yes, Jessie ...?"

"Mrs Monkston, Clive said could you pop along to his office? He has some new figures to go over with you."

Anything was better than opening that folder and seeing those words again. Even sitting with Clive, the subservient creep who ran the other side of the office with a limp and languid air.

"All right, Jessie, I'm leaving now."

Plush carpet caught at her heels, the pale washed walls showed up the perfection of the dark red suit she wore, the snow white tie at her throat, the touches of gold, the expensively cropped gleaming black hair, subdued make-up - it was as if she walked with a mirror beside her, or in front of her, she was so aware of herself, her clothes, her grooming.

Her power.

The offices she passed were lorded over by her; she could look in at any door, dismiss whoever was behind the desk and then find a way of justifying her actions later. It could be done - it had been done - but tell no one of the secret thrills power gave.

Clive's door stood open, he was leaning over his desk, pointing something out to a thin elegant man wearing a bored but amused expression. Clive looked up as Gemma walked in without knocking.

"Ah, the lady herself. Gemma, this is Julian LeRanch, he's just visiting us for the moment, having a look round, deciding whether to invest in our newest project. Julian, this is Gemma

Monkston, head of our systems analysis department."

"Delighted, my dear." A touch of condescension, but the handshake was firm, the eyes calculating, the smile beautiful. An odd word for a man, but it suited this strangely attractive being.

"My pleasure," she responded, aware of the thrills his touch gave her. She sat opposite Julian and crossed her legs, aware of his gaze.

As the talk devolved into figures, strategies, business plans, forward movement and other standard business talk, Gemma found herself more and more attracted to the beautiful person. Tea was served in delicate cups on a silver tray, it all somehow epitomised the elegance of the meeting, which had somehow taken itself out of the standard business range and become something quite different.

Something rare, an experience to be savoured.

As rare as passion in a passionless marriage.

In the middle of a particularly complex set of statistic analysis, Gemma stopped, coughed and went bright red. She had just remembered when she had last had an orgasm.

And what it felt like.

She had just experienced one right there, in the office, under the shrewd all-knowing eyes of Julian.

5.

"Darling, do you remember the fancy dress party the Wiltons put on two years ago?" Gemma sipped sherry and eyed her ageing paunchy balding husband, wondering where the slim dark haired good-looking person she once married had gone to; it was as if fairies had come and left a changeling husband behind.

Charles grunted around the cigarillo he was lighting, and coughing over. "Of course I do. You looked absolutely stupid, my dear. I was positively ashamed of you."

"But when I got the costume, you said you liked it."

"That was before I heard the lewd comments from the men! My God, Gemma, it was awful!"

"Darling," Gemma was seriously alarmed. She put her glass down and went over to him. "You said nothing about this at the time, or since!"

"Didn't want to sound like a wet blanket, then or now. Is dinner ready yet?" A white flag offered, and taken. Gemma went to find out how the roast was doing. She went with a light step and a small, almost secretive smile. She had another weapon to hold over Charles, if he ever proved to be difficult over her work, or over anything, come to that. That outburst had told her a lot.

She had gone to the party as Miss Whiplash, wearing a revealing black leather basque, small wrap around skirt, high heeled thigh length boots, long black gloves and a small cape. She had coupled stark make-up with a severe hairstyle, carried a cat o'nine tails, and had all but stopped the party dead when she walked in. During the evening, flicking her whip at the men - and the women - she had experienced true sexual excitement for the first time since her honeymoon, and by the end of the party realised her panties were soaking wet.

She also realised at least two women at the party were willing to have the whip flicked at them, at least one other was openly eyeing her body, and 95% of the men would have laid down and let her stamp her high heeled boots over them. It was then, reliving the whole thing in bed beside a snoring Charles, that she had the orgasm. There was no way of knowing whether it was the thought of the submissive women, the lesbian or the wimpy men. She had absolutely no idea.

All she knew was, it was a delicious and delightful feeling, alone in her head with her thoughts, with her fingers, with her visions, with her fantasies.

It hadn't happened since.

It occurred to Gemma, as they talked their small talk over dinner, that from that time Charles had been oh so careful to avoid fancy dress parties, or anywhere there would be too much alcohol, anywhere inhibitions might come down and she might once again revert to the role of the Strong Woman.

Surely that was at the foundation of his dislike of her costume and role at that party.

Interesting thoughts.

They took her into a long leisurely bath that night, took her through the scented misted air into her dressing room and into her silk sheeted lonely bed. Charles had long since given up trying to sleep with her.

But tonight the bed was not lonely or cold.

Tonight she shared it with a beautiful man who watched her with all knowing eyes, just as he had done earlier. As if he knew she had come from a relatively lowly background, making the most of a paid-for education and scholarship combined, then clawing and fighting her way to the top, through the racks of Marks and Spencers clothes to the designer ones she now wore. Through the ranks of the junior executives with halfway important jobs, to the real executive power she had now with a very important job.

One which came with power.

Not quite the same power as standing before a cowering wimp of a man, clad in leather and holding leather, dominating by sheer presence.

Near enough, though, she thought, sliding into sleep. Near enough.

6.

Somehow Gemma was not at all surprised to hear Julian on the telephone a week later, and even less surprised to find him inviting her to a very special party. "A fancy dress party, my dear," he all but crooned down the phone in his elegantly modulated voice. "I'm sure you know exactly how you will dress."

And somehow that wasn't a surprise, either.

As promised, the ornately beautiful invitation arrived by courier, accompanied by a stark white orchid, which was a surprise.

There seemed to be undercurrents Gemma couldn't quite pin down; the call, the invitation, the fact he knew with such certainty she would know what to wear, the orchid, it all spoke of something outside her experience, and even more frightening, outside her control. It was disconcerting, to say the least.

Charles was taken aback at the invitation, shunning it instantly. That again was no surprise. "Go, dear, have a good time. I'll go to the Club that evening."

No hiring of costume this time, not with money to buy the real thing, to make it her, to make it a part of her. This time the boots were custom made to fit exactly, the leather bodice cut snug round her curves, of which there were enough to make it interesting. The cape was lined with red silk, the skirt wrapped sufficiently around to remind her of the first time, but the leather was softer, finer, intricately scored and patterned. She added a cat mask for her eyes, and went to a Country and Western shop for a real whip; tooled leather handle, long tapering lash, one which felt right, and which she cracked with impressive expertise the first time she tried.

The man was impressed.

"Don't get many ladies in here that can do that, love." He backed away in the corner, hands up in surrender. Gemma thought only half of it was show.

She deliberated for a long time over the acquisition of a collar, wondering if it was too slavish to wear such an item, changing her mind when she found one studded with spikes. No slave would wear a spiked collar, she decided, they needed collars with studs and rings, to which leashes could be attached, or ropes, or chains, or ...

Or -

That thought led down avenues she did not really want to pursue at this moment, but knew with all the certainty she possessed that she did want to go down those avenues, and she would go down those avenues, with someone other than Charles.

Where the knowledge came from, she did not know, but it was there, it was real, it was -

Needed.

The party was in an exclusive nightclub in the West End. Gemma arrived in time to see a wild haired, blank eyed blind man dressed in rough clothes, like a busker, being escorted into the club by a milkmaid. She carried a keyboard in her other hand. Gemma amused herself by thinking he was the entertainment for the evening, someone pulled in off the streets to play for a few coins.

She walked in the door, smiling coldly, looking for someone she knew - looking for Julian.

"Mrs Monkston?" A butler in full regalia, knee breeches, ribboned wig and all, bowing to her. "Mr LeRanch asked me to watch for you."

Watch for the costume, surely, for most of her face was hidden behind the sweeping black half-mask. She strode along behind the butler, which for once did not feel wrong, down a narrow hall and into the Club itself.

A confusion of noise, music, laughter and wine floated overhead, much as the steam had once hung over the Station, covering everything yet invisible. Laughing mouths beneath half-masks, heads nodding beneath wigs, hands groping beneath skirts here and there - the tone of the party was sexual, hidden and flagrant. Gemma felt completely at home.

Julian, wearing an immaculate 20's gangster suit, rose immediately she walked in and came over to take her hand, to kiss it in a most courtly manner and to guide her through the noise and crush to a small side-table. Gemma thought his gangster outfit most appropriate, although she would never have said so in a thousand years.

"I'm glad you could come."

"I'm glad I came." Fancy dress parties, in the lower social

scale, were tatty affairs, usually Vicars and Tarts, or your average pirate, gorilla, flapper; costumes raked out from some under used closet somewhere, or hastily hired from a local theatrical agency. When money was no object, the costumes became virtually real, everyday clothes.

"You are the only Miss Whiplash, I made sure of that."

Just what power did this man have? Gemma wondered, but would not dare to ask aloud, not under any circumstances. Money probably; money had more power than virtually anything, except positions in Government, behind the scenes positions in Government.

"Charles didn't feel like coming tonight." Gemma sipped the cocktail a waiter on roller-blades expertly slipped onto the table before scooting away, narrowly missing a Superman smooch-dancing with a Catwoman, both incredibly lean, both incredibly beautiful. It took Gemma all of five minutes to realise they were both women.

"Charles had no intention of coming tonight, my dear."

"Well, no ..."

"This is not his scene, not this mixture of outlandish costume and outlandish behaviour -" gesturing to a monk holding a tall drink crammed with ice and fruit. "Your husband is more suited to the afternoon garden parties where power is the aphrodisiac, not outrageousness."

"You know an awful lot about my husband." Gemma managed to make the statement sound like a question.

Julian laughed as he fitted a cigarette into a small holder, matching his costume with his accessories, but did not answer.

"Where are the host and hostess anyway?" Gemma turned around, revealing a lot of leg as she did so, bringing a young Greek god to her feet instantly.

"Madame, oh madame, you are so beautiful, so cold, so hard, so - oh words fail me! Let me worship you! Let this humble being kiss your boots!"

"Clear off, oaf!" Gemma kicked at his chest, sending him

sprawling in the path of the roller-bladed waiter, who with consummate skill, leapt the fallen statue and carried on his way. Gemma laughed, but the laugh did not reach her eyes. The young Greek picked up his laurel wreath and backed away, eyes shining with devoted love, his face expressing disappointment at not being able to serve his chosen goddess.

Gemma laughed again, and this time the laugh reached her face, animating it into even colder planes. She felt Julian watching her every move, every expression, felt he was pleased by her reaction, and was herself illogically pleased she had done something right.

How silly, when every move of every day is always right.

But this is different.

This is -

What is it?

Sexual power play.

People drifted by their table, stopped to chat to Julian for a moment, greeting Gemma and drawing her into their conversations. Food appeared, borne by the same roller-bladed waiter, whose territory appeared to be their side of the club. Laughter hung over everything, reminding her again of the atmosphere in the glass tower; all powerful, all pervasive, all knowing.

The music, which had been more background than anything, suddenly stopped, and a Gladiator leapt onto the tiny stage, causing all heads to turn. Gemma at first thought it was a good costume, then realised it really was a Gladiator, although she couldn't pin a name on the person.

Jokes, laughter, introductions, the party hostess was brought on stage, a truly glamorous Cleopatra, and the wild haired, blank eyed young man in his rough clothes was led onto the stage, his young milkmaid partner still clutching the keyboard as if it were made of gold.

If it was a costume, if he was pretending to be a busker, it worked.

The Gladiator carried the hostess off the stage while Julius Caesar announced the cabaret act.

Gemma had never heard his name, but knew she would never forget the music which began immediately, sending the entire Club into total, rapt silence. The wailing heart-wrenching music wove patterns of sadness and colour into her mind. The most unparty-like music imaginable, but it fitted this wild and beautiful group, who sank down on chairs and bar stools like flocks of drowned birds of paradise. All eyes turned to the stage, where the young man, head thrown back, played his music from the heart.

Between tunes, Gemma asked Julian who he was.

"Kester Reeves," he told her.

"Kester, what an unusual name!"

"Comes from 'Precious Bane', I understand. His mother was a devotee of Mary Webb."

"I've never read it."

"At least you knew it was a book, my dear - many ask who starred in it! The second hero of the book was Kester Woodseaves, as I remember it. Poor heroine had a harelip, and all the paranoia that goes with it, unlike you, my dear, with your cold hard radiant beauty."

"Thank you!"

"It was that which attracted me to you in the first place ..."

Interrupted by music, the strange conversation went on, Gemma remembering to thank Julian for the starkly beautiful orchid, he thanking her for her time and attention, "and the most delightful secret moment" in the office. Gemma blushed deeply. So he had seen, after all ...

When Kester Reeves finally left the stage, the spell of his beautiful music broke, the dancing began again. The dance floor became swirling tie-dye patterns created and broken. Julian stood up, suddenly impatient. He pulled back a cuff, glanced at a Rolex which was most definitely not in keeping with the costume, and leaned on the table.

"My dear, if you can tear yourself away from this delightful gathering, I have something which will please you immensely and give you great insight into yourself. Can you make a trip to Oxford?"

"Oxford? Why, I suppose so. Charles is -"

"At his Club. He won't mind, he expects the party to go on all night."

"Julian, how do you - ?"

"Hush. Come with me. All will be revealed."

"Oh my mistress, do not leave me, my heart will break!" The Greek god was back, imploring, gripping her boots with both hands, kissing her toes. On impulse Gemma brought the cat down hard across his back, making him howl and writhe on the floor, much to the amusement of the other guests.

"Begone, wretch! I have other places to go, other people to see, more important than you will ever be!"

Julian laughed. "Brilliant, my dear, a natural if ever there was! Come, the car awaits."

The dark avenging Angel stalked cold-faced through the colourful crowd, feeling ten feet high, feeling as if every person there had been reduced to the height and status of a Munchkin. Gemma Monkston had found her role in life.

7.

The Jaguar waited at the kerb, glittering under the streetlights, sleek as the animal from which it was named. Classic lines on a classic car. Julian opened the back door, Gemma slid in, immediately aware of leather and richness, of the feel of a car well maintained and cared for.

The driver, a block headed man with no neck, needed no instructions. The moment Julian closed his door, the car was purring into the darkness, predatory, eager, seeking out unwary pedestrians to devour with its chrome teeth and chomping wheels.

Gemma relaxed into leather upholstery as the night sped by the crystal clear windows of the car, a night starred with windows, shop displays, garage forecourts, late night corner convenience stores, chemist for the late night sick, and the homes, from small to large, each with their own secrets, their own burning ambitions, dreams plans and desires.

"What is it you desire most, my dear?" In the luxury of the car, Julian almost purred in unison with the engine.

"Power." She stared at the back of the block head in front of her, wondering who the man was, what he wanted out of life, did he enjoy being a driver, was it his car?

"You like my car." Julian again picking up her thoughts, turning them to suit himself.

"Yes, I do."

"It comes with the power, my dear. First you get the money, then you get the power to spend it as you wish, then you get the car of your dreams. This car, and Harry to drive it, is just one part of my dream, my living dream."

"I've asked Charles about a chauffeur, but he prefers to drive himself - he said."

Darkness now, the houses gone, open countryside. Now the window reflected Gemma herself, with the swept back hair and the stern look, the Gemma who was the only Miss Whiplash at the whole party.

And wondered again at the power Julian LeRanch had.

"Define power Gemma - you running the organisation?"

"One part of it, yes. The higher you go the more influence you have."

"Yes, true, but -"

"And there are other powers, aren't there? Like, controlling a man, making him do what you want."

"But that's new to you, my dear, your young Greek tonight was your first ever, I know that as a fact. It opened a window into your psyche, didn't it?"

Gemma glanced again at the block head, wondering at the silence. Julian saw the look and chuckled.

"Harry's been with me longer than anyone else, soul of discretion, silent as a cemetery full of tombs. You can speak freely in front of our Harry."

Gemma laughed, a little self-consciously. "You're right, I don't know how you know all the things you do -" blushing in the darkness as she remembered her orgasm, "but he did shine a large light into my mind. Many things fell into place."

"My dear Gemma, you are the rare one, a natural dominatrix. Many women think they are, many women act as if they are, but if a man had the nerve to stand up and take the whip from their hands, bind their wrists to the overhead beam and give them a taste of it - there would be far fewer so-called Dominatrixes about!"

A natural. Gemma swelled with pride, feeling the leather outfit become even more of a second skin as she did so. "Where are we going?"

"Oxford. I told you, didn't I? Did I not say I had something to please you immensely and give you great insight into yourself? All will be explained, in Oxford."

The lights bit into the darkness, chewed it up and spat it out behind them. The wheels flattened the darkness into the road as the car flew along the motorway, racing through lighted sections, unlighted sections, dug up sections and whole new stretches still unmarked by litter and fume-blighted plants.

Gemma allowed herself to slide into a semi-stupor, brought on by over excitement and drink. But never slipping so far that she was not very well aware of the intensely powerful feeling radiating not only from the man beside her but the one in front too.

"Here we are." Oxford walls sliding past the windows, walls aged by time and weather, by pupils and learning, by tourists and tv cameras. Oxford universities gave way to ugly suburbanitis, rows of blank faced houses, their only claim to individuality the different double glazing installed. Gemma curled her lip in disgust. Is this where the elegant Julian really lived?

They drew up outside an ordinary terraced bay windowed house that didn't even lay claim to a firm of double glazing men.

Gemma was consumed with curiosity and had to speak, her words sharp in the cold cutting frost-ridden night.

"Is this your home, Julian?"

"Oh my dear, of course not! It's a property I own, and use from time to time for - certain people. Come, I have friends I wish you to meet."

It was so nondescript as to be invisible. Which, Gemma realised, it was designed to be. Whatever nefarious reasons Julian had for needing a discreet place, he had certainly found the right one.

Trouble was, it disturbed her to think of someone so beautiful in a house this cheap and tacky.

Gemma took a fleeting second to ask herself when it began to matter where Julian lived.

"Angelica, this is Gordon, this is Bruce. Harry you know from the car. Gentlemen, this is Angelica Williamson."

"I'm -"

Gordon held up a hand, smiled through designer stubble, radiated calm and friendliness.

"Welcome, my dear. Don't worry about the name - every woman Julian brings here is called Angelica Williamson, regardless of who they are. Saves us remembering a load of different names. We guys find it hard to retain names."

Gemma smiled, while registering the pang caused by the words 'every woman Julian brings here'.

"Lovely outfit," observed Bruce, the twin of the driver. "Lucky old sod, having that in the car!"

"Can't see much when driving, old chap!" retorted Harry, but with a smile. He had seen Gemma get in and out of the car, revealing much, which was more than the others had seen.

"Well, is there no drink for the poor tired Julian? Where's Meredyth?"

"Gone to bed, thought you weren't coming, you're so late." Gordon poured a whisky and handed it to Julian with a small ironic bow.

"Party went on a bit, and we had to listen to Kester Reeves,"

Julian indicated Gemma. "At least our guest enjoyed him."

"Good job someone does, too gloomy for me," observed Bruce. "Well, let's get to it, shall we, give our visitor her surprise? He's in the next room."

"Go on through, my dear," urged Julian. "See what we have for you."

What they had somehow did not come as a surprise, but it was pleasant all the same. A young blonde man waited, naked, hands roped to a hook in the ceiling, feet shackled to rings set in the floor. He was gagged.

By his side was a table bearing a crop, a tawse, a cat and a cane.

For an hour Gemma amused herself with the various implements, stalking around the silent man in her imperious heels, finding out which caused the most reaction when applied in different places, finding out which made the reddest marks and provoked the loudest grunts.

At the end of the hour Gemma was dripping in perspiration and oozing pussy juice, and her right arm was tired.

The young man was covered from head to foot in red weals and marks, his eyes shining with adoration for his Mistress, his penis, against all odds, still standing proud.

The door swung open but no one stood there, an invitation to leave. Gemma dropped the cat she was sliding through her fingers and walked out. Whoever had decreed the session was over was exactly right; the fun had just started to go.

"Enjoy that, my dear?" Julian looked as if he had consumed half the whisky bottle while she had been otherwise employed. Gordon looked the same, Bruce and Harry were asleep in armchairs.

"Very much." Adrenalin still flowed. She rode the erotic high deep inside, realising how much of a thrill it had been for her. "I don't know who your victim is, but he took a lot, and still seemed to want more."

"A true slave, we found him specially for you, borrowed him from another dominatrix who is unwell at the moment and who didn't want her slave getting out of condition. You did her a favour."

"Glad to hear it. You did me a favour, Julian, I never knew it could feel like that."

"Good. Go let the poor chap down, Gordon, would you?" He turned to Gemma again. "I wonder what Charles would make of it?"

So calm, so casually said, yet it started a cyclone of feelings inside her. Gemma sat in the armchair, aware of sagging seat, broken springs, worn moquette, and resenting it even as she sat there; the chair was not good enough for her body.

"What has Charles to do with this?"

"Nothing - yet. I merely made an observation."

"How will he know?"

"Because I videoed it, my dear, the whole thing."

"How much do you want?"

"I will let you know."

An exchange so cold and sharp it almost hurt as much as the frost settling on everything outside, tingeing the overgrown garden with silver.

In the silence which followed Gemma remembered her childhood dream, how she would stand on the railway bridge as the train passed beneath it, covering her with steam, wishing with all her heart that when the steam faded it would reveal a new landscape, a new land, a new world for her to live in.

It never did. Each time the steam faded it left her just where she was before; in a place she hated with a background she hated and a family she hated even more.

The wish passed over her now, the wish that there would be something, anything, that would take her from where she was now; dressed in an outrageous dominatrix outfit in a seedy crummy house in Oxford, where she had been videoed having the time of her life with a young man, putting him through hell.

"Come, my dear, it is time I returned you to your home." He nudged Harry, who came to with a start.

Without a word Gemma walked to the door, slammed it open and stalked out into the coldness.

They didn't speak at all on the drive back.

8.

"Nicely done my dear, very nicely done. A turn around, but -"

"It was the only way to get her."

"Perceptive of you to know that. Well, well, a dominatrix in the making, but with a husband who would not approve. Nicely done. What secrets lie behind glass doors!"

"I am glad Master is pleased."

"You are a valuable slave. Now ..."

"Here it is, Master."

9. Memo.

Contrary difficult creatures, slaves. And submissives, come to that. The last thing we should want to do is annoy our dominants/Masters, for fear of bringing down wrath on our heads, and possibly a punishment more severe than we ever imagined. Yet - the thought of doing that is full of excitement and intense sexual pleasure.

One friend confessed that she had taken ten with a tawse and laughed, so infuriating her partner that he gave her ten real good ones in anger. Ones which left her tearful. And yet, she confessed to walking around all next day with a smug smile of satisfaction and a good feeling.

I've proved this myself. I asked my new Master what I must do, if anything, to avoid his temper. And yet at the same time, the thought of annoying him to the point when he will seriously punish me is fractionally more exciting than any other thing he has said or I have thought so far.

Why?

Is there a key to the slave's mind here? Is she looking for genuine anger, and if so, why?

Do I really want to see his face grow serious, darken with rage, see his lips harden into a line, see the eyes, normally so loving and soft, grow cold and hard? Do I want to feel the full force of his arm? I have no idea of what he would use to be really severe. Do I want to find out?

The gentle oozing of moisture from the secret valley right now tells me yes.

There is something about someone punishing you in anger, so very different from punishing you for pleasure. It adds that edge, that touch of danger, that hint of real threat that is somehow not there during the other times.

Oh, 99% of the 'other times' are fine, good enough for anyone; walking around with a mass of bruises and weals that would satisfy the most submissive of women! But to add that extra edge sometimes, just sometimes, gives a piquancy that is temptation itself.

And I do not understand why. All I can tell you is, it happens. It is a fact. I know it, I have experienced the thrill of anticipating it.

I seek it.

Fool, aren't I?

Part 6.1.

Will it ever end, and does she want it to?

Standing before a full length mirror, feet secured to ring bolts set in the floor at either side, hands captured in cuffs clipped to a bar suspended from the ceiling, arms caught in the tension-tight bondage he has created, winding the winch with its ear-cracking evil sound, notch by notch, until she is bow-string taut from head to heels.

She can look with teared eyes at the red weals running the length of her thighs, at the criss-crossing marks across her belly, at the cat thong weals left around her ribcage, the redness at her pussy. Were she able to turn, she would see the black bruises forming on her abused cheeks, where strap, tawse, and cat had met skin over and over again, for no reason other than he wishes to do it and she is glad to serve.

There are two places left, two unmarked pristine clear targets which even then he is tapping with the cane; testing, tantalising, tormenting. The pain, when it comes, is excruciating, but the scream is stopped by the impenetrable impermeable barrier of the ball gag thrust deep into her mouth.

Only when 12 clear lines stand out across once white orbs does he finally stop, does he lower the bar, unclip the manacles, undo the ropes, allow his slave to fold into a weeping, sobbing mess on the floor.

He stirs her with his foot.

"Go get the last one for me."

2. The File.

Name:	Hartman, Olivia Geraldine.
Address:	79 High Street, Vockston.
Occupation:	Sole proprietor of New Age shop.
Date of birth:	25.12.1957.
Place of birth:	Cheshunt, Herts.
Education:	Standard schooling, no outstanding achievements.
Married:	No.
Children:	None living.

3.

Candle burns down, sad, weary, charred wick rests on melted wax, flame burns still, but flickering now, weakening; too much heat, too much light, too much energy given out to stay strong any longer.

And as the candle weakens and slides, so the woman sobs into her pillow as she too weakens and slides, the woman who cries, the woman who is reached by the candle power.

Olivia Hartman

Olivia Hartman

Olivia Olivia Olivia ...

4.

Another day, another dollar, or in my case, pennies. Olivia sighed, pushed her hair back yet again and unlocked the door to her shop. Damn wind was determined she would eat hair today. Perhaps she should have it cut after all; a bob, a wedge, a nice tidy perm, a middle-aged lady set of waves and curls, anything the wind could not play games with every day.

No way. With the door firmly closed, the wind was trapped outside where it belonged, and her hair could lie down around her face and on her shoulders, where it belonged, and all was right in the world.

Well, no, it wasn't, but -

There was a day ahead, a day of sitting behind a counter, watching the browsers to make sure no rose quartz or other items were slipped into pockets and went out the door for free. A day when genuine seekers came to buy and to talk.

And perhaps a day in which there would be time to think, and in the thinking, decide.

Olivia hung her coat on its hook, took the hairbrush from the drawer and savagely dragged it through her long dark hair, taking an odd satisfaction in the sensation of pulling, of untangling the knots the wind had made, aware that when brushed, her hair swung around her face in a dark cascade of rippling waves. No, no haircut. That was one decision she had made, and the shop not even open yet! That boded well for the rest of the hours stretching ahead of her.

Lonely hours. Empty hours. Oh yes, there were books to read, people to serve, stock to dust and rearrange, salesmen and reps to see and order from, accounts to do, all the many and varied things everyone had to do when running a business, whether it involved other people or not.

It didn't fill the lonely hours.

And the lonely hours were all her own fault.

5.

Once upon a stack of lonely dreams ago, there had been a woman, innocent, alone, working in an office. A little shy, a little mouse, but with the violent passions only a young woman can harbour when not able to release them onto a waiting man.

Her life was simple; a mobile home, single, small, easy to keep clean, not very demanding in its decor. A small car, fit to drive off the mobile home park and down into the town, maybe a mile, maybe a mile and a half away. A small town, small-minded people shopping in small windowed shops, buying small goods for their narrow and constricting lives. She had more than two letters at a time; the local Post Office viewed her with alarm, the lady in the shop on the park viewed her with suspicion. 'You get more mail than anyone else!' comments handed over with the letters too big to be pushed through a letterbox, as if it was a crime. The comment was too big to be ignored. Noses twitched, eyes flicked, ears pricked, but little Olivia lived alone and lonely, chaste and celibate.

Olivia with pen-friends to bring a hint of the outside world into her staid life. Olivia with her letters, and her secret dreams.

Beneath the chaste bed, turned-down sheet, folded blankets, quilted cover, frilled pillowcase, lurked darkness - in the form of books and magazines - with stories which filled the mind, photographs which filled the eyes, advertisements which filled the fantasies, thoughts which filled the long dark lonely hours.

Poor innocent Olivia, struggling with a finger in the dark

hours, longing for sleep and fighting the burning desire which consumed logic and sensible thinking, burned it up and threw it away in the age-old drive for procreation.

Or plain old-fashioned satisfaction.

Charity work filled some hours, planning bring and buy, jumble sales, choral evenings, sponsored this and that, committee meetings with little men in little cardigans, big in their little world.

"All present, Mr Chairman?"

"Yes indeed, Mr Secretary. Shall we begin?"

And the Secretary would read the minutes of the last meeting, minutes laboriously transcribed by Olivia from her shorthand notebook in which she frantically scribbled to keep pace with the discussion ranging around the table as to the wisdom of doing this and that.

Then they all went home, secure in the knowledge that all was right in their neat world.

While Olivia went home, knowing no one had even noticed her existence after the decisions were made, tea drunk and cups washed and stacked away.

The sad thing was, not one man on the committee looked anything like the hero of the books, or even came close to the vision Olivia carried in her head.

For the books contained secret stories and secret photographs of the wonderful world where men were masterly and women got punished for misdeeds, punished by hand, slipper, brush, ruler, tawse and cane. Where the delights came from the glow afterwards, and the joy was in the power of the man to make a woman do what he wanted with a mere look and stern words.

The dreams went on for a long time; dreams contained in brown envelopes which arrived at the shop on the mobile home park where she collected her mail. Dreams which could not become reality until the right man came along.

He walked into the office one day, smiling, chatty, overly friendly, but for once Olivia did not recoil from the advances.

He came again.

And then again.

He told her to let down her hair, and she did.

He told her to wear bright lipstick, and she did.

He told her he would like to sleep with her, and she did.

The tongues wagged at the small firm, of course, as she changed her hair, clothes, cosmetics and lifestyle, as the too young old maid receded and a modern day lady emerged, content to be wanted, content to be 'the other woman', content to take what she could when she could.

Content, because he brought the books alive. No tawse for this man. No school cane with crook handle. No frills attached - but spankings hard enough to make her cry, slipperings to add agony to agony, bamboo sticks to make her cry out and want to run.

Content, because he brought out the love she had long hidden, long crushed, inside her. Love she thought was dead, charred, gone.

She gave up the committee, gave up buying books, lived for the days he came.

Lived for the man she happily called Master.

More changes. A mobile home has thin walls, they needed privacy, she moved.

A small firm has tongues that wag, she gave up the job and did what she had always wanted to do; opened a small shop.

She gave up wearing tights and bras, petticoats and hairbands, looked the role she had given herself; woman in charge of New Age shop. There long flowing hair looked right, wild colourful clothes looked right, open toed comfortable sandals fitted the image.

And he, the man who instigated it all, seemed pleased with his protegee, called her his wonder girl, made sure she wanted for nothing in the way of advice, encouragement and handyman help to put up shelves, create display areas, make her little shop a little haven for all who cared about natural things.

Olivia felt she could not ask for more; everything appeared to be wonderful. How could women not want to be slaves when it felt like this?

Then it changed. Oh how it changed, so slowly, so carefully, so insidiously Olivia didn't notice it for a long long time. How she was slowly coming completely under his control. How she only ate what he wanted her to eat. How she did only the things he wanted her to do.

Still she fought her feelings. Still she loved with an overwhelming, passionate, all consuming love that knew no boundaries, knew no logic, knew no sense. She gave and continued to give.

Even when he loaned her to a friend for a night, a friend who tied her hand, foot, breast and belly to a bench and left her there for three hours, only releasing her to mercilessly use a cane on her bottom, the only part of her not marked by rope.

Even when he laughed when she begged not to be loaned to anyone else again.

"It is part of being a slave," he told her, dismissing her complaints with a wave of his hand, and a dismissive tone which warned her not to pursue the subject. "You can always refuse," he added, and she began to cry at the thought.

How many sleepless nights did Olivia have then? Turning over the thoughts again and again - longing to refuse, desperate not to be handed over to someone else, but knowing that refusing meant the end of the relationship. A slave only refuses an order once. If she was a willing slave, who had entered into the relationship of her own free will.

Olivia could not decide if she was a willing slave, or whether her own obsessive love for the man had led her into slavery.

Could not decide whether she would not mind the slave status disappearing, whether she was tired of doing as someone else wanted and not what she wanted, tired of wearing what someone else wanted and not what she wanted.

Could not decide whether she had, after all, despite everything, experienced a deep secret thrill at being loaned to someone else, a plaything for an evening, an unpredictable and exciting evening.

Could not decide.

As the door bell tinkled and her first customer/browser of the day came in, Olivia sighed, switched on her little portable radio and sat down to watch the newcomer.

"Today the Government announced it had decided -"

"How much are the bottles of oil?" asked the young earnest looking woman wearing the mandatory yin-yang necklet and friendship bands. "I'm just beginning to get interested in aromatherapy."

"They're all different prices." Olivia sighed inwardly, secretly.

Then she would have to decide whether to extend the range of oils in the shop.

In the whole mixed up chaos of her life, that was probably the easiest decision of all.

6.

A party with a difference. A big difference. No mixing of groups here, no circulating with glass in one hand, plate in the other, cigar clutched between fingers holding the glass, cigarette ash dropping to the floor, aromatic smoke clinging to the clothes of those who did and those who did not take in the narcotic nicotine. No silly small talk, no name dropping -

Oh so very different.

"Buy black lace briefs," she was told. "Put your name on them somewhere, somehow, label, embroidery, pen, whatever, just make sure your name is on there somewhere." So she had, inking her name carefully on the washing instruction label. And had gone to the party wearing black: stockings, undies, dress, choker, shoes.

The woman who met her at the door was also in black, but how different this stylishly starkly beautiful being was! Night black hair, expensive clothes, equally expensive cosmetics, all worn with a style and panache which made her look as if she had just walked off the cover of Marie Claire or Elle or some-where. Even Harpers Bazaar would not have been reduced by her reproduction on the cover. Olivia felt drab and cheap in comparison.

"I'm Meredyth," she said in a husky, low, stern voice. "Did you follow the instructions?"

"I did."

"Come in." Just inside the door Olivia met warmth, soft music, chatter of voices - all male, she realised. She also realised Meredyth was standing by a small table graced with pairs of black lace briefs.

"Add yours to the collection," Meredyth said in a tone which stood for no hesitation. "Then go in. Not a word, mind - just stand and wait. Later the men will choose their partners for the evening from these," indicating the briefs, "then you will be free to speak. If you're lucky, your partner may even let you eat!"

Olivia slipped her briefs off, aware they were carrying her scent, wondering if that was how the men would choose, sniff rather than look at the names, but didn't ask. Some things were better left to be discovered later.

"Go on in." The smile was real, the perfume subtle, the sexual allure tangible.

Olivia found herself in a large, elegant room with soaring ceilings, arched windows, fine reproduction furniture, thick carpet and expensively dressed guests.

The men wore fine dark tailored suits, standing together like a murder of crows, sending covert glances toward the women. They in turn were wearing black, but did not seem to be together; aimlessly standing around with glass in one hand, clutch bags in the other, missing that essential item of social gatherings - small talk. Forbidden speech until chosen, they were no more than living mannequins.

Six men - five women.

Olivia stood equally awkwardly, aware of the sherry Meredyth had given her, aware of her knickerless state, knowing the others were the same, wondering if they felt as awkward, as naked as she, aware she was the sixth woman, wondering which of the crows would choose her - and why.

Everyone was a stranger to her, everyone was looking at her, no doubt knowing who her Master was, no doubt knowing she was a slave under orders - thrillingly under orders, for there was no doubting the trickle of dampness from an excited body.

There appeared to be a signal given, one she missed, for the men moved as one toward the door, clustering around the table, picking up the intimate garments and yes, sniffing them, before exchanging them for another.

Then briefs were put into pockets, the men came back, calling names as if the women were dogs, ready to respond to a call.

"Rosalie."

"Jennifer."

"Tanya."

"Olivia."

"Annette."

"Theodora."

Olivia found herself approaching a limpid elegant man with sharp black hair and dark eyes. He took her hand in his white manicured one, kissed the back of it, murmured: "I'm Julian LeRanch," and indicated a seat at his side.

Olivia sat, nervously twisting the glass by its stem, around and around, watching the amber liquid slip with oily ease down the sides. The same ease with which this Julian negotiated cigarillo, brandy and small plate without dropping anything, even ash.

"Would you care for something to eat, Olivia?"

"I would, thank you."

He inclined his head toward the buffet table.

"Help yourself."

As she crossed the miles of soft carpet, Olivia reflected how much of a slave she had become, that she had not attempted to

121

approach the table without an order allowing her to move there. She realised, with a shock which reached the wetness, that the other women were the same.

She returned to the seat with a small plate delicately heaped with triangular sandwiches, a sausage roll, a few peanuts and other eatables snared swiftly from the table, for fear of being away too long, for fear of offending before the evening began.

"Am I permitted to know what this evening is all about?" she asked, aware that women had begun to speak, that the murmur of voices around her had increased in volume, much as her desire had increased. Whoever this man was, he had a powerful air which attracted her, drew her, moth-like, to the flame of his dominating presence.

"Yes, of course. I take it you came in innocence, as all these women did?"

"Yes."

"It's a competition, in a way, but with a difference. You see, when Masters own slaves, they know them, know their limits, know their abilities. But a new slave is just that - an unknown quantity. This evening is for Masters, to prove our ability to read a body, to know when limits are being reached, to show how clever we are, in short."

The laugh was cold, cruel, the eyes hard in the impassive face. Olivia felt ice sweep through her, right down to her core, where it met the burning centre at the apex of the thighs, where it met the heat and was dissolved in love juices which flowed urgently. This, then, was her fantasy come true, the one she had never dared admit to her Master, never dared admit even to the mirror; the fantasy you only took out in the dead hours of the night when little moved but an urgent heartbeat, when a car was a torment of sound tearing past the house, when night killings and rustling undergrowth held their own dark mysteries.

To be truly used.

To be no more than a thing, an object, lower than an animal.

She came back to her surroundings; the party noises, women

122

laughing, men eyeing the women speculatively, Julian's appraising look.

"You have no objections, I take it?"

"Of course not."

"Your Master said you were up for anything, to use his somewhat strange expression."

"I am, if he tells me to."

"My dear girl, he didn't tell you about this. You were entitled to refuse if you wished. His only orders were to come to the party."

"Did you choose me by scent or name?" Olivia asked with a small laugh. She had to know. She didn't know why it was important, only that it was.

Julian smiled, a real smile which touched the sloe black eyes; it changed but did not lighten them.

"I wondered when you would ask."

"You knew I would ask."

"My dear, you would not be a true female if you hadn't. I chose you by smell."

"Thank you for telling me."

"Not at all." He stood up, holding out a hand to her. "Come, the others are leaving for the dungeon."

The first shock came when Olivia found it was a real dungeon, not a made up room. Actual thick stone walls, heavy ironwork, a brazier in one corner, a rack, pillory, stocks, everything a torturer could want. Everything else he could want was hung around the walls.

The women became silent, the men alert, almost evil in their intensity.

Every woman was securely gagged.

In silence, apart from a roll-call of names and the sound of leather on skin, the evening progressed.

During that evening Olivia 'won' the tawsing competition, outlasting her opponent by three strokes of a heavy three-tailed tawse which had blazed its way across all their cheeks without diminishing once in its power, its ability to cause burning agony.

She 'lost' the heavy paddle section by two strokes, Julian withdrawing her at the end with a signal she did not see through streaming tears.

She 'drew' the strap section by equalling two other women, all determined to outlast each other if they could, but having to give way to the wishes of their masters for the evening, whatever their wishes.

She 'won' the martinet section, Julian using it freely on her back, thighs, legs, belly and breasts as she swung helplessly from a hook set overhead, her arms stretched, eyes closed against the pain which threatened to send her into oblivion. But he knew just when to stop, just when he thought she could not really take another stroke.

Julian won the evening for himself by allowing Olivia to be whipped longer than the others, some of whom had been withdrawn by their masters anyway.

Only when the decision to award the evening's performance trophy to Julian did Olivia allow the blackness to overtake her, to slump senseless on the St. Andrews cross, to escape the tormenting agony at long last.

7.

"My dear, I cannot tell you how wonderful you were." The Jaguar purred contentedly along suburban streets, winding past sleeping houses and slumbering offices, past ghost haunted stations and half-lit shops. Olivia stared out at the nightscape, wondering why she had gone ahead with it, wondering if the fantasy would ever be the same again. She felt every line, every teardrop, was aware of red-rimmed eyes and swollen lids, of movement hurting, of a great sense of euphoria, adrenalin rushing here there and everywhere, turning her on. She could have happily accommodated everyone at the party, man or woman, and gone on to look for more. Even the bullet headed man sitting silently behind the wheel looked attractive to Olivia right then.

"It was so cold," she said suddenly, the first words she had spoken since the gag had been removed and she could, if she had wanted to, scream.

"It was meant to be."

"It was as if we were nothing. Lots in an auction. Dummies at bayonet practice. Nothing."

"To us, slaves are nothing, my dear. Mere animals to be used, abused and discarded as we see fit."

The cigarillo appeared as if by magic, was lit, was glowing, and then ash in a moment.

Much as her dreams of slavery were in ashes.

"I thought I knew what slavery was like."

"You have only just begun."

"I want to go further."

"Take your time, let your wounds heal first."

"No. I know what I want. Will you accept me?"

"I might."

"That's good enough for me."

"No sureties, my dear - I have others, you know."

"I'm sure you have." But Olivia had decided. She nestled in the corner of the rich upholstery, smelling money and power; the two irresistible motives for anyone doing anything.

And wondered how she would tell her Master.

8.

"Most satisfying, yes, gratifyingly satisfying. She is caught now in a web of her own making. She is caught with her own sticky strands of desire."

"How did you get that on film, Master?"

"The entire party was videoed. In itself it will make a worth-while film."

"But the woman ..."

"Will now leave the man who brought her into this, and he in turn will search high and low for another willing slave. He will be without for some time to come. And she, poor fool that she is, will find being a slave to Julian to be an entirely different scenario indeed!

There was no trip to Oxford this time."

"There did not need to be. The party video will be perhaps 1½ hours when edited down, oh more than enough for what I need!"

"And what it is you need, Master?"

"Your memo for the day, slave. I trust you have not been so busy with spells you have not found time to write one?"

"There is a memo, Master, as always."

9. Memo.

There is a big difference between a submissive woman and a slave.

This is something many dominants do not appreciate, for a start, and some submissive women do not appreciate, for a second.

The difference is this:

A submissive will seek to submit to cp, even some role-playing for a time. They seek it for physical and a small degree of mental pleasure. Then they revert to 'normality' and resume their life.

However, if you walk away from a session, no matter how painful, feeling dissatisfied, feeling that there could have been more, then you are of slave mentality and need the deeper commitment that slavery brings with it.

Basically, the difference is this:

A submissive will take what she wants to take.

A slave delights in taking it because it gives her Master pleasure.

A submissive will perhaps extend her limits for her own

gratification.

A slave will expect her limits to be stretched for her Master's pleasure.

Now this difference is the reason I, for one, tend to fall out with many dominant men. They come on to me, thinking that, like all submissive women, I will fall to my knees to obey their every wish, allow myself to be spanked/whipped/whatever. And I don't, because they have not touched the chord in me which responds to their domination. I laugh instead, which infuriates them. Then I become tagged as arrogant or difficult. I'm neither arrogant nor difficult - I am merely a slave who has been searching endlessly for the right Master. Until now.

To enter into a Master/slave relationship means commitment by both parties to exploring the needs and wishes of both parties, to finding out what the slave can do to please her Master, and what the Master can do to ensure a contented and happy slave. It involves a deep emotional commitment; there can be nothing cold about such a close trusting relationship. It involves a degree of role-playing into which both freely enter.

My leap from submission to slavery came from reading an article by a true slave, a dear and close friend, who set out to show the males among the readership of a cp magazine the essential difference, having no idea of what light she would shine into my dark corners. It is yet to be discovered whether any males benefited from her words, but I did! It was like a huge spotlight being turned on in my mind. The reasons why I had left cp sessions unsatisfied became crystal clear; I had gone there for my own gratification, not to please another. There had been no compulsion, no obedience ordered, no serving of a Master. Just two people and some discipline.

It wasn't enough then and it wouldn't be enough now.

The path to slavery is a long slow one. It involves looking deep in yourself, it involves much thought and exploring of your own psyche. It isn't for everyone. It is for me. I know it in the total giving which is the normal way for me to carry on.

127

Giving him pleasure, be it with daily letters, small love gifts, an unexpected telephone call, the simple act of buying stockings when I do not normally wear them because I know he will like it, without him having said so, fills me with happiness.

To know I shall be compelled to obey his every command, no matter how light or severe the forthcoming punishment will be, is a source of intense sexual pleasure. To serve my Master is all I desire.

Submission has long since been left far behind.

10.

"Master, as I have pleased you with my spells, my enchantments, dare I ask for the motive behind it all?"

"My slave, you may. Now it is done, now the films are edited and copied, are even now winging their way to their destinations, you may ask.

"Long ago, in a select school where only the best or the rich went for their education, there was a boy; shy, out of place, lonely, seeking approbation from his peers and receiving none.

"He stayed out of trouble, worked hard, had good results, pleased all but the spiteful seniors who wished him to disobey, to rebel, to give them cause to punish.

"They were deprived of that pleasure for a long time.

"Until the opportunity came, most fabricated, which they seized. Six boys, six strokes of the cane.

"It took five to hold me down.

"The strokes burned deep into my mind. I vowed revenge, and vowed it would be terrible.

"Years passed, years when such incidents would be long gone from most adult minds, but in mine it burned on, an injustice, a spiteful act from those with money on one who did not.

"I had money then, a lot of it, and power to go with the money, real power, the sort which changes empires. It took

128

years of work, of struggle, of deprivation, of scheming and dealing, but I did it.

"And having done it, I sought my revenge.

"Through your occult skills, my beloved slave, six women trapped on video doing the one thing their loving partners - those six boys - would hate the most.

"Five women starring in 'The Many Faces of Angelica Williamson', one woman starring in the S&M orgy of the year, and leaving her Master right afterwards. He was the sixth boy, the one with the cane, the one who delighted in it.

"Six videos are on their way to six addresses.

"My revenge is complete."

"Master - the men, Julian, Bruce, Harry, Gordon, the woman, Meredyth, the house in Oxford -"

"All bought and paid for by me. Julian is an old friend, I owed him a favour, he has a new slave, should he care to take her. The others were bought, as the house was, as the equipment was."

"It has cost you so much."

"And it will bring me in so much, slave. Did you think I had not covered that one, too? The S&M Orgy is on its way to Holland right now. the Angelica Williamson tape will follow in a week or so, when the video sleeve is printed. The whole of Europe will be able to buy their indiscretions, the whole of Europe will delight in their submission."

"So my task is done."

"Only insofar as I no longer need your candle spells - at least for a while. I do need your services and your continued devotion. I also need the memos. Is there one?"

"Of course, Master ..."

TWIN PLEASURES

by

JOSEPHINE SCOTT

A. Annie discovered sex.

CHAPTER TWO

Cool September evening, hint of violet sky, touch of melancholy riding the breeze. A night for lovers.

The garage held tools, cans of oil polish, rags and the accumulated debris of years of storage, enfolded by the rough scent of dust, petrol, spider, a silent gathering, mice droppings, and the aroma of disuse.

A silent gathering: Anastasia and Tamasine and Mark Richards, waiting for the church clock to strike the half-hour, the moment Anastasia had decreed it would begin.

Tamasine hung by her wrists from the overhead beam; strong enough to raise an engine, well able to support a slim girl who would not fight or shout. In the naked bulb her naked body gleamed white and ivory, shadowed and lit, crevices and mounds awaited, begged wandering fingers and hands. Anastasia: half naked, breasts bouncing loose inside a skimpy top, erect nipples showing clearly, skirt on the floor in the grease and oil. Mark: good-looking and well developed, muscles rippling under tight ripped sleeve tee shirt, held himself rigid, fighting back need. He knew this body, this girl, wanted her now, wanted so much the pressure became a pain.

But Anastasia's domination was so supreme he waited, not knowing what he would be asked to do, only knowing he would do it.

The church clock began to strike 8.30. Annie at last stirred.

"Here, Mark." She handed him a small whip, coiled and waiting, evil as a small snake. He shook out the coils, and swung it round a few times, unsurprised, ready to carry out her will. Tamasine fought the silencing leather gag.

The garage walls sharded light from racked tools, the shadow of the whip screeched across them, the sound of the lash meet-

135

ing Tamasine's body loud enough to thrill them all. And again, sharp lash on soft body, cutting across her back, her thighs, the tip catching a breast, navel, cheeks exposed and waiting, the lash found them, wrote red lines of pain and tomorrow's bruises.

Tamasine spun and turned, her body crying for freedom. Her eyes showed pain but also complete submission to both her twin sister and the man who held the whip. Had she been free to shout she would not have asked for mercy.

"More, Mark more!" Anastasia excited, fingers massaging her own clit. "Come on, whip her properly!"

Mark stopped and looked at her, saw the fingers busy inside her briefs, shook his head.

"Damn it, Annie, why am I doing this and not that?"

"Because I damn well said so!" Her face contorted with pleasure, orgasm shaking every part of her body. Tamasine hung, watching, envious, aching and longing for her own release.

"I'm stopping." Mark threw down the whip in disgust, lifted Tamasine and set her on the oily patch.

"Damn it, Mark, we weren't through!"

"We were, Annie, and if you feel anything at all for your sister, you'd know it too." Annie went over to Tamasine, untied her hands and then the gag. Tammy's eyes were flooding with tears, she spat leather out and stormed:

"What were you doing there?"

"Enjoying myself, sis, weren't you?"

"No, I wasn't!" Tears flowed, Tammy shuddered a few times, grabbed a dusty rag and wiped her face. "I hate you sometimes!"

"No you don't, kiddo, no you don't, because I know what you're feeling - I get double pleasure."

Tammy held out her arms, turned under the unforgiving light. Lines wove around her, uneven, here light, here dark, here on the verge of blood-letting, here erotic, and here sheer pain.

"Look at me! You let him do that!"

"Yes, and you loved it!"

Mark looked at them, disgusted, ardour cooled, determination flowing away into the dusty surroundings. He pushed open the huge metal door with one easy movement.

"I'll see you girls another time. You're perverted, that's what you are!"

The garage door slammed shut. Annie burst into giggles, after a moment Tammy started laughing hysterically with her. Clutching one another they shook with merriment, picked up the whip and scattered clothes, switched off the light and went back in the house.

"Oh what a picture! His face!" Annie wiped her eyes and started laughing again. "What a wimp!"

Tammy nodded, serious now.

"We need to find a real man, Annie, someone who knows what they're doing. I mean, look at me!" Mark had been the most inexperienced of all the men they had coerced into their garage, and the most disappointing so far.

Annie looked her up and down.

"We do need someone else - you're right, kiddo. No pleasure in that lot, was there? Oh the occasional one, here," tracing a line across small round cheeks, "here," a line from shoulder to waist.

Tammy nodded. "Those were good, but - we asked too much of him. I hope we haven't lost him."

"Mark? He'll be back. Where else could he get such adventures? Come on, we'd better get to bed. We've a long day tomorrow."

Climbing stairs, feet hissing on thick pile carpet. Tammy pulled a face.

"Fancy spending a birthday being nice to all those simpering aunts, uncles and grandparents! If Granny Webster gives us a fiver, it'll be hard going to say thanks, Annie!"

"I know, I know, but enough small bits of money add up to something worthwhile, kiddo. And - who knows what a birthday might bring?"

"Bath salts and undies," moaned Tammy, leaning against the

bathroom door, absorbing coolness. "I'm gonna shower, Annie."

"Sure thing. Listen, see you in the morning, kiddo, and - Happy birthday in advance."

"Happy birthday, Annie."

"I bet I can guess what you bought me."

"What?"

"Undies."

"Wrong first time." Tammy laughed, gently touching her lines. "You'll have to wait for the morning to find out."

"OK. Want to know what I got you?"

"New collar, I suppose."

"Metaphorically speaking, my dear twin, metaphorically speaking. Like me, you'll have to wait for the morning to find out. Night kiddo, and thanks."

CHAPTER THREE

Q. How old were you when Annie discovered sex, as you put it?

A. Seventeen. I knew something was different about her, we - talk to one another, you see, - I mean -

Q. Telepathically?

A. Yes, that's right. Annie thinks at me and I think back. We're that close. So I could sense a restless feeling coming from her to me, a - sudden awareness of her body and what it could do. She had this boyfriend at the time, Niall - Niall Hodgson. Right dish he was, every girl in the school was after him, but Annie got him. And like me, had him just where she wanted him too! He spent his lunch money on her, took her places, did things for her. And he sent away for things for her, got them delivered to his home address so our parents wouldn't find out.

Q. What sort of things?

A. A small vibrator at first. Annie used it a few times, showed me how it worked, offered it to me, but I said no. Then she said it was too small, too thin, it wasn't doing what she wanted, and got Niall to send off for an eight inch big one, and used it to get rid of her virginity. Told me no man was going to take that from her. No man could say 'I had Anastasia Webster first' and get away with it. It gave her the edge over men, which is what she wanted.

Q. What happened next?

A. Annie realised she was what is called a dominant. Niall was getting catalogues for her, sex toys and clothes, and she was turned on by pictures of women in black leather with whips and things, and fantasized about it. Niall was a wimp, despite being the hunkiest guy around school, and before long Annie had him tied up and was whipping him - Niall Hodgson! The school would die if they found out! His parents would too. And as for all his adoring fans -

Q. And you?

A. With the history of domination I'd suffered from Annie, I had to be a submissive, didn't I? So before long Annie got other people, boyfriends who adored her, to hurt me. Wimp Niall started it, got a ping-pong bat and spanked me with it - me bent over the workbench in the garage.

Q. Did you like it?

A. No, I hated it. But Annie insisted, and as she got my feelings, she knew underneath my hating it was the feeling - a tiny feeling - of pleasure. I got that from obeying, rather than from being hurt.

Q. Your parents never found out?

A. No, they nearly always go out Friday nights to some dinner or party or something. The garage would be empty, we would ask someone round, and Annie would devise a session. Sometimes it would be me getting it, sometimes Niall, who was a real submissive man! It moved from ping-pong bats to heavier things; a riding crop can hurt a lot, I had to be tied down for that. We had this one guy, Mark, who

139

liked fucking and would do anything to get into Annie's pants. He used to bind me, wrists and ankles, large knots, take ages over them, making sure the knots were large enough for me to see so I could know for sure I'd never get out. Rope round and round my wrists, my ankles - I can see them now, those huge knots, can remember the edge of the workbench cutting into my stomach and breasts. Then he would beat me with the riding crop, whatever amount Annie said. Six, twelve - once it was eighteen times. I think I'd displeased her over something. If I made too much noise she'd stuff an oily rag in my mouth. Later we got a leather ball-gag.

Q. What were your feelings about all this?

A. Getting to like it, as Annie knew I would.

Q. And Annie?

A. Annie loved it all. You see, it was me being subdued, punished she'd call it, and she would have my feelings coming through, mixed-up with her feelings of domination, her having ordered me to take it, her being able to watch me take it, and my pleasure at being ordered to take it. Twin pleasures, she called it.

CHAPTER FOUR

"It isn't often I get the pleasure of photographing such lovely girls." Above the clink of glasses and scrape of silver on china the sound of legs snapped on the tripod. Professional smarm, thought Tammy, sitting on the bench waiting patiently, watching the photographer set the equipment in the centre of the floor and begin to fix the camera onto it, saw her father watching, knew he was envious of the equipment, knew he would be useless if he had any of it himself. Father could just about manage the disc camera, but even then regularly cut people's heads and feet off.

"I know, we're proud of our girls." Father being predictably father. Tammy smiled blandly, wondering where Annie was, if she, Tammy, had to be the focus of all the attention until the moment came to press the shutter. Aunts, uncles, and assorted relatives stopped eating and drinking, admiring again her pose, her charm, her 18 years sat firmly on blonde head.

"OK girls?" The photographer waved to Annie, summoning her from a corner, deep in conversation with an uncle Tammy hardly recognised. Annie smiled, hurried over to the bench and sat down.

Look at us. Anastasia and Tamasine posing on a bench covered in deep red velvet, wearing identical dresses, long flowing skirts, full billowing sleeves, scooped necklines, one dress white the other black. Waist length straight blonde hair shining in the lights the man set up. Patiently re-arranging us, a hand laid here, an arm lifted there, crossed feet in black patent and white patent shoes.

Finally - look this way! Family and friends gathering round the perimeter of the room, smiling, chatting, complimenting aloud. Worse than blowing out the candles and having everyone applaud. What for? We've been doing it for 18 years! We ought to be able to do it by now, two of us, together, breathing as one.

"Eighteen day!" he shouted, making them both smile, snapping the moment instantly and forever.

"Again," moving their heads, one looking to one side, then the other, the shutter clicked, recording it. "Now with the proud parents." Father crossing half-mile of carpet, no doubt feeling every eye on him. Mother glancing his way, approving for a change, and they sat down, mother with Annie, father with Tammy, the way it had always been.

The photographer pushed them here and there, arranged a skirt, held the shutter release, looking for the smile, the look, the movement that would captivate the customer.

Family held its collective breath, waiting -

"Don't they look alike - parents and daughters?" Granny

141

Webster, tone whining as always. The shutter clicked as she added:

"What a surprise, as they're adopted."

Silence instant and deafening. The photographer knew something profound had happened but didn't know what it was; uncles and aunts responded, shocked, embarrassed, nervous.

Adrienne was furious, blonde hair shaking with suppressed rage, eyes black with the effort of not throwing a scene right there and then. She contented herself with hissing to the speechless Martin:

"Your damned mother!" Rubbed Anastasia's shoulder. "We'll explain later," said through clenched teeth.

Annie grabbed Tammy's hand, squeezed it, whispered: "I think I always knew."

Tammy nodded blindly, shocked to her core.

Her parents were not her parents.

These relatives were not her relatives.

"Well, if that's the photos ..." the photographer trailed off, knowing the session was lost, began winding-on the film, putting the lens cap back on, unsnapping the camera from the tripod; a backward run of everything he had done earlier, anxious to be gone before anything else exploded into the afternoon.

They were left sitting alone, still the centre of all attention and eyes.

"I'll see to your bill -" Martin tried to speak but the sound was lost in the bubble of voices and over loud laughter trying to cover the embarrassment of a family skeleton suddenly tumbling from the closet into the centre of the party.

Tammy heard her father trying to rescue the situation, turned and saw Granny Webster sitting, gloating in her wheelchair.

"Hey, kiddo, what do you think of the pressies?" Annie caught hold of Tammy's arm. "Didn't know you had such an eye for a good gift!" Fingering her present from Tammy, a heavy Celtic pendant, worn in place of the gold locket their parents had given them, whispered: "We'll get the truth later,

142

won't we?"

Tammy avoided the subject, repeated her statement of the morning, shaking her wrist to make the bracelet jangle. "I like yours a lot." She looked around the gathering, saw cousins and offspring running here and there, precariously balancing glasses of squash. Mother would be having heart attacks by the second.

"It isn't every day we get to be eighteen, and old enough to vote." Annie grinned, smiled at Uncle Phil passing by. He stopped.

"Along with everything else you can now do legally." Uncle Phil, the one she had to watch. Smooth. Sharp. Barbed like the wire which separated their garden from the farm next door. Uncle Phil meant hands that wandered when near ladies. She had no intention of letting him anywhere near her, even if she had just discovered it wouldn't be illegal.

"Oh, thank you for the tokens." Annie, rescuing Tammy from an embarrassing silence. Why couldn't she recall what it was Uncle Phil had given them? She remembered the moment Annie opened her mouth; £20 each.

"That's all right. Say, you girls give me a ring some time, we could go out somewhere in the car."

"Good idea, Uncle Phil." Annie grimaced at Tammy, silently telegraphing: 'Remember it, we might -'

Mark left a group of giggling, gossiping friends, interrupted, pushing between them and their Uncle.

"Sorry about last night, Tam, Annie." Embarrassed flush, not realising he might be stirring up yet more problems for them. Annie flashed him a savage 'shut up' look.

"That's all right, it was OK, the dress hides the marks," sharp as barbed wire.

"And what were you youngsters up to last night?" Uncle Phil still pushing in, reluctant to leave, openly eyeing nubile young ladies. Annie flaunted her neat bust, smiled provocatively, pushed her tongue between her teeth, tapped Mark's arm possessively, noted how he picked up the conversation,

143

wondered -

"Enjoying ourselves, weren't we, Mark?" She turned away, whispered: "Go talk to Granny Webster," pushing Tammy toward the garden. "Go!"

Tammy moved, leaving Annie to small talk friends and relatives, to try and pick up the mood which had gone so dead with the sudden announcement, and her mother's flash of temper that threatened to explode the party right off the face of the earth.

Someone had pushed the wheelchair out onto the patio. The afternoon sun was gentler now. The old lady's hands lay still, wrinkled, sketched with blue veins, almost transparent.

"There you are, girl," a cackle, a sharp look. "Nice dress, did your mummy buy the matching outfits? Did Annie say, 'go talk to Granny Webster, keep the old girl happy'?"

"Yes, Gran. That is, yes to Mother buying the dresses, no to Annie telling me to come and talk to you."

"Sit down here," tapping a footstool someone had left. Tammy gathered up her skirts and sat, staring out across the soft green lawn. Saw younger cousins running and rolling, felt it was inviting her to roll on its delicate softness as well, to breathe in the scent of growing things, of wildlife and nature, not musty old lady smell tinged with some flowery scent.

"Don't fool with me, girl. You've been jumping when Annie says jump since you were old enough to do it."

"Did you enjoy the party, Gran?" Change the subject, she knows too much, sees too much.

"I see you use the past tense, because you know the party's dead on its feet. And I don't think you mind, either. But to answer your question, once I got everyone going, I did."

"It shocked a few people."

The old lady cackled again, the folds of her face moving concertina-like around a mouth toothless and pink.

"I meant to. God help us, girl, your father standing there with that insipid look, trying to pretend you were the fruits of his loins! He can't father children."

Tammy said nothing, watched the swifts dart in great flocks, tea leaves thrown across the soft blue sky. September, they'd be leaving soon for far off places, where the leaves were green and the skies were a deeper blue, and nothing would stop their endless flight.

Like my thoughts.

"Your mother was so upset about it, she couldn't have the world thinking they weren't a normal family - she wanted to be Mrs Superwoman, you know that, of course. Perfect decor for your home, perfect decor for herself. Husband hand-picked to fit the image, and even the girls came hand-picked to finish the picture. Well, it looks like that from my angle. The angle of years."

It was the longest speech Tammy could ever remember. Granny Webster was a feared visitor. Mum rushing around to ensure everything was perfect; that they were perfect, not a spot of dust or a hair out of place, they were told to be polite to Daddy's mother. Tammy realised they had missed a lot over the years by not making friends with the old lady, to find out what lay behind the crust.

The voice cracked a little. Gran snagged a glass of champagne from a small silver tray Tammy only just recognised. Mother had pulled out all the best silver for this do. And now it had been spoiled.

Or had it?

"She was just lucky, your pompous, stuck-up, snooty, snobbish mother. There - I've said it, what I've been waiting to say these 25 years and more. When Martin brought her home I said to him: 'Listen to me, boy, that woman will drain you dry to keep a picture of what she and her family should be', and I were right. Damn it, I were right."

Yes, thought Tammy, leaning her elbows on her knees, chin in her hands, staring across at the trees edging the land, shielding the home from unsightly cows doing unsightly things in the middle of the fields as they chewed and cropped and produced the milk which mother said was so essential to their fair skin and strong bones. Yes, old lady, you are right. That's just what she's like.

"So, I thought to myself, all those years ago, when she brought you twins home from the hospital, right out of the poor woman's womb! I thought then I'd wait my chance and if God let me live, I'd tell the world when you were 18 years old. And I done it."

She leaned back in the chair, old, frail, tired, hunched under the weight of sunlight.

"You all right, Gran?" Tammy was genuinely concerned. For the first time a flicker of feeling for the old lady, she didn't want to lose her, not now!

"I'm all right." She sipped champagne, burped, ignored it, went on. "Damn it, girl, I never meant to spoil your day. I thought the foolish woman would have told you and your sister, but kept it from the family. I saw by your faces you didn't know, either." A chuckle from somewhere deep and probably evil. "Well, I certainly shook them up, didn't I?"

"You won't be invited again, Gran!" Tammy put a young healthy hand over the withered one, feeling the blood moving sluggishly through veins. "Does that matter?"

"Course not. I won't be here much longer anyway, my duty's done now. I'll be with your grandfather soon enough." She shifted impatiently in the chair. "Take me in, girl, get your mother or someone to help me to the lavatory, would you?"

"Sure, Gran."

"Your mother preferably, she hates it! You're an all right kid, to use an expression I'm sure I heard someone use the other day! Not like your sister. Let me tell you something, Tammy, don't thrust Annie in everything, she don't always know right."

Tammy got up, stretched, and took the handles of the chair.

"I don't have much choice, Gran."

"No, I rather guessed that."

Tammy pushed the chair in, found her mother, told her what Gran wanted, saw her mother's face cloud and then show disgust. Tammy smiled and went to find Annie. They had so much to talk about - perhaps Annie wouldn't demand impossible things of her tonight.

Would she?

CHAPTER FIVE

Q. You said before you were ordered to take the beatings - were you also ordered to take the sex?

A. Oh yes, at first I was. I didn't want to lose my virginity, I hadn't touched the vibrator like Annie had, I didn't want anything to do with it. But Annie said do it and I did.

Q. Who was your first man?

A. Mark. Wimpy Niall wouldn't come near me, kept saying he was scared, but he got it up all right for Annie, but then, she dominated him, and he didn't dare do otherwise. Two submissives together, no way. It was Mark, he got turned on by hurting me, and wouldn't admit it, but boy, could you see the bulge in his jockey shorts! In the end, well, I fancied him half to death anyway, so we went into the back seat of his Escort and got on with it.

Q. And you liked it?

A. Sure did. And I got Niall to order me a vibrator of my own after that.

Q. So, what you're saying is - both you girls were sexually active before your 18th birthday?

A. Yes.

Q. Can you tell me what happened on your birthday?

A. That was when it all began to change. It was a good party, we were enjoying it, or at least I was. Mark was around, he'd whipped me the night before, which had put his back up a bit, well, not his back, you know what I mean. See, he'd made up his mind he wanted Annie not me, and she refused, and worked herself off in front of him. That was the sort of thing she did, denied him her body, left him with an erection and nowhere to go. So, he was pretty grumpy with her during the party, but all right with me.

And then Gran Webster dropped her bombshell, told the whole party we were adopted, not natural children of our parents. Whatever anyone might tell you, Annie near burned up with rage over that - because everyone got embarrassed and shocked and uncomfortable and the party broke up. Mark went home without saying goodbye, relatives had a good gossip and then left us, and I found out Gran wasn't a bad old stick after all.

But Annie had different ideas.

CHAPTER SIX

"Well, that was a bombshell and no mistake," Adrienne smiled encouragingly. The girls pushed together on the settee, blonde hair intermingled. Annie felt Tammy was half asleep, felt her twin's eyes closing. Around them the party debris; glasses, half eaten food, curling sandwiches, overflowing ashtrays despite Adrienne's injunction that:

'Those who care to smoke use the garden - please!'

The fact there was party remains still around them betrayed eloquently their parents' agitation. Adrienne had normally had a perfect Interior Homes lounge.

"We didn't intend you to find out like that," Martin's hand reached out to touch his wife, voice weak even to Annie's ears. She despised her father, even more so now.

Annie wasn't sure how Tammy could even think of sleeping! She was burning up. An old lady spoiling the party. She had looked forward to it for weeks, planning what to say at her birthday speech, who to ask so there would be some talent around - only to have everyone disappear like mercury out of a test-tube as the words left the old lady's mouth.

Rage consumed hatred, burned a hollow core so hot it was a

148

wonder Tammy couldn't feel it.

"Well, it was like this." Adrienne smiled at Martin, smiled at the girls, took a visible hold of her emotions. "We - couldn't have children, your father and I, and we so wanted children. So we applied for adoption. There was this very poor family, oh my dears, you would never know how poor! Rough house, almost a slum! And there this poor woman was having twins! And she already had four children! No way could she cope with twins! So, the moment you were born you became ours."

"We have loved you as if you were our own," added Martin, reddening under Annie's steady gaze. "And believe me, we were going to tell you, weren't we, Adrienne?"

"Of course! Do you think we would have gone through life not telling you? Of course we were going to tell you, but in our own way and at our own time."

Like hell you were, thought Annie viciously. Tammy stirred, put a restraining hand on her arm. There was a time and a place, and this wasn't it.

"Just tell us who we really are and where we came from," said quietly, convincingly calm.

Adrienne smiled.

"I knew you'd understand! And just think what awful names you had too! Oh, we haven't told you. Your mother, your real mother, named you Mary and Audrey. She had to put something in the register at the hospital. You're Mary, Tammy, and Annie you're really Audrey, or you were. We changed your names legally by deed poll, from Mary and Audrey Gibling to Anastasia and Tamasine Webster."

A quiet fell over the room, profound as the one which had descended earlier. Tammy all but stopped breathing. Annie panicked until she felt her twin's heart pumping like mad. Tammy was controlling her emotions. Annie had never gotten hold of the meditation bit, just let her emotions boil over.

"We gave you a proper home," Martin offered feebly. "You'd have grown up on the streets otherwise, rough, talking slang, probably getting into drugs and all sorts of problems. I mean,

London is one hell of a rough place."

"Instead you live here with us in this good home," added Adrienne. "Your own rooms, good friends, food, family to support and care for you. And never so much as a hint of scandal or problems round either of you - you've been such good girls! Such perfect daughters!"

Tammy smothered a giggle, Annie felt her shudder with the effort. If only they knew!

Annie knew she had to end the conversation. There would be other times, other opportunities to pursue the things she wanted to know.

"It's been one hell of a party." Annie moved Tammy gently off her shoulder, stood up, gestured almost unseen to her twin. "Whatever happened, it was a good party, and we thank you for that and for the gifts, don't we, Tam? Listen, it doesn't matter about the news, we can talk about it another time, can't we?"

Tammy struggled bleary-eyed and went to kiss her parents goodnight.

"Thanks for everything."

"We're only sorry it got spoiled," Martin hugged Tammy and held out an arm to Annie who went instead to her mother - as always.

"Don't worry about it, we learned a lot - things we didn't know. And it gave *them* something to talk about for weeks! After all, we're still one family, aren't we?"

Adrienne nodded.

"Of course we are, Annie, thank you for saying so. I knew you'd understand. I said to your father, my girls will understand. Goodnight, darlings. Oh, we might be going out again Friday."

"That's all right. Coming, Tam?"

"Sure."

They climbed the broad staircase in silence, thinking their individual thoughts yet reaching out to one another as always. Silently Annie thought:

'Come and see me later,' picked up Tammy's equally silent response:

'Sure.'

Annie closed her door, crossed the expanse of dove grey carpet and stood at the window looking out at near darkness, band of light bordering the horizon, a tree standing black and sentinel silent on the boundary, hoot of an owl, protesting cow in the field, dog barking - somewhere.

Annie gripped the window-sill with both hands, knuckles threatening to pierce the skin.

Adopted. It solved a million mysteries, it had been hard to see any trace of domination in either of her parents, or their immediate family, so where had it come from? And they weren't smart enough to have been able to pass on psychic ability, the link with her twin, the trick of conjuring things - She turned, pictured a giant spider in the middle of her bed, watched as it formed, its hairy legs, saw the heaving body, concentrated on holding it there until Tammy came in, heard her start of revulsion and let the vision go.

"Getting my own back."

"No you're not, you did that to scare me!" Tammy walked over to the chair suspended from the ceiling, flopped into it.

"Well?" Annie sat at the dressing-table, drew the brush down her gleaming hair.

"Well what?" Tammy stared at the spot where the vision had been. Annie knew she hated, detested and was repulsed by them.

"What did Gran Webster have to say for herself?"

"Oh, Gran. Ann - we missed out on something there. The old lady sees a lot, knows a lot, has our family just about sized up."

"I'm sure she does, but she damn well spoiled my party!"

"Hey, hold on, it was mine too!"

"I know, I know, don't get yourself in a state, kiddo." Annie clamped down her temper. "Tell me."

"Well, she said she told Father the day he brought Mother

151

home for the first time that that woman will drain him; keeping up appearances. And she's so right, Ann! Look how we all match; our house, our lifestyle - even us!"

"I've know that for years."

"I guess I have, too, but didn't want to say."

Annie crossed to the bed, laid down, put her hands under her head. "What do you think, kiddo?"

"What about?"

"For starters, what do you think about going out of here right now, walking down the road, accosting the first man you see, saying to him:

"Sir, I am in dire need of a good spanking, would you do me the honour of putting me across your knee and spanking my bottom until I cry, until I am so red it looks as if I'll be bruised for a week? And if he refuses, going on to the next one and asking him."

Tammy's breath came faster. She shut her eyes tight, went red, her fingers restless, sliding on her own long shapely legs. Annie continued:

"And not coming back until you find one to spank you so hard you'll be bruised for a week come Tuesday. Well, are you going to do it?"

"Annie -"

"No, I won't make you, not tonight." Annie sat up, stared at her sister with all the force of her personality blazing out of her eyes. "What you do instead is go dig up a worm and eat it."

"Annie!"

"Go!"

"Annie - please! You already did the spider -"

"And tomorrow we'll talk about what we do about this adoption thing. I'm too angry, too tired, and too wound up to think of it right now."

"Annie!" Pleading, begging, longing to be let off this task. Annie was immovable.

"Go, I said."

Slowly and reluctantly Tammy trailed across the [t]
eyes down, loathing and love mixed and trailing back t[
who took in the emotions, wrapped them around her own hates,
and smiled evilly.

"I'll know you've done it when I hear you being sick."

CHAPTER SEVEN

Q. Can you tell me what you meant by 'Annie had different
ideas'?

A. I told her Gran was an all right person, but she said no,
Gran had deliberately wrecked the party, her party - but of
course it was mine too. Thing is, I didn't mind, I thought it
had gone on long enough, and anyway we all had a lot to
think and talk about. We sat around after everyone had
gone, and Mother sort of got herself together to tell us we
were adopted, that they couldn't have kids. Didn't tell us
who was at fault there, just that they adopted us from this
poor poor family, and we had their awful names. I think
we were supposed to feel grateful to our parents for rescuing us from the poor poor family and the terrible names,
Mary and Audrey.

Q. Do you think they're awful names?

A. They sound awful, after we've grown up being Tamasine
and Anastasia. My name means little twin, by the way.
Mother put a lot of thought into our names!

Q. What does Anastasia mean?

A. Resurrection. Reborn. Reborn with a new name. It all fits.

Q. What happened next?

A. We went along with it, smiled a lot, said thank you for the
party and the gifts, were told we'd be alone again on Friday evening, and went upstairs. Annie called me into her
room, well, what she did was ask me to come in when we
were going upstairs, so I did, and she had a horrid spider

153

sitting in the middle of the bed. She'd pictured it just for me. Then, as she always does when she's in a foul mood, started on about me doing something terrible. She'd been on about walking the streets, approaching the first man I saw and asking him to spank me until I cried. And if he refused, to go on to the next one until I found someone to do it, and then I'd have to come back and show her what he'd done to me. I was terrified at the thought, but -

Q. But you found it exciting as well.

A. Yes, terribly exciting. I mean, it could be a real experience, couldn't it? All I'd experienced up to then was Annie's boyfriends, who weren't exactly part of the scene!

Q. Did you do it?

A. No. Because we knew we had Friday to ourselves again, Annie promised to get someone else to come along. But she didn't let me off. She told me to go and get a worm and eat it.

Q. Couldn't you have faked that?

A. No, she said she'd know I'd done it when she heard me being sick. And I was.

CHAPTER EIGHT

"Darling, I heard you being sick last night, are you all right?" Adrienne laid a caring hand on Tammy's forehead, looked to her eyes, registered motherly concern. Tammy nodded, knowing she was white and drawn this morning, results of a night tossing and turning waiting for the worm to regurgitate itself - which it did.

"Ate too much rich cake, I think. Don't worry Mother, I'm all right."

"Good, good." Tammy stole a look at Annie, caught the gleam of pure lust, knew she had heard and approved.

If Mother heard me, Tammy thought, why didn't she come

and find out if I was all right? She wondered if her real mother would have been more caring.

Odd how the thoughts changed from one day to the next.

Her real mother.

Her adoptive mother.

Suddenly Adrienne didn't seem so much the perfect wife, mother and house owner. Suddenly the superbly cut blonde hair seemed a sham, rather than a naturally beautiful asset.

"We've - been invited to a dinner on Friday evening, is that all right?"

"Is what all right?" asked Annie, with a malicious gleam her mother missed entirely.

"Leaving you girls alone again, we seem to be doing a lot of that lately."

"Actually, you mentioned it last night, it's fine by us, isn't it, Tam?"

Tammy nodded, not ready to speak. As they were going to be alone on Friday, Annie would dream some devious scheme, but at least it wouldn't mean walking the street looking for a man to punish her. Yet.

Annie pushed her plate away, traditional fried breakfast consumed; fried bread, tomatoes, sausages, egg and bacon. The cut-off rind sat on the edge of the plate, a squiggle of brown looking like a -

"Excuse me," she pushed her chair back and left the table, toast half eaten, coffee untouched. She felt Annie's tentative enquiry:

'What's the matter, kiddo?' but ignored it.

Her bedroom was cool, the morning sun didn't touch this side of the house. She could sit in half shadow and look out across green gold richness of September and let her feelings flow out, regardless of whether Annie picked them up or not.

The village church began tolling the calling bell, summoning people to church. Perhaps she should get to church, approach the vicar, ask him for confession - but he would be surprised, perhaps offended, by her sins.

"I have sinned," she would say. "I have laid with a man not my husband - well, several times actually. I have been whipped by at least one person. Someone else used a strap on me. Yet another a ping-pong bat to smack my bottom until I was crying. And I loved it. I loved the giving in, the feeling of being controlled, the sensation of someone else being responsible for what happened to me. And even more, I loved the knowledge my twin was sharing the feeling while I glimpsed something of her feelings, her desire to dominate, to control, to direct. Yes, to give pain, but she dare not lay a hand on me. I would like her to, oh believe me I would like her to! I would lie down at Annie's feet and let her beat me - I would kiss her feet and worship her as she deserves, for she is the stronger twin, the older twin, the more intelligent twin. I love her and would do anything for her."

And the young vicar, with theological college stars in his eyes, would reel back in shock and demand she go to the police or the social workers - or someone.

Annie crept into the room, looking around, wrinkling her nose as always.

"How can you be happy in here with all this blue?" gesturing toward the frilled blue duvet cover and pillowcase, blue walls, darker blue drapes and royal blue carpet.

"I like it. It's calming."

"Oh, you and the calming meditation and all that! Where does it get you?"

"Less wound up than you are, Anastasia."

"Oh fine, Tamasine." Annie sat on the window seat, looked out of the window, fiddled with the tie-back. "All right, are you?"

"Now I am."

"Sorry about that." The apology seemed sincere, for the first time ever. "I didn't really mean you to be sick like that. You were so sick, kiddo."

"I know, I was the one doing it!"

"How big was the worm?"

"As big as the rind of bacon you left on your plate."

Annie laughed softly. "So that's the reason for the hasty departure! Never gave it a thought, kiddo."

"You never do."

"Oh but I do, you are never far from my thoughts. I plan all your penances very carefully indeed."

"But I won't have to walk the streets looking for someone, will I? We've got Friday to ourselves."

"Oh, you remembered that, did you?" Annie gave Tammy a knowing and understanding look. "No wonder you're tired, used up the batteries in the vibrator, did you?"

Tammy flushed. "Yes, I did - actually. You can buy me some new ones!"

"Not likely, it was your pleasure, not mine. I wonder who you fantasized about, or was it a faceless stranger? Someone passing through Salldown, a businessman on his way to a conference, stopping overnight at the Coach and Horses, wandering around to walk off a late dinner and too many drinks. What would he think if he saw a girl looking as young as you do, kiddo? All the long blonde hair shining in the streetlight, that short short skirt, you know, the one we made together, the black one, with the slit up the side, the one that makes your behind stick out, would he think twice at your offer to give you a good tanning? In the back of his company car, a big one, upholstered seats, plenty of room, skirt up, pants down, hand coming down again and again, you wriggling and writhing and wanting to be free, knowing he won't let you free, knowing he'll give you a good fucking afterwards, and knowing I'll want to inspect you when you come in - is that what kept you and the vibrator busy all night?" She watched Tammy go red. She knew the answer before it came.

"Yes."

"I know, kiddo, I felt it. I was right in there, directing his arm, his hand mopping up your tears, holding your wrists so you couldn't get away, feeling myself go red and sore in sympathy, but kiddo, I didn't need the vibrator, you did that for

157

me, slick and wet with your juices - it suited mine too."

Tammy stared at her. "Were you sick with me as well? When that damned worm came back up and hit the toilet bowl? Were you there then, big sister?"

"No, I pulled out and left you to it. What do you think I am, some kind of masochist?"

Annie stood up, paced around the room, touched the Stephen King novel, looked at Tammy and smiled.

"Gerald's Game. Bondage. We'll try that some time when we can get the guys in here, get you tied to the bed instead of in the garage, see what they do to you then. In the meantime, what are we going to do about this adoption business?"

The sudden change of subject took Tammy by surprise.

"Can we do anything?"

"Sure we can." Annie crossed the floor again, grabbed Tammy's shoulders and shook her lightly. "Listen, kiddo, they gave us away! Those people - what was the name? Gibling. They gave us away! We have a whole family out there, brothers and sisters, aunts, uncles, cousins and grandparents! We don't know who they are, what they gave to us. Did one of them have dominant desires and pass it on to us? How did we get to be psychic? Don't you want to know?"

"Well -"

"Sure you do." Annie paced again. "And another thing. These two who call themselves our parents, they took us in, fine, they're to be let off a lot of things for that, but kiddo, they didn't tell us! They deceived us! Let us find out from that vicious nasty old lady! That I don't forgive!"

"But Annie -"

"Don't 'but Annie' me! Think about it. Work on it. Let's see where we go and what we can do with this knowledge!"

"You mean - blackmail someone?"

"I didn't mean that, but anything and everything is up for grabs, kiddo - and I mean everything."

Tammy became infected with Annie's enthusiasm, as she knew she would. Sooner or later, whatever Annie thought and felt, came over the psychic link, became part of her, too.

"Where do we start?"

"Well, I can scour the telephone directory and see what I can find. And you can find out where we send off for birth certificates."

"I feel better already." Colour had returned to her face, life to her eyes. She had something to do.

"And Friday to look forward to," added Annie, as if reading her mind.

"Yes, and Friday to look forward to." What game would Annie devise this time? Who would Annie find, that wimp Mark again?

"Find me someone strong for Friday," begged Tammy, putting on her shoes and finding a jacket.

Annie grinned. "You bet I will!"

CHAPTER NINE

Q. What happened next, Tammy?

A. Something odd. I was walking in our churchyard, before you laugh, it's a good place to escape from Annie and family at times! Those who go there are silent; mourning over graves, arranging flowers, clearing weeds away. And I discovered a grave with Gibling on it. Then I found some more. We might have been born in London, but Giblings are from Salldown, for sure. Annie came with me on another visit, and we began building a picture of our family. The real family. It was like a game, nothing really meant anything, and we put them in some kind of order. We knew, for example, that there was a baby buried there, lived for three months. A Loving Husband and Brother, so that was an uncle who died. One set of grandparents. We didn't have the other name, I only looked for Giblings. There could have been other family members, I couldn't do anything about that at the time.

Q. And?

A. Annie got busy with the phone books for the area and the adjoining area. She got the number of other Giblings around the area. Unusual name, had to be the same family.

Q. What happened then? Did you use the information? Did you get your birth certificates? Did you get in touch with this family?

A. No, that was the odd thing. It took Annie some time to think about doing anything about it, and then when it happened, it all happened by pure accident. Because before then she had other ideas, did Annie, about getting revenge on our family, what we thought of as family No. 2, and she started with Uncle Phil.

CHAPTER TEN

"Wait until Friday." Annie said it over and over, sometimes without Tammy asking, other times in answer to her question.

"Have you found someone? What are we going to do Friday?" It all got the same enigmatic answer. Friday was a lifetime away, an eternity of being nice to parents, avoiding the over solicitous hugs, kisses and enquiries after health and mental well-being.

"Why can't she just leave us alone?" Annie demanded after one particularly sickly session of mother-love. "We were all right before!"

"Before, we thought she was our real mother," Tammy had invincible logic. Annie found it hard to accept.

"Much more and I'll be really rude to her!"

"Oh give her time, Ann, give her time, she'll get used to it."

"Give her time! All right, I'll try and be good."

"Tell me about Friday."

"Wait until Friday," and that's all Tammy could get. But there were whispered telephone calls which stopped when she got close, and a general air of mystery which intrigued her and nearly drove her mad.

She guessed Annie knew exactly what she was doing. Most likely laying traps which no man could resist.

Friday came at last. Adrienne and Martin got themselves ready, kissed and hugged the girls, drove away to a chorus of 'take care', 'see you later', and other meaningless expressions.

Tammy and Annie raced upstairs and changed. Tammy into a virtually backless low-cut tight black dress, as Annie had ordered. Annie into tiny cut-off shorts and cropped top. When the bell rang they were ready and waiting. Annie opened the front door slowly, smiling her most inviting smile.

"Uncle Phil, do come in."

"Thanks Annie. I must say this all sounds highly mysterious and interesting, what's going on? Didn't I see your parents going off down the road?"

If you did you were hanging around, watching. Annie smothered her thoughts, smilingly inviting him into the lounge.

"You did. Tammy, Uncle Phil's here."

Tammy got up from the settee, aware of her twin's prickling of excitement and lust, and did some deep breathing to control her own feelings.

"Have a seat, Uncle Phil. Drink?" Annie crossed to the drinks cabinet, stood with a bottle of whisky in her hand.

"Just a small one, Annie, thanks."

"Here you are."

With the glass in his hand he looked more relaxed, but still studied both of them carefully. "So, tell me what this is all about."

"Well -" Annie sat on the arm of his chair, making him go slightly red as her hip came into contact with his arm and shoulder. "We know what you're like, Uncle Phil."

"What's that supposed to mean?"

Tammy smiled.

"You keep a pile of - interesting, shall we say - magazines in your closet, don't you?"

Phil looked at Tammy and then at Annie, saw knowing smiles, knowing eyes, and blushed deep red.

"Who's been talking? Tony? I'll kill my son when I get home!"

"Don't do that, Uncle Phil, it wasn't his fault, we know you men always have a secret store of magazines, so we mentioned it, just casual like. If you had, he'd know about it, and of course he did. We were right, weren't we, Tammy?"

"As usual." Tammy smiled. They hadn't asked Tony to do anything, they had gambled on Phil having the magazines. He was someone who sought every opportunity for hugs, kisses on the lips rather than the cheek, a hand sliding here and there, a quick pat on the backside, he had to have magazines - and it got Tony into trouble, Phil would have a go at him as soon as he could.

Phil began to panic, began to look very uncomfortable, tried to move away from Annie's warm body - and failed.

"Look, don't tell your Aunt Phyllis, will you? I mean, if she knew -"

"We won't tell anyone, don't you worry about a thing, Uncle Phil."

"Look, we know now I'm not your real uncle, don't we? Can't we drop the uncle bit?"

"If that's what you want." Annie let her arm fall naturally to her side, touched his arm, let her fingers walk along his hand, painted nails gleaming wicked red, slid back to his wrist, held it lightly between her fingertips.

He tossed the whisky down his throat and held the glass out, silently asking for another. Tammy got up, took it from him - making sure her fingers touched his, and went to pour another drink, a larger one this time.

"So, what do you girls want with me, other than to tell me my guilty secrets?" Blustering, still afraid, yet intrigued enough to stay.

"We want you to do us a favour, Phil." Annie trailed a finger

162

round his ear, down his neck, round his collar and under his chin. It was all he could do to sit still. Tammy could see his emotions ready to boil over. "Tammy here, she's developed a taste for discipline, and you see, we don't know where to go to get some! I mean, boyfriends are all right, but they're bit wimpy, get scared if we talk about spanking and things like that."

Tammy watched Phil go even redder. He clenched his fists and pushed them into the cushion. Annie had scored a direct hit; it wasn't just girlie magazines, it was discipline, too.

"So we were wondering, as we're alone here, and no neighbours can hear us, whether you'd like to put Tammy across your knee and tan her bottom for her?"

"You're not serious!" Blurted out through virtually ground shut teeth, his expression defying her to disappoint him.

"Yes, we're serious."

Tammy stood up, walked gracefully over to him, stood in her tight clinging dress which revealed everything, including the fact she wore no knickers.

'Go, go, go!!' came from Annie, silent, impulsive, urgent. Tammy reached out a hand, nails flashing in the light, blonde hair gleaming, face deliberately wistful.

"I've been such a naughty girl, Uncle Phil, such a naughty girl. Won't you punish me for my bad deeds?"

"I don't believe I'm hearing this." He tried to stand up. His legs gave way and he fell back into the armchair. "You're having me on. Adrienne? Martin? Are you there? The joke's over!"

"No one's here, Uncle Phil." Tammy knelt down, gazed into his eyes with her own large soulful ones. "You said you saw them leaving. No one's here but us girls, and I'm the naughty one. Do you know, Annie was so mad with me she was thinking of spanking me herself? Now she's not really strong, but if she used a ping-pong bat or a leather strap, or perhaps borrowed a riding crop from one of her friends, do you think she could make some impact on me? But that would be a waste, wouldn't it? I mean, there are people - men - around who like doing it, who get pleasure out of doing it, and who can do it a

163

lot harder than Annie could."

Phil went even redder, his face began to swell, hands twitching violently. Annie grinned from behind his shoulder, saw the rising lump in his trousers, touched him and he jumped.

"Go on Phil, she's begging for it, aren't you, Tammy?"

"Spank me, Uncle Phil, spank this naughty girl." With one graceful, slithering movement Tammy prostrated herself over his knees as Annie got up, moved slowly and silently away.

"Damn it!" Phil raised his hand. For a long, long moment Annie thought he was going to hold out against temptation, but Tammy was just too much to ignore. Even as she thought he would resist, he brought his hand down with a resounding thwack! Tammy jumped, but didn't cry out. He spanked her again, then tugged the dress out of the way, exposing her cheeks, small, round, creamy white, flushed with pink from his first smacks. He groaned, a long meaningful sound, and began to spank her hard, smacks ringing out around the room. Tammy squealed and jumped, wriggled and kicked, but made no real effort to escape.

Annie pressed a button and began the tape recording that would ensure she had Phil forever in her grasp. Not that it would be needed, she was sure of that. Tammy's cheeks were turning bright red under his onslaught, his stinging hand finding every inch, her cries urging him on to hurt her even more. The red became intense, her cries became real, and she finally broke down, sobbing and lying limply over his knees, tears dripping into the carpet. Only then did Phil stop, run his hands lovingly over her bottom, his fingers sliding between the crack, finding her moistness. He stood up, tipping her ungracefully onto the floor as realisation hit him.

"OK, so I did it. Now what? I suppose you report me?"

"Another drink, Uncle Phil?" Annie appeared as if by magic at his side, whisky in hand. He saw her nipples pushing against the top, saw her thighs grind together in the cut-off shorts, knew she had found the experience exciting, a real turn-on.

Tammy laid on the floor, bottom red and angry, weeping

into the carpet, the picture of contrition. But his fingers had found the truth. She too had been turned on.

He snatched the whisky and drank it in one.

"God, you girls are something else!" There was admiration in his voice this time.

Annie eyed the sleek, too-smooth man, saw the slicked hair, pampered skin, clean-cut nails and white hands, and smiled.

"Would you like to come again one day, Uncle Phil?"

"I'd like to come now." He grinned, pressed his crotch, tried to adjust the bulge.

"Tam, Uncle Phil is uncomfortable."

Tammy got up on her knees, dress around her waist, revealing her small blonde bush. She smiled tremulously, reached for him.

His cock sprang free as she lowered the zip, and as she took him into her warm mouth he sighed with happiness. Annie took the opportunity to stop the tape, the sound of so much sighing, sucking, and groaning covered the small click the recorder made. She smiled behind Phil's trembling back, giving Tammy the thumbs up.

One down - no, two down. How many to go?

CHAPTER ELEVEN

Q. Did you get Phil to come round again after that?
A. Oh yes, regularly. We progressed from spanking to a slipper. From that to a leather belt Annie bought in a charity shop. 75p well spent, she said. A cane too. Annie got Niall to send away for a cane, would you believe! And she used it on him too! I don't like the cane too much, it causes terrible burning lines, especially when you've been spanked first, as I often was. And he never gave me less than twelve. But Annie got a real thrill out of seeing me caned.
Q. Did he ever - have sex with you?

A. No, never. He drew the line at that, but I always gave him relief afterwards, by mouth or by hand, either way he enjoyed.

Q. So what did you do about your own feelings?

A. Retired to bed with a vibrator. Sometimes Annie would come in and watch. Sometimes I'd be alone. Surprising what you can do with an eight inch vibrator and some lubricant. I had some good sessions alone, reliving the sessions.

Q. Did Annie get more of a thrill watching than doing it herself? You said she caned this Niall.

A. I think she got equal pleasure out of it, to be honest. Imagine, we'd wait until Mother and Father were going out, then Phil would come in, he'd be waiting somewhere down the road, and immediately he'd get down to it, whatever it was Annie had devised for the evening. We'd be hard at it by say 8.15 - and he'd be gone by 9, and Annie and I would be in bed. Sometimes in the same room, sometimes in our own rooms, busy with vibrators and fingers, having the time of our lives.

Q. Was that all that was going on at that time?

A. Oh no! I had Mark - still - and he was useful for a quick fuck now and then, and I used to let him spank me occasionally, or use a strap on me, just to keep him in practice. Phil was better, he was a genuine devotee, he loved every last moment of it. It was the sessions which turned him on, rather than what came after, which is what turned Mark on. A difference in thinking. Sometimes Annie would jerk Phil off for a change. That's when he started calling us his 'twin pleasures'.

Q. What was happening with your parents at this time?

A. Nothing. The mother-love bit quietened down, as I knew it would. We went on as normal. I felt a sense of unease for a while; Mother obviously thought we had taken it too well, was waiting for the time-bomb to explode, and when it didn't, she got a bit nervous for a while. Then it all went

166

very quiet.

Q. And your real family?

A. Family No.1. Finding them, as I said, was an accident. Annie hadn't done much about compiling any more records. She had an idea of sending off for our birth certificates and things, but didn't do anything about it, we were too busy with Uncle Phil!

Q. So, how did you get in touch?

A. Accident. The games with Phil lasted all through September and most of October. Kept us occupied, you might say. Then Mark invited us to a Hallowe'en party in the village hall. We had fun with that - got ourselves dressed as cats; put our blonde hair up under black curly wigs, painted whiskers on our faces, put cat masks on to cover our eyes. Black leotards with long tails, and black high-heeled boots. Our parents didn't even recognise us! I danced with Mark a lot, because I still fancied him even if he was head over heels in love with Annie, and Annie tormented him by going off with a man. Very tall, very good-looking guy wearing a close fitting black costume with a skeleton painted on it. I thought she had a 'cat and cream' look about her halfway through the evening, so I got close and telegraphed 'who is he?' and she sent back 'Daniel Gibling'. I could have fallen over with shock. Was he brother, cousin - who was he?

Q. Who was he?

A. We found out later he was our brother. From then on there was no holding Annie.

CHAPTER TWELVE

"Nobody loves me, everybody hates me, think I'll go and eat worms." Annie sang, giggled as Tammy turned a hard face.

"Lay off, Annie! I felt bad enough then, and still do when I think about it!"

"Got you, kiddo - no matter what I say, you do it, don't you? And you love it too."

Tammy stared hard, trying to conjure a worm, a snake, anything - but nothing happened. Her will wasn't strong, she tried hard but nothing ever appeared. Annie had all the abilities - it seemed.

"I've got a new game for you, kiddo."

"What now?" Tammy felt her stomach turn and ripples set up that sent scared erotic thrills everywhere. What devious scheme had Annie come up with this time?

"You'll like this one." Annie threw her a small printed card. It caught the air currents and ended up under the bed. Tammy had to scramble to find it.

A name and address in heavy black type, in the corner a telephone number. Tammy looked at it, and then at Annie.

"So - ?"

"So that's an ex-headmaster, kiddo. He gives - private lessons. You go get one." Annie's look said lust and stern words, said obey me or else.

Tammy went cold. "You mean?"

"Mean he dons his gown and hat, produces a nice swishy cane, and canes young people's bums. I want you to go and get caned. Tell him twelve at least."

"Annie -" Tammy let her arms fall, despair and dismay writ large.

"Annie what?" A surge of anger hot enough to scorch Tammy's mind. She shrank back. Annie thought at her: 'Do you want to be punished by wimps like Mark all the time?'

"Uncle Phil's doing a good job on me." Spoken to hear the sound, fretful, reluctant and - scared.

"Uncle Phil's getting himself entrapped in my web, that's what Uncle Phil's doing. And anyway, you know what to expect from him. You won't with Mr Wrayland."

Tammy stood looking at the carpet and her feet, wondering why they didn't move. If - no, when - Annie gave a command

Tammy was gone, but there was the distinct feeling Annie wanted more. And she was right.

"You can go there the long way round, have a good look at 47 Kensington Drive. Flash name for the lower end of town, but then I suppose it wasn't always the lower end of town. Tell me what the house looks like; the garden, what age the car outside, the lot."

"I guess that's where -"

"Part of our real family lives. Right first time. Kill two birds with one stone, kiddo, get me some info, get me some thrills at the same time."

Tammy walked slowly to the door, looked back. Annie was already sprawled across the bed with earphones in her hand, ready to indulge in some music.

"You won't feel me if you go musicing." Tammy was still reluctant but knowing she would go. And in knowing, felt all the thrills, felt herself go moist, felt her legs go to jelly. Whatever the man offered she would take, and allow Annie full access to her mind while she did. Annie grinned.

"My dear twin, I'll feel you all right if Wrayland's as good as they say he is."

"Can I really - just go there?"

"Well, it isn't usual. If he's busy I suggest you make an appointment, give yourself plenty of time to think about it. I'll enjoy that."

The earphones were slipped on, Tammy effectively cut off. She tried telepathy but met a wall of music.

There was no escape. Anastasia had spoken.

The edges of the small card cut into her palm. Tammy left the room, closed the door quietly behind her, and went downstairs. No time to waste. She lifted her coat from the hook, calling to her mother.

"Just going to the shops!"

"All right, darling, don't be long, wrap up warm!"

Cold wind bit at her ankles, wrists and exposed skin. November sweeping in off the fields, catching the unwary.

169

Cold kept people at home. Tammy walked empty streets, blonde hair streaming out behind her as the wind tugged and played with it. Her mind was obsessed with the thought of visiting this - Wrayland, of being ordered to bend over a desk or a chair and being caned by someone who had done it all his working life. The feelings intensified, became a serious ache. Tammy groaned, thought she heard an echoing laugh in her head. Annie was enjoying this; her discomfort, her apprehension, and her secret pleasure in submission.

The long way round. Out past the shops, past the lengthy car showroom and yard, pennants fluttering in stiff wind, cars dripping condensation and money. Rusty cars hidden at the back, showroom shiny only at the front.

The neighbourhood became considerably shabbier. Here the fences were broken. Gates hung by one hinge, if at all. Litter grew in gardens in place of flowers. Cars abandoned, rusted, crashed, sat in driveways or on the pavement.

Tammy hurried, cold now, cold with apprehension and the weather, casting a swift look at 47 Kensington Drive, taking in the peeling paint round the window frames, the tarnished knocker, the boarded lower glass pane. Outside, no colour or genteel flower beds here, just weeds, grass, and a drooping laburnum that swayed in the cold.

Look, absorb, telegraph it to Annie. If she was listening.

And on to the smarter area away from this end of town, where cars were gleaming and new, where trees lined the street and not just appeared occasionally in front gardens, where double glazing firms had earned their keep.

Mr Wrayland's house was smarter than the rest; hanging baskets with winter pansies and ivies, huge tubs with conifers and heathers, paved front garden, immaculate white net curtains, elegant glass front door. Tammy rang the bell feeling small, stupid, and very afraid. She heard the echo of a laugh again, knew Annie was absorbing every moment of this.

A tall, severe faced, balding man opened the door, bent steel blue eyes on her, said nothing.

"Excuse me. Mr Wrayland?" At his nod she stumbled over her words. "My sister -" settled for blatant honesty. "My sister ordered me to come and see you. Could I please make an appointment for a - private lesson?"

"4.00 p.m. tomorrow."

The door was closed abruptly, giving her no chance to say I cannot make it then, because of course she could and she would. But there were a hundred questions. Would it cost, and if so, how much? What should I wear? Must I come alone - ?

'Come home.' Annie's voice clear in her head, as clear as if she held a mobile phone to her ear.

"I'm coming," she said aloud, startling an elderly lady struggling by with two large shopping bags.

The chill was total now. Her blood ran cold. Her feet hurt as she hurried along the iced pavements, shuddering as blasts of wind caught her.

Home seemed a long way away.

But tomorrow was even further away; there were many hours to wait, to anticipate, to brood, and to fear.

And Annie knew it.

CHAPTER THIRTEEN

Q. And you went back the next day?

A. Of course, I had no choice! It was a long walk, shivering in the cold, nervous tension roiling up the stomach, the old mound aching like a mad thing -

Q. Go on.

A. Well, I got there, and stood on the doorstep for three minutes in the biting cold wind, ringing the bell precisely on 4.00 p.m. I'd been well trained, you see! Annie had seen to that. I thought I detected a grunt of approval when Mr Wrayland opened the door. He was wearing his gown, flowing black thing, made him look taller and larger than be-

171

fore - more intimidating. He took my arm, led me into a
sort of lounge where there was a huge wooden desk, all
carved and solid looking. He said: "Take your coat off,"
and I did. I was wearing a short flared skirt and a huge
sweater. And even then I was cold. He said: "Your sister
telephoned me to confirm it was a valid order, that you
weren't trying to catch me out. I understand you're over
eighteen," and I nodded. Annie had made sure I didn't get
away with anything. I sent a violent message in her direction, got back that laugh again.

"Hm," he said. "Very unusual, finding someone submissive to their sister, but I suppose anything goes in this world.
I shall have to take your word for it, though I still feel
there is something odd here. I'm not entirely happy."

I said: "We're identical twins. Only she's dominant and
I'm submissive. She gets a lot of pleasure out of setting
me up for discipline."

"I see," he said, taking a cane out of the drawer and flexing
it in his fingers. I expected him to swish it through the air
but he didn't, just flexed it and looked at me. And I felt
myself going wet for the first time. Really wet. "Your sister said twelve, is that right?"

"Yes Sir," and I couldn't help myself, he was so cold, so
stern, so unforgiving!

"Well, as it will give me a considerable amount of pleasure
to cane someone so pretty and so - willing, there will be no
charge. Bend over the desk, please."

And I did. I felt the edge dig into me, knew I was pressing
too hard, but couldn't help myself. I reached for the other
side to have something to hold on to. And I waited. It
seemed like forever, he walked around, he smoothed my
briefs down, felt my bottom, took his time. And I thought:
of course there's no charge, nor should there be! And I
waited.

He said: "One," and the cane landed at the same moment.
And then I knew what Annie meant. I knew how Uncle

Phil did it, and this was different. This was a master. He caned hard, every line counted, and how! But he never let the tip come round and cut into my hip as Phil did at times. I got six good hard strokes. I cried out at every one! And then he let me think about it, let the lines burn and scream agony at me. I waited again, sniffling a bit, hanging on with all my strength, determined not to get up, not to wriggle, not to escape -

Not to miss a single moment. He moved around the other side, changed hands no less! And did it again, six more times. I yelled at every one. I felt the lines overlap; they have to with twelve. Six you can place without touching; create six individual lines. But twelve, they overlap. And then he added two more, on the tops of my thighs, just where the bum curves down, you know? Right there - and then stopped. And I stood up and held my poor cheeks with both hands, asking -

"Why?"

"Because you are too submissive, too good," was the odd reply.

But he didn't know how I'd been trained for the best part of eighteen years to obey my sister and her friends, come what may.

I wonder what he would have said if he'd have known Annie was linked to me while he caned me, and was enjoying the experience.

Q. How did Annie eventually find out so much about the Giblings, Tammy?

A. It took me a while to realise she did know a lot. We'd be talking about something, and suddenly she'd say something like 'when they came back to Salldown', and it slowly dawned on me she knew a great deal about them; that they'd left London and come back to their home town.

Q. Yes, but how did she find out?

A. Eventually she got around to telling me she'd been seeing Danny Gibling in the local record shop, in the disco, in the cafe. And she never let on once that we were related. She saved it for the right moment to drop the bombshell - and that took some time in coming. That was when I realised that Annie was no longer open to me all the time, that she had learned to shield some things from me. I knew nothing about Danny and her seeing him, or the things she found out.

Q. What effect did that have on you?

A. I felt really left out for the first time.

CHAPTER FOURTEEN

"It's time to start calling in some debts." Annie paced the lounge floor, thinking hard. November pressed against the windows, rain, strong wind, cold draughts that even in this rich warm house found their way in to chill the body - or was it Annie's talk?

Martin was, against all common sense according to Annie, playing golf in the rain, and Adrienne had disappeared to her beauty parlour - keeping back the years. Annie sniffed contemptuously.

"Where do we start?" Tammy didn't question Annie's decision, just wanted to know where to go from here.

"With Phil of course. It's time we started turning the screw just a little. Aunt Phyllis - how did he get to marry someone with the same sort of name? - will be wondering soon what he's up to round here every other week. So, an anonymous letter might find its way through their letter-box, all cut out letters from the paper, you know the sort of thing. And we'll start on the Giblings too, we've been ignoring them. Go order a pizza to be sent to their house, a large one," Annie directed, eyes blazing. "Go on, let's start some aggravation there!" She paced again, getting angrier by the moment. Tammy could feel the heat swelling out from her, a huge cloud of red fire. It burned her mind, and she drew back.

"I never asked them to come back to Salldown, did I?!" Annie went on. "They've probably not even given us a thought after all these years! Handed us over, never a thought of what we might have, or be, or become! Did you know that Danny's a year older than us? Just one year. God! Didn't waste time getting flat on her back again, did she?"

"What do you think she's like, our real mother?" Tammy edged closer to the door, knowing at any moment Annie would flare up if she didn't go order the pizza.

"Don't know, can't get a picture of her yet. But I will. Now go call them, make it a large pizza with anchovies - go!"

Tammy hurried out of the room to the kitchen. Annie pulled a pile of old papers toward her and began scissoring out the individual letters, arranging them on the table. She smiled, knowing there was nothing she liked as much as stirring up trouble.

While an anonymous letter proved nothing, it would put Phil on edge, might make Phyllis ask some searching questions, might stir him up just a little. He'd become too complacent about the whole thing, coming round here, getting his rocks off beating Tammy - No, things had to change.

She paused, scissors raised, as Tammy came back in the room.

"It'll be there within the half-hour."

"Great. Listen, kiddo, we could go spy on the Giblings, they wouldn't recognize us because we had such brilliant disguises at the Hallowe'en party, didn't we?"

"Yes, but you've got to do your share of spying!" Tammy objected, looking out at the cold rain. She saw the car sweep into the drive too fast. "Mother's back."

"Oh, is she?" Annie swept the letters and cuttings into a pile, shut them in a paper, and ran for the stairs. "I'll finish this in private."

In the safety of her room Annie swiftly cut out a mass of letters and began to arrange them on her chest of drawers. She had enough letters to make a note for Phyllis:

ASK PHIL WHAT HE DOES AT THE LAURELS ON FRIDAY NIGHTS.

And another for the Giblings:

ASK DANNY HOW HE FEELS ABOUT HIS TWIN SISTERS.

She smiled maliciously, thought a mouse into the centre of her room, and then a snake. That ought to do it, first the letters, and then casually strolling by, imagine something horrid in their houses. That would stir things up a little.

But before then - Annie went to her telephone extension and called Niall.

"Find a place for us all to meet Saturday afternoon. Get Mark there, we're having a session." She put the phone down before he could argue, and smiled again - an evil, sadistic smile. She went back to the chest of drawers, found a sheet of paper and began to glue them into place - the letters would finish it off.

CHAPTER FIFTEEN

Q. Did the letters work?
A. Oh yes. Phil came round almost immediately, contrived a visit, talked to Mother and Father, and slid out to talk to us as soon as he could.

"Who's been sending letters?" he hissed. "Phyllis is asking all sorts of questions!"

"Letters?" We looked so innocently at him. "What letters?" and he sort of grunted.

"Might have known it was nothing to do with you girls, after all, you enjoy it, don't you?" And Annie said oh so sweet and innocent it was like pure glucose being dripped: "Sure do, Uncle Phil," and she laid a hand on his arm; gentle, enticing. "Don't you think it's time Gran Webster went into a home?"

He looked shocked and horrified, and then he sort of sagged, like a deflating balloon. He said:

"I gave it all away, didn't I? You don't know a thing about the letters, but I've given you a weapon, haven't I? You know Phyllis is getting suspicious now. And your price for quiet is Gran Webster in a home. I don't know why you want it, but I'll have to see what I can do," and he left, all unmanly and drooping, and Annie skipped around the hall and danced up the stairs and I knew - just knew - there was more to come.

Q. And was there?

A. Oh yes. Phone calls to the Gibling house. "Have you asked Danny about his twin sisters yet?" and shouting, "you DO know what I'm talking about!" and slamming the phone down. Then one time she strolled into the pizza place with Mark - she told me about this afterwards - and someone was in there raising hell about pizzas which were being delivered which they hadn't ordered, and the man behind the counter shouting back:

"I get the phone call - I get the order - I bring the pizza - you pay - all right?! Or get the person to stop phoning!" And I knew then she'd gone on ordering the damn pizzas until they were going crazy.

And Mother and Father went around muttering about Phil. Was he going crazy or something, wanting Gran Webster in a home? All right, she was in a wheelchair, but she had the nurse morning and night, and wasn't that enough? And then it began to change. I remember how it began to change to why should we go round there every day and why should the nurse go in twice a day when she had enough money to be in a nice home? And slowly the pressure began to build. Just as Annie wanted.

Q. What was the reason for that, Tammy?

A. The one thing Gran Webster feared more than anything was not dying in her own home. And she made the mistake of saying so when Annie could hear.

Q. You said you liked the old lady. Did you see her much?

A. I had to, Annie told me to, she wanted to know what effect it was all having on Gran, but wouldn't go visit herself. I could see what it was doing; dragging her down, taking away her will to live. I liked going round there, she had a mile of stories of Father when he was young, then when they were first married, what Mother was like colour matching the wedding presents, returning anything that didn't fit the decor. I enjoyed just sitting and listening. And I'd report back to Annie that the pressure was wearing Gran down, which it was. Each time she'd say things like: "I don't want to go in no home, Tammy, why should I? I've lived here all my married life." And I'd say things like: "Well, Gran, it's hard on the family, and it would be nice to have a nurse and warden to call." And she'd sigh and say I was right but she didn't want to go. I got to visit my Gran, Annie got to know what was going on - we all gained out of that.

Q. Didn't you feel guilty? You were contributing to her decline, you were helping it!

A. Of course I felt guilty! But I was being punished for it, wasn't I? Phil, Mr Wrayland, Mark - oh yes, Mark. He got more into it as time went on, and he knew how to hurt. Whatever I got, it was punishment for what I was doing to Gran. And the Giblings, and Phil. And for deceiving Mother and Father and obeying Annie instead.

Q. Do you really believe you were deceiving your parents?

A. Of course I was. We both were. We were acting innocent and loving at home and all the time Annie - we - were scheming things.

Q. What happened at the session Annie ordered Niall to arrange, Tammy?

A. That was wild! I mean, like wild! Annie excelled herself that time! Niall found a place, an abandoned barn. No one around for miles. Nothing in the barn but a few bales of straw and some rats and mice - Annie didn't mind them, but Niall did. We all turned up there, Niall and Mark, Annie and me, and Annie had a bag which she pulled out of the boot and carried into the barn. In the bag were ropes, implements, and a Polaroid camera. This was for real - I mean, for real. She got Mark to tie me up, hands over my head, toes just touching the ground, the most uncomfortable pose she could devise for me. And she tied Niall the same. She got Mark to pull my panties down and arrange my skirt so it didn't get in the way, and she did the same with Niall; got his underpants down and shirt out of the way. Damn fool hung there shivering, he hated the pain, just loved giving in to Annie. Me, I liked both, and was prepared to admit it too.

And there we were, Mark with me, Annie with Niall. She handed Mark a tawse; thick leather, solid, heavy - and had one for herself. And for every stroke she gave Niall, Mark gave one to me. How that leather wraps itself around you! The impact is enough to knock the breath out of you. Three inches wide leather creates a three inch wide band of pure agony and leaves pure agony behind. The end comes around, strikes the stomach, the hip, the pubis. For Niall it was worse, sometimes he yelled out if the end caught his tackle, but he should have known better and should have worn a jockstrap of some kind. He should have known Annie's beatings by then! Ooops, Annie doesn't approve of the word 'beating', says it indicates pure sadism. She prefers to call them sessions. Not that she denied she's a sadist, mind!

We got ten strokes each from one side, and then Annie moved round and we both got another ten. Because Mark was mirroring Annie exactly, whatever she did he did, whatever Niall got I got. We were both yelling after fifteen, and nearly had enough by twenty. Damn that leather hurts! Stroke after stroke landing one on top of the other, hurting ... hurting ...

Anyway, we had a breather, Niall and me suspended there, Annie and Mark having a quick roll, his hands down her pants, her hands down his pants, kissing like kissing was going out of fashion. Niall revolved on his toes and looked at me.

"What are we doing her, Tam?" he asked, and I could see he was pretty much in a state. But I could also see a gleam of pure pleasure behind the pain and 'I want to be free' face he wore. Much like mine, I guess. I still fancied Mark, you see, and to have him deal with me like that - well, it was something else, I can tell you! I said:

"Doing what we're told, Niall," and he just nodded.

From tawses Annie progressed to riding crops; nasty vicious things. My bottom was burning from the tawse, I knew the crop would be agony, and it was. Mark slashed it across my thighs. At one point he forgot to mirror Annie and swung me round, bringing the crop down across the front of my thighs, leaving me screaming. Niall was screaming, but for a different reason - he'd seen a rat. It fled the barn at the noise we were making.

I don't know how many we got; my bruises were blurred and indistinct afterwards. But I knew I was riding an adrenalin high that would be hard to beat for some time to come. When Annie stopped thrashing Niall and Mark stopped thrashing me, he sent me spinning round and caught his hand between my thighs and stuck his fingers into my slit, which was dripping. He pressed his fingers against a nerve or something and even as I cried I shrieked and writhed and had the biggest orgasm in the world. And then he fucked Annie.

And Niall and me had to watch.

CHAPTER SIXTEEN

"For Christmas I'd like a smart computer," Annie dropped the comment lightly into the conversation after dinner. Mother looked surprised and then smiled. Father just looked sad for a moment.

"What happened to surprises?" asked mother, looking at both of them.

"Surprise? I thought that went out when we stopped believing in Father Christmas!" snorted Annie. Her hair trailed over her scarlet sweatshirt, gleaming under the chandelier. Tammy knew hers should look the same, but somehow Annie had more shine, more enthusiasm, more energy, as if she, Tammy, was a pale imitation of the overwhelming twin.

Which is only right, she thought with a swift touch of bitterness.

"We'll have to see, darling." Mother cleared the table, stacking dishes on the silver tray which had stayed in use after the birthday party. Father spread leaflets all over the table when the plates were gone. Tammy leaned forward, caught sight of 'home' and 'sheltered accommodation' and beckoned to Annie to leave.

"I borrowed a record for Niall," she told Annie as they left the room. "West Coast group called Love."

"They're ages old!" Annie was scornful. "Who cares about people from the past?"

"Plenty of people, look at the Doors film! Anyway, I thought they might be good, I like the sound of them. Want to hear?"

"Might as well, nothing else to do."

"Did you see what Father had there?" climbing the stairs, almost arm in arm, almost Siamese twins. Tammy looked back, saw mother watching them with a soft, almost soppy look.

"No - what did he have?"

"Old people's homes leaflets."

"Good." Said with such viciousness Tammy was taken aback. Then she felt the flare of anger from Annie, knew the party had not gone away; that it rankled still, and nothing would be settled until Gran Webster had been paid back.

"That's not good." Tammy led the way into her room, put the Love CD in the music centre and set it going. The melodic sharp sounds filled the air.

"Dated stuff," Annie dismissed the music. Tammy turned it down a little. Wind slashed the windows. Sharp bites of sleet tapped icy fingers, demanding admittance. Annie closed the curtains, shut out the winter weather, turned to Tammy. "That's the old bag taken care of, they won't rest now until she's in a home."

"You're shortening her life, Annie."

"She's got pots of money. We could all do with some more, it will be good all round."

"What if they use the money to pay for the home?"

"Doesn't matter." Annie shrugged, blonde hair shimmering. "All that matters is she gets paid back for ruining our party and our lives."

"How will she know?" Tammy took the CD back; Annie wasn't interested, wasn't impressed.

"She'll know. I'll get Phil to tell her. Talking of which, are you missing his attentions, kiddo?"

"A bit," and it was true, she was. Phil's sessions were painful but exciting; any moment mother and father could come home for whatever reason, illness, anything, and find them. It added spice, and that spice was sometimes missing with the sessions with Mark and Niall.

"Then we'd better find you someone else." Annie parted the curtains, looked out. "I'd a good mind to send you walking out there tonight, but it's still sleeting, so I won't. Not yet anyway. But I will, kiddo - I will."

Tammy felt the familiar secretive thrill run through her, felt the fear clasp an icy hand around her heart, knew she would both love and hate it at the same time. A strange man, a hard man, who knew what he might do?

"In the meantime, you'll do it yourself." Annie threw a plastic belt across the room to Tammy. "Here, try it, whip yourself. And I'll watch to make sure you do until you hurt. I mean it, until you hurt."

Tammy took the belt, wrapped it around her hand, looked at

it, looked at the mirror, and slowly removed her jeans and briefs. She looked at Annie just once, and then concentrated on the mirror and her own anguished face as the plastic slashed at her hips and back, her bottom and her legs.

She was crying after ten minutes - sobbing after fifteen.

Annie just stood, and smiled.

CHAPTER SEVENTEEN

Q. It's hard to believe you would beat yourself, Tammy.

A. Why? I just did what Annie told me, regardless of what it was.

Q. But this was different - this was self-abuse!

A. And deep down I loved it. You see, you have to understand, pain and pleasure are mixed, inseparable, real. To feel pain, to know it is coming, to anticipate it and thrill to the anticipation, even as you hate it - there's no way of explaining it, not properly. But to bow to someone's wishes and do what they tell you and do it well, and at the same time to know I was giving Annie pleasure because she was linked to me, she knew my thoughts and feelings, she had double pleasure - well, it made it all worthwhile.

Q. Didn't your parents hear you crying?

A. No. Annie made sure of that! Loud music, rock music; covers a lot of sounds.

Q. You haven't mentioned Danny Gibling for some time, did Annie go out with him again?

A. On and off. She had trouble keeping him at arm's length, so she deliberately discouraged invitations. But he was after her all right, I could see that when we met up, in pizza places or discos or wherever. And we were going out a lot, with Niall and Mark - once we double-dated guys from the College, but that didn't work, as they both lusted after Annie and took no notice of me. So she refused to see them again.

"You take me *and* my sister," she told them.

Q. How did the - vendetta - against the Giblings proceed from there?

A. Annie stopped ordering pizzas and began filling in every single form for brochures and leaflets that she could find. I don't know what effect that had on them, but it must have driven them crazy. It would me, anyway.

Q. And your parents knew nothing about it.

A. Nothing. But Annie started on them, gently dropping hints about things like Aids. Did they know anyone who had it? What would they do if we had it? That kind of thing. Then one day she dropped the big bombshell, said she was thinking of going for an Aids test and I should go too. Mother and Father sat there at dinner with their mouths open, shocked rigid. Then Annie burst out laughing and said she was joking and they relaxed, but not completely. She sowed a few seeds of doubt in their mind, you see. And perhaps they realised for the first time we weren't so innocent.

Q. What happened next?

A. Annie went walking by the Gibling house and thought some creatures into it. She said she heard the shrieks from outside!

Q. And you?

A. What do you mean?

Q. How did you get involved?

A. Oh, I didn't, not then. It was down to Annie what she did next, the vendetta was entirely hers, nothing to do with me. I didn't feel a thing toward the Giblings. Then or now.

Q. Not even -

A. Not even then.

Q. What time are we at in the history?

A. About two weeks before Christmas, I think, if I remember right. Everyone had their decorations up, in the houses I mean. Shops had put theirs up weeks earlier. It was bitter cold, and felt very wintry. The lights and trees all decorated made it feel very Christmassy. Unfortunately it was

184

too cold to arrange sessions in the garage, we'd have frozen to death, so Annie came up with something else.

Q. What was that?

A. Sent me back to Mr Wrayland. Annie came with me - to watch.

CHAPTER EIGHTEEN

47 Kensington Drive was everything Tammy said it was; run down, shabby, tasteless and graceless. Garish coloured lights winked on and off in the window, a tree overladen with ornaments stood just inside.

Annie paused, pretended to be tying up a shoelace, and listened. She could hear raised voices and slamming doors even through the closed windows. My family, she thought, my family, cheap nasty lower class people! And I come from them! Her hatred spilled out, and she imagined a large spider in the front door. She heard a shriek, grinned and moved on, feeling much better.

"So easy," she whispered. "So easy to terrify people!" and smiled evilly. An old lady passing by glanced at Annie's face and immediately crossed over the road. Annie smiled a little more, feeling even more pleased with herself. Control. Power. That was what it was all about. Power could overcome anything; class problems, money problems - no, not money problems. That was something she wanted to work on; how to get money, lots and lots of money. There had to be a way to use her power, her sexuality, her dominance, to get money. Even as she questioned it, hurrying along the broken pavements past rusting cars and run down houses, she knew how she would get the money. An advertisement in a contact magazine.

"Me or Tam," she mused aloud, startling a dog wandering around a pile of rubbish bags. It barked at her and ran off. "I could sell my services or Tam's. Not sure what she'd think of it."

A cold wind blew round the corner, making Annie shiver. Tammy had better be on time, she thought, I'm not hanging around in the cold!

Tammy was on time, waiting on the corner of the road where Mr Wrayland lived. Annie could sense her fear verging on terror, sensed the anticipation which made it all worthwhile, felt the clenching of the muscles in Tammy's rounded cheeks, felt the wetness that permeated her knickers, and knew Tammy was excited, no matter what she might say. She hurried to Tammy and hugged her.

"Oh my twin, don't I know you better than I know myself?" Annie drew Tammy close as they walked along together.

"This one's for me and me alone, kiddo."

"No, it's for me too, I did get such a thrill last time," and it was true, she had.

Mr Wrayland opened the door as they walked up the path, his eyes going wide at the sight of the two of them.

"Do I get both of you?" he asked, as they walked past him into the warm hall.

Annie laughed. "Definitely not! I want to watch this time, that's all."

Mr Wrayland eyed her closely. "You're a very strange young lady, if I might say so."

"And you're a strange man, Mr Wrayland; it's an odd way of spending your time. Good job there are some of us who enjoy it." She pushed Tammy into what she guessed was the lounge.

Tammy hadn't spoken. She stood in the centre of the room, her legs perceptibly shaking, her eyes wild with fear and delight. This man was an expert, and it wasn't often she got punished by an expert.

Annie slumped onto the settee, absorbing Tammy's apprehension and anticipation, feeding on it greedily, adding it to her own vicarious thrill of being able to watch. So often she was involved in something herself and wasn't able to be more than an onlooker. This time she could.

"I'm not happy about this," Mr Wrayland looked very uneasy, despite having the cane in his hand already.

No way are you unhappy, thought Annie. I've got you where I want you, old man! If you were unhappy there'd not be a cane in sight!

"Tamasine is my twin, my identical twin in every respect, Mr Wrayland." She spoke soothingly, approving as Tammy removed her coat and skirt. "We just have this difference of sexual inclination. I prefer to be dominant, she is a submissive - in case you hadn't noticed. Well, it isn't for me to punish my own twin, so I get someone else to do it. Last time I couldn't come, this time I want to watch."

Tammy still hadn't spoken. Her gaze flashed from Mr Wrayland to Annie, and back again. Annie flashed her a silent message.

'You're doing all right, kiddo, and I've got wet knickers too.' And she had, she wasn't lying.

"Let's make it twenty-four this time," she said aloud. Tammy gasped, and then groaned very slightly. Annie tut-tutted under her breath.

'Kiddo, you're not supposed to come before you get caned!'

Another silent message which brought a grin to Tammy's face.

Mr Wrayland took a deep breath, straightened himself to his full height, and nodded.

"All right, if that's what you want."

"I do, and so does Tamasine."

"Then bend over the chair, young lady." He touched Tammy with the cane, and she went obediently to the settee, leaning over the end, briefs stretched tight across her cheeks, identical to Annie's in every way except Annie's never bore bruises of any kind. Ever.

And then he began the caning.

187

CHAPTER NINETEEN

Q. What was it like, Tammy?

A. Twenty-four? Horrendous - but so thrilling it wasn't true. I almost melted on the spot. I certainly had an orgasm as Annie said! And she knew, of course. Anyway, I leaned over his chair and waited, knowing he was flexing the cane, knowing it would strike at any moment, knowing too that Annie was sliding one hand inside her own pants beneath the loose coat she wore, and fingering herself. My quim was twitching like mad ... and then the first one landed. I never remember how much it hurts and jump every time. My head comes up as the band of pain sears across me - he does it right across the middle first time, and I'm sure I'll never take them all. Never! No way! But I stay there getting lower and lower, pressing myself harder and harder to the chair, longing to roll over, to throw myself at his feet and beg for mercy, and yet -

Q. Why don't you?

A. Because deep down it's what I want. I know I'm basically bad and need punishment. So, I get it where I can. And Mr Wrayland, for all his headmasterly nonsense, is a man prepared to give it and give it good and hard. Twenty-four. Oh my! The thought of it! They overlaid once and then twice and then again. I was screeching into the cushion by the time he was done, flooding the upholstery with dark stains from my eyes, and burning everywhere - but I'd come again. Oh yes, I'd come again, as Annie had, we both had wet knickers. And we walked out of there leaving Mr Wrayland with an uncomfortable bulge to take care of.

"He had a strong right hand," Annie commented as we walked down the path, me carefully, she bouncing down the flagstones. "He'll get rid of that when we're gone." But he was standing at the window, looking out. I looked back, just once.

Q. How did you hide the beating from your parents?

A. Mother and Father are easy to hide things from! They don't ask questions, they don't demand your presence every evening in front to the TV. They're busy with their lives, watching their videos of nature programmes and comparing notes from the natural history encyclopaedias they buy. They don't worry about us. We put our heads round the door and say:

"We're going out now." And Mother says:

"All right darling, have a good time. Be good and don't be late." And Father grins stupidly and says:

"Have a good time, girls," and we're gone. They don't know where, and I don't think they realise they don't know where.

Q. But twenty-four! You must have walked a little stiffly for a few days!

A. No. I'm used to being punished, the muscles are well used to it. I walked around as if nothing had happened, and after a day or so it was as if nothing had happened. I winced a bit when I sat down.

Q. What happened next?

A. Christmas happened next. Danny Gibling had got the message, he hadn't asked Annie out for ages, just ogled her from across the floor in MacDonalds when we went in there, or if we met when shopping, that kind of thing. He started dating someone from our street, a long thin streak of - well water, called Gloria. Fancy name, not so fancy person. But they seemed all right together. Mark and Niall were our escorts still. Niall and I made a good pair, submissive to both Mark and Annie. They had a lot of fun at our expense, ordering us about.

Q. What about the family vendetta?

A. Our family? Gran Webster was very ill, depression they said. Phil went around looking as if the cares of the world had ended up on his shoulders, and even Mother commented on how he didn't come round so much any more.

Trouble was, Phil had got used to the sessions with us, he missed it terribly, which was part of Annie's plan, of course. I didn't see it then, I only saw it later. He was in torment, it was in his eyes when he looked at us, longing to get his hands on me and couldn't. Because he was too damn scared of what else Annie might ask him to do. I think he worked out Annie = sex with me = keeping quiet about the whole business to Aunt Phyl and also - getting Gran Webster into a home for whatever reason Annie wanted her in a home. And he didn't like it one bit. He cornered me in the hall one time, when he did come round to see Father about something, and whispered: "God I miss you," and walked off before I could answer.

Q. Did you miss him?
A Not while I had Mr Wrayland. And that's something else. I found out Annie was making sly visits to Mr Wrayland on her own. It was some time before I found out why.

CHAPTER TWENTY

Christmas came in a flare of silver designer-matched Christmas tree, sparkly but oh so refined decorations, and a whole lot of hypocrisy. Annie raged against it all as she leaned against Tammy's window-sill and stared out at strong winds, scudding black clouds and cold cold rain.

"Look at it all," she swept her arms around in a huge circle, taking in Tammy's carefully wrapped gifts, the new dress waiting for Christmas morning, and Tammy's few attempts at decorating her room; a shining star suspended from the ceiling, a few bits of holly here and there, tinsel draped round the mirror. "You've made it look halfway homely, but downstairs -"

Tammy knew precisely what she meant. Downstairs was mother's domain, where everything had to be matched or it wasn't allowed. Cards with cheerful Santas on them were tucked to the back, the elegant snow scenes and Victorian prints brought to the front.

"Is homely a compliment?" she asked, picking up a sprig of holly and tucking it behind the hands of her Victorian doll.

"Yes, of course it is! I bet the Giblings have a traditional tree, pine needles dropping everywhere, lights, tatty old fairy, the whole bit, things they've loved forever which come down from the loft year after year - while we get designer trees."

"But they're lovely," objected Tammy, trying to visualise a tatty tree strung with lights and old ornaments, and failing.

"You're missing the point, kiddo." Annie swung round and round, throwing her arms out, almost touching the glass lampshade suspended from the ceiling. "You're missing the whole fucking point!"

"Don't swear," Tammy spoke automatically, registering her twin's distress and rage.

"I'll fucking well swear if I want! Listen, Tams, listen and look. Every year Mother goes out and buys - buys a damn tree fully loaded with ornaments. Other people, normal people, get their decorations from their lofts, and say things like 'oh look at this, I remember this!', and 'isn't this old now?', and it's loved. It isn't sterile and new and shiny bright! It's loved!"

"As we are."

"I wish! I think we were bought, paid for, brought home in new white shawls encrusted with lace and ribbons because that is what was needed to complete the picture! Gran Webster was right there, damn her soul!"

"How do you know all this, Annie?"

"Know what? About the decorations and things? I was there when the Jeffersons got theirs out. Amanda invited me round, remember? I never got over it."

"We have our own traditions; Mother buys a new tree." Tammy picked up a package and handed it to Annie. "Here, an early gift. Don't let Mother see what I've bought you."

"A surprise? How did you manage to get a surprise without me knowing?" Annie pulled at the brightly patterned paper with the glee of child. "Oh no!" She looked at the cover of the video with a mixture of dismay and surprise, then burst out laughing. "The Experience. You bought me The Experience!"

"What's funny?" demanded Tammy, feeling hurt that the secret her carefully closeted mind had concealed should be laughed at.

For answer Annie hurried out of the room and came back clutching an identical package. Tammy took it, suspecting what she would find.

"You didn't!" She had, the same video.

"But how - ?" they began together, stopped, laughed and tried again.

"Who got - ?"

"You first," Annie gestured toward Tammy. "You first, you gave me your gift first."

"And I got Mark to get this for me. The suppliers must have thought Christmas had come - oh it has!"

Annie began to laugh so hard she rolled on the floor, holding her stomach and shaking as tears flowed down her face. It was infectious. Tammy found herself joining in.

When they finally stopped laughing, Annie picked up her video and looked at it.

"I'll give this to Alfred, the original dirty old man."

"Who's Alfred?" Tammy reached for tissues, dabbed her wet face and flopped out on the bed, a lifeless rag doll, exhausted with laughter.

"Wrayland." The answer prompted a further question in Tammy, one she had wanted to ask and didn't like to. Perhaps deep down she knew the answer before it came.

"Why do you still go there, Annie?"

Annie sobered up, put a finger to her lips, whispered 'sssshh', and flashed Tammy a series of vivid and erotic pictures; young men and young women bent over the chair in Mr Wrayland's study, being caned.

"And where are you while this is going on?"

"In his kitchen. Would you believe he has a mirror in the

hall, directly opposite the chair where you bent over, kiddo? And you can see that mirror from the kitchen. And it works, damn me, it works!"

"Really?"

"I wouldn't lie to you, my twin. I wouldn't dare - you'd see through it." But Tammy wondered if she would. Annie had learned to close her mind to all probing and touching.

"How do you know when to go?"

"Questions, questions! I don't, I just go, and if it's a good day he'll have a visitor, you know, someone who's answered the contact ad. This woman the other day, she must have been 50 if she was a day, all saggy bum and drooping cheeks, wanted to be really roughly treated. He got her bent over, caned her six times, hard mind! Whistling that cane down across her white flabby cheeks. How they bounced when the cane hit them! And then made her stay there for ten minutes, gave her another six, waited another ten minutes, gave her another six, and then called me in. She was shocked rigid! But he ordered her to stay there and gave her another six with me watching, and she was bawling when he'd done."

"What did you think?"

"Tam, my dear twin, I loved every second, even if I couldn't bond with her like I can with you. So I have a good time at old Wrayland's, and there's the other thing -"

"The other thing is, you've got him where you want him."

"Right first time. I'm not sure yet how I'll use him - but I will."

And Annie said it in a cold hard voice that sent chills down Tammy's spine. Then she added something that sent more than a chill down her spine.

"New Year's Eve, kiddo, you go walking. Remember, the first man you see -"

"How could I forget?" A sweep of feeling went through Tammy, making her almost climax right there, on her own bed, without a single fantasy thought to help, just the mere knowledge she would obey Anastasia, come what may.

CHAPTER TWENTY ONE

Q. Tell me about the video, Tammy.

A. You're as bad as the rest of them, I swear you are! The Experience. A video about a girl who is tied up by her boyfriend, wrists and hands tied, and is whipped on the pussy and breasts until she is red raw, and loves every minute of it. So she finds a place where she can go, where she's put in stocks and beaten with leather straps and paddles. We see hot wax dripped on breasts, especially nipples. People hanging in awkward positions, quite a bit of beating going on, but really it was a disappointment to me. I don't like the hanging scenes, or the hot wax. I prefer straightforward videos of punishments. I've got quite a collection. You can see them if you like. You know where they are, on the shelf next to the video at home.

Q. You had no idea she'd bought the same thing?

A. No. But we were that close, telepathically close, it would have been a surprise if she had found something different from me. After all, it was all I could do to keep it from her, to keep that part of my mind shuttered from her prying thoughts. It was easier for her, she didn't have me probing all the time, only occasionally. I got scared by that kind of activity and usually backed off.

Q. Did you share videos?

A. Yes. One or other of the guys would get hold of one and slip us a copy, and Annie and me would watch it.

Q. And you were turned-on by them?

A. Oh yes.

Q. Tell me about Christmas.

A. Not much to tell really. It was a quiet occasion, Christmas Day various family members came round for sherry and mince pies, leaving gifts, or in Uncle Phil's case some more cash - buying us off still, I think - and we hung around home. Annie got her computer and played with that most of the day. I hardly saw her. My big gift from Mother and Father was a new hi-fi system. I had a lot of fun with that, fixing up the aerial to get good reception for London radio stations, things like that. I miss that, being here. My real gift to Annie was another piece of Celtic jewellery, and she bought me a CD I particularly wanted; full price import job, very expensive. It was good of her.

Q. How was the family at this time?

A. Gran Webster was very ill, too ill for us to visit much, so we just made brief duty visits on Boxing Day. I felt bad about that, but Annie was full of it, I could see that. "Silly old bag," she kept saying. "Silly old cow, teach her to spoil my special birthday!" Thinking back, I realise it was about that time I got an inkling that Annie wasn't - quite all there. A little bit of her was out to lunch, if you know what I mean. And I got scared, because she could so easily influence me. And did.

Q. And after Christmas?

A. You know what I'm going to say, don't you? All these other questions are a device to keep me from revealing what you really want to hear, what happened on New year's Eve, until you are good and ready to hear it. I told you, you're as bad as the rest of them! You want details of the spanking Tamasine got? I'll tell you, I got spanked, and damned hard too!

CHAPTER TWENTY TWO

Mother was a little wistful.

"Are you sure you girls don't want to celebrate New Year down here with us?" Smiling her 'let's all be family together' smile, which made Annie sick.

"No thanks, Mother, we'll be all right. The New Year can come in without us, we're a bit tired, aren't we Tam?"

"Yes." And it was true. Tammy was very tired, having laid awake night after night visualising New Year's Eve, visualising walking along the road, accosting the first man she saw, the whole scenario re-enacted over and over again until she finally fell asleep, sometimes with fingers buried in her slit, waking in the morning wet, stiff and very tired.

"Too much Christmas partying," father smiled a benevolent 'don't I know all about it' smile, that made Tammy sick.

"Happy New Year," chorused Tammy and Annie, without so much as a look at each other.

"Happy New Year, darlings." Mother raised a crystal glass of sherry toward them and smiled.

11.30. Tammy glanced unwillingly at the grandfather clock on the landing, felt a chill run through her, felt the familiar and welcome surge of eroticism that preceded any adventure, any obeying of Annie's orders. How did she know just what to pick, what to say, what to order her to do to send thrills and excitement through her?

"Get changed, kiddo," the words were whispered but Tammy heard them, hurried to her room, found the short tight skirt and cropped top and struggled into them. It would be cold, it would be very cold, but she could throw a leather jacket around her shoulders and still reveal her body to the men who were out celebrating New Year in Salldown.

There were men out celebrating New Year in Salldown, weren't there?

Annie suddenly appeared in her room, smiling her knowing smile. "Happy New Year, kiddo."

"I wonder."

"It will be. Oh, we'll have such adventures! You see if we don't." Annie approached her, flicked her long blonde hair, tugged at the cropped top, exposed a little more cleavage. "You leave here 11.50, and get out there and knock 'em dead. You hear? You understand?"

"I hear. I understand."

Tammy flicked a look at the clock. 11.45.

"Enjoy yourself, kiddo," and Annie was gone.

Tammy walked slowly and silently to the top of the stairs, clutching her leather jacket and a small plastic bag with her keys. Annie would have the back door unlocked for her, but just in case -

As the hands of the grandfather clock touched 11.50 Tammy carefully yet rapidly descended the stairs, feeling Annie's probing thoughts, feeling her own excitement wet through the black lace briefs she wore.

There was starlight bright enough to equal the moon, which hung low and full in the night sky. The street was still alive at five minutes to midnight, families staying up to welcome in the New Year with drinks and crackers, with high hopes and a lot of wild dreams, most of which would be shattered by February, if not sooner.

She started to walk along the street, casual, but her knees were shaking so hard it was a wonder she could stand upright.

The first man.

It was as if Annie had spoken to her directly, the voice was so clear. Tammy knew Annie was lying flat on her back on the bed, probably naked, one hand at her slit, the other rubbing her nipples round and round, sending shivers of excitement through her as she saw what Tammy saw; the silent cold street, the lit windows, the stars - some still, some twinkling, the huge moon staring coldly down at her, wondering what she was doing.

What she was doing was walking the streets at midnight.

Her footsteps echoed in the cold silence.

Other footsteps. Not her own. Tammy drew in a sharp breath, felt fear clutch her heart, wondered if she could go through with it.

Knowing she had to.

She stopped under a lamp post and leaned against it, the picture of whoredom, the picture of innocence.

"Tammy, what are you doing out here?"

"Hello, Uncle Phil. I'm -" She felt Annie's touch, her surprise, and her sheer gurgling pleasure.

"I'm looking for someone to spank me."

"God, girl, I've been looking for a chance, come on."

He needed no encouragement or invitation. Before Tammy knew what had happened she was being escorted to his car, a dark estate parked in a side road. Tammy registered surprise and interest that he should be out, that the car should be in a side road at midnight on New Year's Eve, when he should surely have been at home with Aunt Phyl.

She said nothing, but felt the worn upholstery beneath her thighs, wriggled a little which caused him to groan, and watched as he swiftly and deliberately drove to a small clearing in the nearby woods.

She'd been here before, but said nothing.

The engine coughed, spluttered, and died. Phil turned in his seat, arm around the steering wheel, staring at her in the cold moonlight.

"This one of your games, Tamasine?"

"Yes."

"What is it tonight?"

"Ask the first man I saw to give me a spanking."

He shook his head. "You girls live dangerously, don't you? It could have been anyone, a murderer, rapist, whatever. For God's sake why?"

She lifted her chin defiantly, and stared at him.

"Life in Salldown is unutterably boring, Uncle Phil. We escape, Annie and me, we escape to College a few times a week, but mostly what is there for us? Nothing. So we have to do something to liven up our lives. So, we live dangerously. Every adventure survived is another for the memories."

"You're right." He looked down at his groin, saw the bulge, saw the throbbing movement. "There is nothing for you, or for me, come to that."

"But what were you doing in that street at this time?"

"Can I - I mean, will I do?"

"Of course!" Tammy opened the door, went round to the back door of the car and climbed in. "What are you waiting for?"

With another groan Phil got in the back, pulling her roughly across his knees, wrenching at the tight skirt, staring down at the black briefs with a longing that was almost a physical pain. Tammy twisted her head back, stared at the carpet littered with tiny specks of grit and crumbs, wondered where they had come from.

"God, I've missed you!" He brought his hand down hard, making her yelp in surprise at the severity.

And then he shifted slightly, pulled her closer, wrapped one arm firmly around her waist and began to rain spanks down on her cheeks, harder and harder, stinging, burning and hurting. Tammy wriggled and yelped, and then began to cry, surprising herself and him. He smacked the tops of her thighs, the small of her back, the curve of her cheeks over and over again, savagely hurting, bringing out all his pent up longing and frustration.

When he was finally tired, when his hand stung too much to go on, he sat her up, pushed her back on the seat and thrust his fingers deep into her slit, bringing her to instant orgasm. As she shuddered over his hand, tears coursing down her face, she automatically reached for his erection, releasing him and jerking the engorged penis with both hands. She lowered herself to his lap, and kissed and nibbled until a fine spray of semen splattered over her clothes.

"OK, I've done what you told me," she mumbled, sensing Annie's laugh deep in her mind.

"What was that?" Phil kissed her tearstained cheeks. "What was that, Tammy?"

"Nothing." She shook her head, reached for tissues from her bag, and dried her face. "Take me home, Uncle Phil. Annie's waiting for me."

CHAPTER TWENTY THREE

Q. What did Annie say when you got back?

A. She was torn between being furious her plan didn't work, that I didn't end up with a stranger but a family member, and delighted that we had yet another hold over Phil. "He'll be so useful," she kept saying, and I didn't know or understand why - not for ages. She was red-faced and a little breathless, so I knew she'd been there when I got spanked. I envied her that ability. Imagine, being able to dominate and submit at the same time! Must have been multiple orgasms going on, while I only had the one.

Q. And your parents never found out?

A. Do you know, it seems odd these days to hear them called 'your parents' when we knew they were adoptive parents. But never mind, no, they never found out.

Q. Don't you find that odd?

A. No, of course not! I told you, they had no real interest in us, we were decorations, additions to their perfect lives. Mother had her salon visits, her afternoon soirees, her Oxfam hunger lunches and all the other fund-raising things she was into. And Father either had 'conferences' in the evenings with clients, or he was at the golf club. Mother joined the golf club too, became part of a ladies team, and we saw hardly anything of them. She got our cleaning lady to come in more days and to cook dinners as well, would you believe. Mind you, we didn't mind, we got to eat things like sausages and chips, beans and beefburgers. Mother would have died if she'd known! But we enjoyed it.

Q. I assume Annie hadn't stopped the vendetta?

A. Oh no, it increased. She switched tactics, having made sure old Gran Webster was on her way out, she started on the other grandparents. We had both of them still, Gramps and Gran Livitt, who after all were responsible for Mother not being able to have children, or so Annie reasoned. She began a campaign against them, the whispering phone calls, the occasional pizza delivery in their home town, the brochures through the door, the whole bit. We knew about it because they would come round and complain bitterly about the campaign being waged against them. They blamed it on next door, because they'd fallen out with them, or Gramps had, shouting over the fence, all that kind of thing. All over the cars they insisted on working on in their front garden. All right, it lowered the tone of the neighbourhood, but there are other ways of dealing with it rather than shouting over the fence for half the street to hear! Gran said she had never been so ashamed in her life as that day.

Annie said later she wished she'd been there, she could do with learning some new swear words. I didn't agree with her, I thought she knew plenty. I'd heard most of them usually directed at Niall when he knelt at her feet after a whipping - and she did give him some terrible whippings!

Q. Where were these?

A. In the garage as before. Worked quite well, nice overhead beam to string people up.

Q. Did you get whipped?

A. What a silly question! Of course I did, it was what I lived for!

Q. You said when you came back Annie was angry but pleased, because she had another hold over Phil. Did she make use of that?

A. Not immediately, what she did was ...

CHAPTER TWENTY FOUR

"So you see Mr Wrayland, I need somewhere to have the mail sent." Annie was all innocence, standing primly in her clinging jersey wool dress of emerald, the deep green making her blonde hair look even more blonde. The dress clung to her curves, and she was aware of his eyes; knew he wasn't as rigidly controlled as he liked to make out.

"Sit down," he indicated the overstuffed richly upholstered settee and sat down in an armchair opposite her. "Now, tell me what this advertisement is."

"A contact ad, we want to get some guys to write to us about sex."

"And no doubt you're going to offer yourselves as submissives."

"Of course!" Annie giggled, an erotic sound starting deep in her throat. "But only one of us. I go along for the ride, as it were."

"Just what hold do you have over your sister?"

"Nothing you need worry about," she told him tartly, wondering where the question was going.

"I'm just curious. You seem to enjoy her coming as much as she does."

"No point in not telling you. Tamasine and I are telepathically linked. I can sense what she is feeling, and so I get double enjoyment from her discipline sessions. I get the dominant side of me thrilled to pieces, and the submissive side of her to balance it. Nothing like it."

"Curious. You're a very forthright young lady, aren't you?"

"I wouldn't be here otherwise."

"And you've brought me a lot of pleasure."

"I know that."

Annie tilted her head to one side to look at him, let one of her smiles turn up the corners of her mouth, let him look at her crossed legs, uncrossed them so her panties winked at him.

The doorbell rang and he got up.

"That's the other reason you're here, isn't it? To watch someone else getting theirs. Go on, in the kitchen with you."

Annie snatched up her bag and disappeared into the old fashioned, almost quaint kitchen. She looked around in disbelief as she did every time. A gas cooker nearly 50 years old, all rounded edges and worn away knobs and rings. Wooden drain-ing-board, whoever had wooden draining-boards these days? Old fashioned square sink with one cold water tap. A battered old kettle sitting on the stove, waiting for someone to light a match and set it going. A table covered in some kind of plastic cloth with a material backing. A coconut mat under the table, and scuffed chairs.

Old. Old as Wrayland. Nothing changed. Living alone, he had no reason to change anything.

Annie moved closer to the door and looked at the mirror. Alfred Wrayland had all but shut the lounge door, but there was enough of a sight-line for her to see the man who had called, a thin bookish looking man, glasses and long floppy hair, twisting his hands round and round in nervousness as Alfred Wrayland lectured him. It was apparently part of the service, this lecturing. Annie could swear she saw a gleam of pleasure in the man's eyes.

The lecture went on, interminably, a jacket was discarded, then a sweater, then the trousers were lowered, and he bent over as Annie heard the inevitable swish of the cane through the air and saw the man flinch, even before the cane came near him.

It was a long and severe caning, Alfred Wrayland landing each one perfectly across the taut cheeks, underpants up and then down, caning hard, leaving distinct fine lines across the skin, bringing a howl of protest every now and then as they overlapped, blood specks springing to the surface. Annie counted 24, 30, then a further six. It was the most she had seen Alfred Wrayland give anyone. 36, and the man was clearly suffering. And clearly aroused. His erection thrust up in front of him, and it was all he could do to pull up his pants, stand, and zip up his trousers.

He left, red-faced and walking stiffly, as Annie slid out of the kitchen and back into the lounge.

"Magnificent performance," she said, with a small bow in Alfred Wrayland's direction.

"Glad you thought so, my dear, nothing like praise from a connoisseur. Now, about this advertisement -"

"Tammy and I want to put an ad in a sex magazine, for men who want someone to spank to contact us. We want to mull over the answers, see if anyone is worth responding to. We need an address to have the mail sent to, even though it's a box number. Would you oblige?"

"If that's all it is -"

"Good." Annie snatched up her coat. "Didn't he wonder who's this was?"

"I don't think he even noticed!"

Alfred Wrayland slid the money from the table into his wallet and restored it to his jacket pocket. "Let me know when to expect the letters."

"Oh, I will." Annie went to the front door and opened it. "Take care, Alfred," said with a touch of menace so he would be sure she meant what she said. She had a hold now, and nothing but nothing would make her let go.

On the way home Annie stopped off at Phil's house to ask Uncle Phil if he would be so kind as to teach his nieces to drive - to save father the money for a full course, you understand. While she was there the phone rang, and they learned that Gran Webster had died that afternoon.

CHAPTER TWENTY FIVE

Q. So you had a funeral to go to.
A. We did. Very demure we were too, in matching black dresses and little hats with veils, and black handbags hanging with black ribbons. Oh Mother knows how to dress for a funeral - she excels at it! One day she'll make a wonderful widow - when Father finally dies, I mean. Uncle Phil was very subdued, as if it was all his fault. In part it was, but we know whose fault it really was, don't we? Anastasia

204

Webster. And I wanted to shout it to everyone - I liked the old lady.

Q. What else happened around that time, Tammy?

A. Oh you've heard! Or maybe you haven't, you're just guessing. Well, we found out we were being pretty damn stupid, Annie and me. We thought - and don't ask me why we thought it - that our original parents had no idea who or where we were. It should have occurred to us to wonder why they came back to Salldown! It wasn't just because they had some relatives there, was it? No, it was because they knew we were. All the time we thought we were spying on them they were spying on us!

Q. How did you find out?

A. Danny gave it away. We were at a disco one night, Annie, Mark, Niall and me, and Danny was there with a guy we didn't know. No girlfriend around. Anyway, Annie saw him and started her usual pouting and come-on looks and he came over. He pulled her to one side, and said:

"Listen little sister, it's no good me getting involved with you, is it? It's illegal," and walked off. Annie could have fallen down on the spot! All I felt was a rush of fear, shock, amazement, and then fury.

Q. What did she do?

A. Typical Annie. Stalked after him, grabbed his arm, pulled him round and said:

"Explain yourself, Mr Gibling." So they went to the bar, got Cokes each and sat and talked. That was when we found out they knew who we were. He knew he had twin sisters, he had been told the day someone told his mother who he'd been seen with. She'd warned him off. And told him why. And admitted they'd moved back to Salldown so she could see the two precious girls she'd had to hand over.

Q. What did you and Annie make of all this?

A. I was amused, to think the old lady cared enough to come back, but I don't believe that was all there was to it. I don't think somehow that was the true reason for coming back.

After all, if you were heartbroken at giving away a child, would you want to see that child grow up? Worse when it's two girls, surely!

Q. So you were amused - and Annie?

A. Even more furious, if that were possible. To think her plans had been thwarted in that way, that her moves toward revenge were being wasted, that the time spent gluing the letters, was wasted, not to mention the phone calls! We had a whole evening of her ranting and raving around the bedroom. Driving me mad, she was. Vengeance, that was all she was after.

"How could they live here and us live here and they not care to try and see us or anything?" She slammed my books around, nearly damaged my new hi-fi until I stood in front of it to guard it with my life. Then she quietened down and sat on the bed, and said:

"We'll get them, Tams, we'll get them. Kiddo, I tell you, we'll do it if it's the last thing I ever do." Prophetic words, weren't they?

Q. And your parents still knew nothing of this?

A. Nothing, and it was just as well. I feared Annie more in that quiet mood than in her ranting and raving.

Q. And?

A. Annie went to see them.

CHAPTER TWENTY SIX

"Hello, I'm Audrey Gibling,"

The words sounded harsh - alien. Annie had to spit them out to the drab woman in curlers standing in the doorway.

"Yes, I know." The door didn't move, the fixed blank look didn't move, only cigarette smoke drifted upwards and out into the sharp Spring breeze.

"Well, aren't you going to let me in, Mother?" Impatient,

tossing the glittering blonde hair back. Mrs Gibling moved away from the door, threw the cigarette into the weed-encrusted garden, and motioned with her head.

Annie stepped over the muddied doorstep and into a smell of smoke, bodies, old musty furniture and cheap food; grease and cabbage somehow combined. She sniffed and looked around. The wallpaper was stained, peeling here and there.

"Come in."

The lounge door was thrust open, the smell stronger. A two bar electric fire glowered in the grate, worn flex trailed across the carpet. A kitten played with the torn remains of the frill around the armchair. A dog looked up as she entered, and then looked back at the rug.

"Are you alone?" Annie looked round, saw no one. "Where's Mr Gibling, Danny and everyone?"

"Football."

"Oh yes, it's Saturday." Annie sat gingerly on the edge of a cushion. The kitten looked at her and fled under a dining-room chair, staring with slitted eyes from the safety of the legs.

"Cuppa tea?"

"No, thank you, I don't drink tea."

"Gin, sherry, whisky?" Another cigarette appeared as if by magic, a cheap plastic lighter flicked, a stream of smoke directed toward the brown ceiling.

"No, thank you. I just -"

"Wanted to see what we looked like. Well, you've seen us." Mrs Gibling sank into the other armchair and stared at Annie through eyes slit against the smoke. "Wondered how long it'd be before you came around, after I done told Danny to keep his hands off you, that you was his sister and all."

"Good of you."

"Wasn't it?" A harsh laugh broke through the smoke barrier and cleared it away. Annie could see in the ruined remains of a face drawn by poverty, work, and probably drink, outlines of her own fine bone structure. Once Mrs Gibling would have been a fine looking woman. Once.

"Where's your sister?"

"Mary?"

"Nah, you ain't Audrey and she ain't Mary, is she? You got some fancy names your fancy mother made up."

"We're Anastasia and Tamasine."

"Like I said, fancy names."

"They mean something, you see. Anastasia - reborn, new name, new life. Tamasine - little twin, which she is. Smaller than me, weaker than me. We like our names, they make us different."

"Better than Audrey and Mary."

"Of course."

"Upper class accents and all. Fancy, my little girls all fashioned and fancy talking. You'd never have made it without that fancy mother of yours."

"Who's to say?"

"Agreed." Mrs Gibling nodded. "Agreed. You might have made sommat of yourself, looking like you do. Does your twin look like you an all?"

"She does. Identical we are, in every way except she's slimmer and smaller and less strong, like I said. Stand her next to me and you'd know who we were, alike as two peas. Same blonde hair -" Annie lifted a strand, let it slide through her fingers, let a corner of her mind go walking, created a mouse. It ran across the carpet, the kitten ran after it. Mrs Gibling shrieked and burned herself on her cigarette. Annie let it go, smiling. "Scared, are you?"

"Don't like the things." Hand on heart, which was probably pounding like mad, she sank back in the armchair. "Don't like snakes much either."

Good, thought Annie, I'll remember that. She stood up suddenly, unable to bear another moment in the awful house. Her abrupt move startled the kitten and Mrs Gibling all over again.

"I'd better be going. Mother doesn't know I'm here. If I can, I'd like to come again, bring Tammy with me. Will that be all

208

right?"

"Of course. Let me know, I'll make sure to have Danny here, and perhaps Mr Gibling would like to see his girls."

"That would be nice," murmured Annie moving toward the door. "It's all right, I'll see myself out," and in a moment she was gone, standing outside, breathing deep lungfuls of fresh Spring air. The house had smelled worse than ever after being in there for a while; she hadn't adjusted to it at all.

The curtain moved. Annie waved and hurried down the road, anger pulling at every part of her. So casual, so offhand, they didn't care at all! Couldn't care less! Not a real offer of hospitality, nothing! Tea, gin, whisky, pah! You'll pay, she vowed, standing staring at a damaged lamp post. You'll pay all right, and it won't be just mice and snakes. I'll work out something for you. Something you'll never forget.

In the meantime -

She hurried home and called Niall, ordered him to call for her, took him to a local wood and whipped him until he bled.

Only then did her anger subside, and she allowed genuine thoughts of revenge to take over.

CHAPTER TWENTY SEVEN

Q. Did you go and visit your real parents?
A. Yes. About a week later, Annie phoned, made the arrangements, and we went. We deliberately dressed in identical clothes; shoes, bags, coats, everything, we do that sometimes - sorry, we did that sometimes - to confound people. Only those who know Annie is taller and bigger than me can tell us apart when we do that. Mr Gibling stood with his mouth open. Danny had such a look of lust when he saw the two of us it just wasn't true.
Q. Did you get to meet other relatives then?
A. Did we! We'd only been there five minutes when some

younger kids came in, our brothers, no less! Horrid little brats. No girls. And then two sets of grandparents! Oh God, you should have seen Annie, charming the birds out of their nests for these old people! Smelly old people, nasty old people, except for one grandmother who looked very much like Gran Webster, I almost broke down and cried. Only a sharp mental jolt from Annie stopped me, and I knew I'd pay for that later. And I did. Annie punished me, pushed me down on the bed and spanked me with her hairbrush. Told Mother we were playing, when she asked what the noise was. Playing! If she was playing I don't want to be on the receiving end of an angry session! God, she hurt!

Q. Why didn't Annie want you to display any emotion?

A. She said we had to show the Giblings how we upper-class people really live; can take anything, stiff upper lip, control our emotions and our thoughts, you know the kind of thing. I was doing all right until I saw a Gran Webster lookalike. But I have to admit, the old people, the kids, the house, all smelled as bad as Annie said they did, and it was all we could do to pick at the sandwiches and drink the foul stewed tea.

Q. What did you think of your parents?

A. Hated them on sight. Simple as that. No bonding there!

Q. But you stayed for a while?

A. Yes. Got Annie wound up creating a huge spider, making Danny and the other boys run to kill it, then a mouse and Mrs - Mother - said:

"That happened last time you were here, I'm so embarrassed!" and the mouse disappeared. I thought she'd do the snake but she didn't.

On the way home she said:

"Aren't they the most awful people you've ever met in your life? And they were. Then she said:

"You nearly broke down, you nearly gave way in front of them, I don't allow that, you'll pay for that," and like I told you, I did, flat on my bed, face buried in the pillow, hair-

210

brush coming down again and again. I was scared, Annie had never punished me before, and I didn't know whether this was the start of a new regime of pain for me. It wasn't, it was a one off, but I can still remember the feel of that hairbrush and the look on her face, and the sheer anger radiating out of her to blast my mind while she blasted my bottom.

Q. What happened next?

A. Uncle Phil started driving lessons for both of us. And Annie pulled her master card; got Mr Wrayland to go round to the Giblings and pretend to be from the Council, made them clear up the garden and get rid of their junk cars. He hated doing it, she loved it, stood on the corner out of sight and took it all in. His reluctance and embarrassment as he went storming around pretending to be hard, and their fear at Authority coming down on them. Me? I waited at his house for him to come back and cane me.

CHAPTER TWENTY EIGHT

"Darling -" Mother seemed very embarrassed, almost afraid to speak. Tammy waited patiently, tapping a spoon on the worktop in time to the dance rhythm coming from the small portable radio in the corner. "Darling - I've been meaning to ask you, what Anastasia said about Aids tests and that -"

"Just a joke, Mother."

"I know that, there's no way my darling girls would have Aids, or any other such horrid disease!" she shuddered theatrically. "But - you are - still ..."

"Mother, don't ask!" Tammy smiled, dropped the spoon and came round the worktop to hug her mother. "Don't ask, and you won't ever be hurt, will you?"

"I know, but - I would so like to know that my girls are pure and clean still ..."

"We live in the 20th Century, Mother, and it is usual for girls to do that kind of thing, you know."

Disappointment, almost hurt, swept over her mother's face, and Tammy felt as if she had committed murder of some kind. But better that, than let her mother go on thinking they were innocents, and so needed protection. Who knows? They might take it into their heads to start locking them up at weekends and at night, then what would she do for a regular session of the sting of the cane - so desired, so hated, so feared and yet so loved and longed for?

Tammy slipped away, knowing there was nothing else to say, it was best to leave mother to get on with her thoughts. Annie was sitting on the top of the stairs, hands around her knees, looking very young and very innocent. No one would believe that inside that head were schemes and devilish plans. No one would believe she had not been eavesdropping. Mother's current feelings were all part of the Master Plan; put them through hell, as Annie said. Pay them back for not telling us.

But really, having seen that awful house and that awful family, would she have preferred to be a Gibling?

"The screw's turning," Annie grinned, whispering as Tammy went by. "Now I'll have to think of something else to drop into the quagmire of emotions!"

"Got to go," Tammy reached her bedroom and gripped the handle. "I've a driving lesson in fifteen minutes."

"Good, stir old Phil up a bit for me, kiddo. It's my turn later."

"You girls are driving me mad!" Phil groaned, as Tammy expertly swung the car out into the street and headed toward the woods. Somehow she knew that was where he wanted to go, or perhaps it was just her own mind which wanted it. Wrayland was all right, Wrayland was more than all right, he caned hard and expertly, but he concealed his emotions too well. It was almost clinical. Phil on the other hand showed all his feelings.

"Why don't you give Aunt Phyl a good spanking, Uncle

Phil?" Tammy indicated, turned right without being told, pushed the car through the gears, and ignored the agonised look she glimpsed from the corner of her eye.

"She'd leave me, kid, that she would."

"But wouldn't you just love it?"

"Sure I would. She has a big arse, well rounded, plenty of it, no doubt it could take a rare lot -" He groaned, leaned forward, pretended to look for something in the glove compartment. "You girls are driving me mad!"

"Are we, Uncle Phil? I wonder why!"

"You know why. You and that Annie, you're up to some fiendish trick. You got me to get the old girl into a home, didn't you? God, it took some arguments, but I did it, and I did it for you!"

"Not me, for Annie. She was the one who wanted it."

"Why?"

"Because of our birthday party. Remember? Gran Webster spilled the beans about us being adopted."

"She thought you knew."

"Well, I don't know about that, but we didn't, and it was one hell of a bomb to drop into the middle of a party. Annie resented that, you see."

"Annie is a strange young lady." He lit a cigarette, blew smoke out of the half-opened window. "Go for the woods, Tam."

"I was."

"I know, just thought I'd say it anyway. What do you want of me, Tamasine?"

Tammy didn't speak until she had the car half hidden up a small track in the woods. Then she killed the engine, turned in the seat, and put a hand directly on his groin. He gave another groan.

"I want you to give me a hiding, Phil, because you do it with passion."

"Get in the back," said through clenched teeth, as if in pain.

Tammy slid out of the door and climbed into the back seat. Phil followed, and had her over his knee in seconds. He peeled down her briefs and gasped as he saw the cane weals, vividly red and leering at him. Tammy felt him harden even as he gasped.

"Who in heaven's name did that?"

"An ex-headmaster," muffled voice, coming from the depths of the seat. "I go there sometimes for a caning."

"You want me to spank you over that?"

She knew he had no option. Once she was sprawled across his knees he could no more not spank her than he could of his own accord stop breathing. Phil was a sadist, through and through. Not dominant, he knew nothing about dominating women whatsoever, if he did, he would have Phyl where he wanted her. But sadism, that came naturally to him.

Tammy wriggled happily as he began to spank her, his hand finding every single cane weal, every line, bringing a double intensity to the pain that thrilled her through to her deepest soul.

She sent a message - Annie, enjoy this - and felt an answering chuckle.

Phil was lost to them, completely and forever.

Even as she writhed under the hard relentless hand and over the hard relentless groin, she wondered - what would Annie ask him to do next?

CHAPTER TWENTY NINE

Q. Did you place the advertisement in the magazine?

A. Oh yes. Annie worded it so carefully: 'Submissive lady (over 18) wishes to find a Master. Provide details of training on offer with photo. ALA', which of course was a lie, she had no intention of answering all the letters.

Q. What sort of letters were they?

A. Oh, slagging us off, or rather, 'she' - she wasn't a lady, but a slag or a whore for offering herself in that way. Someone else wrote saying how he would never touch her but direct someone to do it - sheer nonsense. They thought they were being big tough dominant men, but all they did was make us laugh.

Q. Were there any Annie was really interested in?

A. An odd way of phrasing the question, we were supposed to be doing this together, and yet - you're right, it was Annie who read the replies first, and who picked out the ones we would later respond to. Have I come over that weak?

Q. Not really, but how did you feel about that?

A. About Annie doing all the choosing? I've got so used to that over the years I hardly notice any more. Why do I keep using the present tense about my sister?

Q. What was happening in the family at this time?

A. Mother and Father were spending more and more time away from home. Not sure if it was us, might have been. Mother was really bothered by our attitude to sex and Aids and everything - hated being made to think about us as women. I'm sure she was jealous; she began to spend more time at beauty salons having facials, wax treatments. She played less golf and spent more time in a gym working out, improving her health, she said. A new wardrobe of clothes arrived, younger looking than before, and too young for her age and figure. She began to look slightly ridiculous wearing short skirts and higher heels.

I must tell you about this. There was a dinner party one night for some clients of Father's, real posh guys. Mother laid on the whole bit; the candles and the best food, best wine from the cellar, the whole lot. Annie and I were asked to please wear our best cocktail dresses, and Annie, out of some kind of spite, put our hair up in great curls and we put on our make-up, just that tiny bit too much that makes the difference between being demure and being startling. You know where the line is, you must have seen it! And neither of us showed our faces until the guests arrived. Then we walked down the stairs together. The look on

215

everyone's faces was a treat - Annie nearly burst with suppressed hysteria. We had matching red dresses, silky, very sleek, very tight, our hair up in swirls and curls. Our make-up was moss green eye-shadow, blusher, and vivid red lipstick. And we both painted our nails an identical shade of red. Add black high-heeled shoes and seamed stockings, and the men nearly burst out of their trousers just looking at us. It was no surprise to us to learn Father scored a direct hit with the company after that, and got all sorts of commissions and cash out of it. But it was down to us. All through dinner they could hardly take their eyes off us. Mother, delicate in her pale blue and silver, couldn't hold a candle to us. And she knew it, and she resented it. Needless to say it was the last of the dinner parties with us present. It was like an open declaration of war, but nothing was ever said.

Q. This must have pleased Annie.

A. It did. Since we'd been told they weren't our natural parents, I realised she was fast falling out of love with them, if ever she loved them in the first place, which I doubt. She somehow went from just living with them, to actively stirring them up. But she wasn't entirely satisfied, even with that.

CHAPTER THIRTY

"Are you going to let me see any of the letters?" Alfred Wrayland handed another packet to Annie, who slipped them unopened into her bag. She smiled at him and walked around his room, touching the bobbled table-cloth, the fraying edges to the chairs, the dropped hem of the curtains.

"You ought to tidy this place up, Alfred, get someone in, get yourself a woman to do some mending around here."

He frowned at her. "I like it as it is."

"I don't. And as I've come here -"

"No one asks you to come."

"Oh, but they do, Alfred," she walked over to him, stood close enough to see his face go red with suppressed feeling, knew she had him where she wanted him. "You ask me to come, every time I'm here, you ask me to come back, with your gestures, your stance, the way you look at me, your whole body language cries out for me to come back. Admit it, go on." She moved closer, knew her perfume was filling his senses, knew her personal musk was penetrating to his basic instincts.

"God, I'd give a lot to have you under my cane!" He turned away with visible effort, sat down in a chair, put his head in his hands. "However did I get mixed-up with a woman like you?"

"By being weak." She strode to the radio, turned it on, changed stations, turned it off again, touched a sepia photograph of a stern looking couple, and turned back. "And because you're weak, you do what I say, not what you want to do." He moaned slightly, just enough for her to hear. "Incidentally, you did a first class job on the Giblings, thank you. They've cleaned up their act something wonderful."

"I hated doing it."

"I know that. It made it all the more enjoyable for me."

The doorbell rang, stopping Annie from saying anything else. She slipped quietly into the kitchen, turning up her nose in distaste. I'll have to do something about this, she thought, get him to spend some money on the place or something. Perhaps even find somewhere else; this is awful.

But with an ear pressed to the door, and the sound of a cane falling hard on an upturned backside, Annie forgot her distaste. There was something about the sound of punishment, the sound of cane or strap coming down on flesh, the solid THWACK of punishment instrument on living skin. The sound of a voice crying out in pain, in suffering, in terror at more to come, that underlying fear that there would be more, that the recipient would not be able to stand it, it would be terrible.

217

Fear and longing and sheer surges of need combined to make the most evocative sound in the world. For a dominant.

And for a submissive too, she thought. I'll have Tammy here next time, see how she reacts to the sounds of a good solid caning. Instead of her being under the cane I'll get her to listen to it, and feed on her feelings.

She leaned against the door. It was a man being caned, not as interesting as a woman. Annie knew in her own heart she preferred the women being punished; they cried more, they begged for mercy more, they gave more under punishment than the stoical men.

A devil-may-care mood swept over Annie. She heard the man cry out as the cane whacked down again. She smiled, hitched her skirt a little higher, and walked boldly into the room.

"Alfred - oh I'm sorry, are you busy?" Alfred stood, cane raised, eyes wide in shock and sheer annoyance. The man looked round and groaned.

"Yes, I am busy!" Alfred Wrayland snapped. "Would you leave?!"

"Well, no, I'll just stay and watch - now I'm here," and Annie sat on the arm of the chair, crossed her legs, letting her foot swing idly backwards and forwards.

"Excuse me!" Alfred snorted, and went on caning the man, slowly and hard. Annie watched, saw the lines being created, felt the thrill of domination. That could be me! She thought, why don't I do that? A stranger. Yes, I'd like to do it to strangers.

The man got up, pulled up his trousers, glanced at Annie again and mumbled something as he left, leaving the usual money on the table. Alfred saw him to the door, and stormed back, face red, eyes wild.

"Damn you! Why did you have to come in?!"

"Why not? I have as much right as you to be here, don't I?"

"Well no - !" Then the anger began to drain and he smiled. "You did an excellent job on humiliating him. He's pleading to come back and do it again!"

"We could make a good pair, Alfred, you and I together."
Annie moved close to him again, sensing his emotions as she
did before. She straightened his tie, smoothed his hair, ran a
finger down the side of his face. It was the first time she had
ever touched him, and he reacted violently. His arms shook
and his lips trembled with suppressed feelings. She lifted his
lifeless hands and pressed and shaped them over her breasts.
She held them there, watching the turmoil in his eyes, feeling
her nipples swell into his palms - feeling him feed off her
strength.

"Listen," she eventually murmured, stepping back. "Let's
get this place straightened up, shall we? Get someone to come,
get the curtains fixed, get the furniture polished, get the kitchen
modernised. Alfred, we're in the last half of the 20th century!
Yours looks like something out of the 40's!"

"It is something out of the 40's," he said, tucking the money
into his wallet. "But you're right, I do need a cleaning woman."

"Do it. And put a new ad in the magazines where you adver-
tise. Say there's a mistress here too. I'll deal with your wimpish
men for you, you deal with the ladies. And sometimes I'll deal
with the ladies too." She paused, waiting to see what effect her
words would have. His eyes lit up, he began to look very excited by the whole idea. Then, as she stood with her hand on
the door ready to leave, Annie landed the knockout punch.
"One day I'll cane you, Alfred, just as you secretly want. All
right?"

She turned her back and walked out.

CHAPTER THIRTY ONE

Q. It seems there was some disaster in the family around this
   time, Tammy, is that right?
A. Disaster? Tragedy, yes, there was. It was Annie's fault. You

219

see, along with her ability to conjure things, she could thought-fix someone; ill wish them, to use an old term.

Q. How did she learn to do this?

A. Projection. She had learned to project her thoughts to create the literal images of things, so it was one step on to project her thoughts to a living person and affect what happened. She could, for example, put Father off his swing, if she was in the golf club when he was out on the green. Mother too, she could put her off very easily. She was like a jinx of some kind; if she was around, things went wrong. Everyone knew it, and joked about it, and no one took it seriously.

Q. So what happened?

A. Annie had been brooding over the 'walk in the dark', as she called it - my walk out to find someone and I'd met Phil. Uncle Phil. For some reason that got to her, whether it was because her plans for me finding a stranger had gone so wrong, or because she was disappointed it was him, I don't know. But what really got her was the answer to the question - what was Phil doing out at that time of night?

Q. What was he doing out at that time of night?

A. Well, first we had to find out. Annie got Wrayland on it. Poor devil didn't know what had hit him with Annie, she had uncovered his darkest secret. She told me all about it, giggling like a lunatic when she got home. She said it was a wild stab in the dark and it had gone home, drawn blood, to use her terms, but I don't think so. I think she knew her men too well, and knew that under the bluster lay a submissive man crying to get out. With that secret, with his shocked reaction to her comment, she had him even more under her control. So she said to him:

"I want to know where Phil goes at night," and gave him the address.

Q. And what happened?

A. Annie couldn't have known anything about our relations' habits, you see, or she'd not have phrased it like that. I know that's what she said, she told me. But Phyl and Phil if you say them, sound the same. And where does Phyl go at night? To beauty salons and beauty parties and things like that. She was a demonstrator for a cosmetics company.

Q. But Annie didn't know that?

A. No. She didn't like Aunt Phyl. If anyone talked about her around Annie she switched off. I could feel it, it was like a huge shutter coming down. She didn't take any notice. If she thought about it at all, I bet she assumed it was cosy afternoon chats - not evenings out.

Q. So Annie got the message -

A. Their car was seen here and there and everywhere all over Salldown.

"Hm," she sniffed to me. "Phil's leading a rare life here! I'll do something about him," and I wondered why, because he'd done everything we wanted; got Gran into the home, given us driving lessons, given me hidings. Everything she could want, but for her it wasn't enough. So, she thought-fixed the car. Affected the steering. The Police said the car went out of control, but no other vehicle was involved. And Phyl, dear Aunt Phyllis, whose only crime was to have married our Uncle, was dead of a broken neck.

Q. Another funeral?

A. Another funeral. Black clad twins, demure and delicate, with Annie secretly delighted, if not absolutely thrilled to bits, that her thought processes worked, but shocked rigid that it was the wrong Phil.

Q. Did you ever find out what Phil was doing out that night?

A. No, we never did. And we couldn't ask, not after that.

Q. And then what happened?

A. She sent me out for that walk in the dark again. Only this time there was no Phil there to rescue me.

CHAPTER THIRTY TWO

Spring touched everything, from the new unfolding buds to the sound of birds nest building and calling each other in courtship rituals. The sun slid slowly from the sky, leaving behind a coolness touched with sadness.

Tammy walked along the roads of Salldown, heading for the centre, where shops held their fascination for those who had little money and plenty of time to gaze into the elaborate displays and wish. Her instructions were precise, repeated at intervals silently in her head by Annie, lying flat on her bed at home, earphones on, listening to music and picking up Tammy's fear and trepidation of the ordeal ahead.

First she was to walk. Just walk, just be seen, to see what reaction she got from passing cars and strolling men.

The build-up to the walk had been almost as overwhelmingly thrilling as the walk itself. Time and again Annie had described her emotions - the fear, the stark naked fear of what a strange man would do, how hard he would hit her, how long the spanking would last, how long the bruising would last, with Tammy squirming in pure sexual excitement in her bed night after night, picturing it.

And here she was, walking in her tight red skirt and black cropped top, small plastic bag swinging at her side, high-heeled shoes tapping out their own rhythm 'come and get me ... come and get me', over and over, as her feet found the flagstone pavements.

"Hey, doll, doing anything?"

Tammy smiled, shook her head, walked on. A wolf-whistle from the other side of the road. Unintelligible shouts from a gang on the corner outside The Plough. Smell of drink and staleness wafting to her. God, don't ask me to approach one of them! she begged Annie silently. There was no response. Tammy walked on, relieved.

Suddenly Annie's voice spoke in her head.

'The next man, whoever he is, the next man!'

Tammy felt her breath catch in her throat, her heart begin to pound, as a man walked along the road, heading toward her.

Then she recognised him.

Her real father!

The leather cracked and moved under her weight as she shifted on the bench, waiting for Mr Gibling to come back with a drink for her, busy inventing a story that would satisfy him; he was bound to ask. The pub was full, voices raised in loud dispute and laughter, thud of darts hitting the board, eyes watching her every movement.

"Here, kid."

"Thank you." Tammy took the glass and sipped the drink. Too much gin and not enough tonic. Never mind. She put it down on the table.

"Well, go on, tell your old dad what you was doing walking the streets looking like that?"

"An experiment." Tammy began to tell him about her non-existent social study, how she wanted to assess sexist remarks by walking along the road. He seemed to buy it, for a while.

"Damn strange things you girls get up to! You could have been took off and raped and all sorts!" He shook his head, downed half his pint of dark beer, and smiled at her. "The old woman's been that set up since you and your sister come around, you know."

"Has she? What about you?"

"What about me?" He stared at her, hooded eyes peering over a glass. Tammy noticed how dirt lay in the creases of his face, how watery his eyes were, and shuddered inside. Was this really her father? Was this man responsible for part of the genes that made her?

"How did you feel when we came round?"

The rest of the beer disappeared, he got up and ambled over to the bar, slamming coins on the top, collecting another pint.

He came back and sat down.

"I needed that small break from you, kid, to make up me mind what to tell you. And I decided to tell you the truth, because I think you're a truthful girl." A coldness began to creep up her neck, creeping up into her brain. She was not going to like what she heard.

"I ain't your father. The reason my old woman give you girls away was because some Yank fathered you two. Well, she said it were some Yank, but I never proved nothing. Reckons she met him at the pub one night."

"Where were you?" Tammy was surprised to find her voice was calm and steady. It should have been shaking after a revelation like that. Not only had they been given away, they were also illegitimate!

"Me? Long distance lorry driving. Off heaving me old lorry around the Continent. Come back to find me old woman up the spout, bun in the oven, you know what I mean. So, I said to her, get rid of the kid or get rid of me, one or the other. But she's a bit religious, you know, old soft-hearted thing that she is, and she weren't having none of that abortion. Let some poor buggers have them. And that's what happened. Mind, she got a bit of a shock when they told her it was twins! 'God', she said, 'glad I decided to be rid of them! Fancy having two mouths to feed!'"

"I have to go." Tammy drank a little of her gin and tonic, pushed the glass away. Mr Gibling took hold of her hand.

"You asked how I felt when you come round. I felt like I do now, ready to stick one in you any time. You're a delicious pair of - well, you are and you knows it."

"I have to go," Tammy repeated, and stood up.

"Not wanting to stay with me now, are you? Bit scared of me, I think. Yeah, that's what I think. Go on, kid, get going, before I do sommat I shouldn't. You're jailbait if ever I saw it."

Tammy smiled weakly, shook his hand off, and made for the door, sliding past the gathered men, ignoring their comments.

One of Salldown's taxis was touting for business outside the pub. Tammy hailed it and got herself driven home, feeling as if stone had taken the place of her feelings. Dead inside, dead to everything. Wait until Annie finds out! Was all she could think, over and over, a litany of unhappiness. Wait until Annie finds out!

Annie's response was immediate and savage.

She phoned Mark and got him to come round and watched as he whipped Tammy until she could cry no more - a punishment for disobeying orders. Father or no father, stranger or not, he should have been asked to spank her. Annie told her that as the whip found Tammy over and over again.

Even as she felt the lash curl round her, even as she cried out, Tammy knew that Annie was only giving half her attention to the whipping. Annie, for sure, was planning her revenge.

CHAPTER THIRTY THREE

Q. Was there ever a moment when you realised things weren't - quite right - with Annie?

A. Yes, and I can tell you exactly when it was. Phil came round one night, a broken man. He sat talking about Aunt Phyl, reminiscing, saying things about how they met - she'd said 'I'm Phyl' and he'd said 'so am I' and they laughed about it and - got together. And how she'd been his only love and he was devastated without her. And Annie just sat and laughed, inside, but it was welling out of her and into me. She was revelling in his misery. A look passed between them, and I think he could have killed her right there on the spot, even though he didn't know she had anything to do with it.

Q. But he wasn't her only enemy, was he?

A. Oh no. Alfred Wrayland would have killed her too, if he'd had the guts.

Q. You're saying he didn't do it?

A. I'm saying he didn't do it. He didn't have the strength. In almost every bossy man there is a weak man trying to get out, but is too weak to get out. He hated Annie because she revealed his secret weakness, and because she did, just once, cane him to please him, and he knew he'd never be the same person again.

Q. Who else hated Annie?

A. Who didn't? Our lecturers at college hated her because she could outsmart them, or if she didn't do that, she would create some diversion in class to annoy the hell out of them. Danny Gibling hated her because he loved her really and wanted to get his hands on her but couldn't, because she'd led him on and got him wound up before he found out she was his half sister. Or did he think she was his full sister? Whatever, it was illegal. I don't know how Mr Gibling felt, he never admitted it.

Q. But none of them hated her enough to kill her?

A. They might have done, but they didn't have the strength of mind, or the necessary anger or rage. It's very hard to kill someone, no matter what crime-writers might like to tell you.

Q. What about Mark and Niall?

A. What about them? In their way they were both wimps; Niall for allowing Annie to dominate him to the point where she had drawn blood, and still he sat at her feet and worshipped her. Mark, while being able to give someone a good whipping if she said so, did it because she said so, so he was dominated by her in that way too - even if it did give him a huge erection that I had to deal with afterwards. She ruled our lives, you see, in every way. And that was before she destroyed the Giblings.

CHAPTER THIRTY FOUR

Sometimes Annie felt as if the world was against her, that everything conspired to turn itself back and annoy her. First, you get used to the shock of being adopted, that the elegant and expensive creatures you had called mother and father weren't your mother and father after all, even if they had provided for you, loved you, and kept you.

Second, you find out your real parents are slum dwellers, lower class, pig ignorant people who knew nothing, read nothing, felt nothing but their own basic instinct for survival. Fancy being related to Danny Gibling! He was one step away from Neanderthal Man!

And then, as if that wasn't bad enough, you find out that the man you had reluctantly come to accept as your real father wasn't your father at all, but some unknown person, possibly an American, possibly an Englishman, and that your mother, your real mother, was and probably is nothing more than a slut!

Annie paced her bedroom floor, anger burning through her, demanding a release; angry at the perfect summer day outside, angry at the emotions churning her up. She had Alfred where she wanted him, had Mark and Niall where she wanted them ... but the Giblings! They were the rogue card, they were the ones destroying her peace of mind.

Then I'll go and see the Giblings, she decided, snatching up her bag and clattering down the stairs.

"Going out, darling?" Mother, clad in leotard and leggings, on her way in, red-faced and sweating after another work-out at the gym.

"Mother, why don't you give this up and grow old gracefully?" Annie demanded as she eyed her mother with disdain. "You're making a fool of yourself."

"Just keeping fit for my old age, darling." She disappeared

into the kitchen as Annie slammed out of the house.

Her Mini stood in the drive, sun-roof open, headlights staring. Annie started the engine, and with a vicious spurt of gravel swung out of the drive, sensing Tammy's thoughts racing after her - 'Where, why, and what do I do?'.

'Nothing', she shot back silently, pounding the horn as a pedestrian jaywalked in front of her. 'Nothing. Just wait'.

Kensington Drive drowsed under the summer sun, wilting plants and litter offended her eyes, angered her even more. She slammed the car door, felt the Mini rock on its wheels, patted the roof and apologised.

Mrs Gibling - mother - opened the door as Annie stormed up the path.

"I wondered if you'd be round again," she said by way of greeting, the cigarette bobbing dangerously in the corner of her mouth. "The old man said he'd told your sister, it was your sister, wasn't it? Not you. He said it was the quiet one, and you ain't quiet. Anyway, he said he told your sister what really happened."

Annie pushed past into the smelly house, feeling the dirt and poverty wrap itself around her. She stood in front of the fireplace, back to the crinkled tissue paper and few dried flowers and grasses, looking at the woman who had given birth to her.

"Who was it?" she asked, cool and calm, controlling her temper. "Who is my father?"

Mrs Gibling stabbed out her cigarette and collapsed into an armchair.

"I've gotta be honest with you, girl, I don't know. Me old man was on the Continent, see, and the old fires were burning, you wouldn't know about that, would you?"

"Oh yes, I know," Annie spoke slowly, with deliberate cruelty. "You could call us sluts too, as I think of you. But I know who my lovers are, *Mother*." The word was spat out.

"No," the dyed hair in tight ugly curls moved around her head as she shook it vehemently. "No, you girls don't know a thing. Wait until you've had a regular old man poking you, then go without and see what happens. After a few weeks you go crazy, and my old man was caught up on the Continent with them foreigners, not knowing when he'd be home. So, I went out one night with a few girls down the pub, and we got roaring drunk. She said, my friend that is, said I went off with three or four of them, but I don't remember a thing. It could have been any of them, because a week later I was suspicious, and a month later I knew."

"I was right, you are a slut."

The woman's eyes narrowed and the hands clenched tightly together in her aproned lap.

"At least I had an excuse for what I was doing, but you and your sister, well, walking the streets in clothes like that for a 'social study' - are we supposed to believe that? We ain't that stupid, you know, just because we live in Kensington Drive! Sluts, both of you, no better than I was at your age!"

"And you gave us away." Annie ignored the insults, pressed on with her questions.

"Course I did! Think I'd keep two brats from a father I didn't know? No way, Jose!"

"But you didn't know what you'd be giving away. You didn't know if we'd be clever, beautiful or what!"

The cigarette appeared from a capacious pocket, the cheap plastic lighter flicked and lit it, a cloud of smoke drifted to the ceiling.

"Kid, like I said, you know nothing. My Danny was enough for me. The others, the boys, well, they're all right as kids go, but I had my Danny, and be sure nothing else matters to me. You girls were just babies, that's all. I had you in no time, easy as shitting it was, pushing you out. And I never saw you again until you walked in here."

Annie leaned against the chipped tiled fireplace, looked at the woman who was her natural mother, looked at her with hatred and anger so bad it almost consumed her.

"So it never occurred to you we lived here in Salldown? You

never gave us a thought when you moved back?"

"No, not for a moment. Mind, I was a bit surprised when you did turn up. I never thought you girls could be so stunning! Right proud of you I was - I am! But you ain't mine, you belong with your fancy names to your fancy parents."

"Thanks for telling me." Annie walked across the threadbare carpet to the door, hesitated with her hand on the latch. "Is Danny around?"

"Nah, gone to the amusement arcade in town. He'll be back later. Why?"

"Oh nothing, I just like to see my brother occasionally, that's all."

"Keep your eyes off him, girl, you're half sister to him!" But Mrs Gibling didn't move from the chair, and her expression didn't change. Annie got the impression that it wouldn't matter if she did get her eyes on Danny, this woman wouldn't care, didn't care about anything.

"No hard feelings, eh? I didn't mean to call you a slut," the words followed Annie into the hall. She slammed the door after her, but felt it was a wasted gesture.

Out in the street Annie felt rage surging through her, felt consumed by it, and invigorated by it at the same time. She rode the anger as others would an adrenalin surge, felt the sweet taste of revenge coming closer, delighted in it.

She got in her car, and headed for home.

CHAPTER THIRTY FIVE

Q. How did Danny die, Tammy?

A. I don't know for sure, but I know Annie had a lot to do with it. I think she liked him. I think it was a hard thing for her to do because she did like him, but - what better way to get back at the Giblings?

Q. I think you do know how he died.

230

A. If you know, why ask me? Oh I see, you're guessing. Well yes, I did have a lot to do with it, and yes I do know how he died.

Q. Can you tell me about it?

A. Why not? I have nothing left to lose, have I? Well, it was like this. Annie hung around the local burger bar, drinking coffee and stuff, until Danny came in. She knew he would, she knew his movements probably better than he did. I was around the corner, in our Mini, waiting. We had both passed our tests, in case you were wondering! She enticed Danny out of the bar, not a difficult thing to do, he had been at the amusement arcade and was restless, all those flashing lights and things. He came round the corner, hand in hand with Annie, she looking up at him and muttering things about 'sisterly love', and crap like that. Anyway, he got in the car, said "Hi," to me, and Annie got in the back with him. "Where to?" I asked, as if I didn't know, because it was in my mind already, Annie had flashed it to me.

"The lake, kiddo," just like that, and I drove away.

"Hey, where're we going?" Danny asked, amused, laughing as he said it. Annie patted his face, I saw that in the mirror.

"Don't worry about it, big boy, we decided we weren't going to take any notice of that sister/brother lark. I've been to see your mother today - did you know we're not fully related, only half related?"

"Are we? That's news to me." And his eyes got all big and round.

"Some other poor bastard was our father," Annie laughed, enjoying the thought processes that went on behind his eyes. "Ha!" he snorted. "Never thought the old girl had it in her!" and he said it with some pride. I felt Annie's blast of contempt as clear as if she had said it.

You know the lake? Pretty spot. Lovers go there a lot. We drove in, and were the only car, by luck. Annie got out, giving Danny a good view of her behind as she did, and

231

then he climbed out as well. I locked the car and wandered over to where they were sitting by the side of the water, throwing pebbles, watching the ripples, saying nothing. I knew what I had to do, she'd telegraphed it to me in a split second, and I had no problem doing it. I despised Danny Gibling. The thought he was in any way related to me made me feel sick to my stomach. I picked up a rock and hit him on the head with it, hard. He went down like a sack of cement. Annie grabbed his arm, I grabbed the other one, and we dropped him, face first, into the lake.

Then we got in the car and drove away.

Q. No sense of remorse?

A. What for, ridding the world of another Neanderthal Man look-alike, a sponger, a scrounger, a loser? Of course not.

Q. No one saw you?

A. No one. That was a miracle in itself! Our tyres are common as mud, it hadn't rained so there weren't clear impressions anyway, and a number of other cars apparently went there that evening, drove over what we'd left. No, no one saw us, no one suspected us.

Q. Was Annie satisfied with that?

A. No.

Q. So what happened next?

A. After she went to the funeral? Yes, before you ask, she had the nerve to go to the funeral! Stood on the edge of the group of mourners wearing her delicate black, touching her eyes with her hanky. I saw her from the car, I couldn't go near. Mrs Gibling was fair broke up, nearly fainting at the graveside. It should have been enough but it wasn't.

She left it for a week and then went to visit Mrs Gibling, all black clothes and demure face. She told me later how it went, how Mrs Gibling thanked her for going to the funeral, how devastated she was, and who would do such a thing? If anyone had done it; the Police weren't sure if he had fallen and banged his head then rolled in the lake, or whether someone had hit him in a fight and left him, they didn't know. Then Annie stood up to leave, imagined a snake, sent Mrs Gibling into a state.

Annie walked out, got halfway down the road, turned round and saw nothing. I believe her too. If she had seen smoke she'd have called the Fire Brigade. She thinks - thought - Mrs Gibling dropped a cigarette which fell down the side of the armchair while she was rushing around screaming about the snake, and - well, it all caught fire, didn't it?

Q. Would she have called the Fire Brigade, really?

A. Sure. She's a fine upstanding citizen - was a fine upstanding citizen, pardon me - was my sister Anastasia. But it wasn't smoke and flames when she left. That came later. We read that the Fire Brigade had pumped gallons of water into the house. First wash it had ever had, she said afterwards. Everything ruined. Mrs Gibling - Mother - got out but lost half her home.

Q. Insurance?

A. No. People like that don't insure their homes!

Q. Was that the time she destroyed Alfred Wrayland?

A. If you're asking questions like that, you know the answer. Yes, it was. She told the police in an anonymous letter to check out the 'Headmaster' who punished people in his home. They raided him and found the latest batch of letters the magazine had forwarded. They found a dress in the cupboard - that was lucky, we didn't know about his cross-dressing! But it all came out at the trial. Funny how it all fitted together, as if Annie had planned it. His explanation that a couple of girls (he didn't name us) had asked him to receive the letters was completely disregarded, after all, it was a pathetic story, wasn't it? Why would two girls ask someone else to receive their letters? What nonsense! Or so the Prosecution Counsel said, and do you know, he's right, it's a pretty silly story, isn't it?

Whatever, he got put away. That'll teach him to believe innocent young girls!

Q. Then what happened?

233

A. Annie sent me out for another walk. Only this time it happened just as she'd visualised.

CHAPTER THIRTY SIX

Summer pressed against the windows, a breeze moved languorous leaves on the huge tree in the lawn, sent Granny's bonnet flowers nodding in their sleepy old fashioned way. Bees kept working, droning seriously around the flowers, in the foxgloves. Tammy stood at her window, breathing in the scented air, a vibrator firmly clenched in her slit, feeling the buzzing, reminding her of the busy little bees outside.

Annie had ordered her out for another late night walk, and the emotions had been too much to suppress. She would walk better, look better, be better, if she wasn't dying for a climax. Even as she thought of a stranger's hand descending, the orgasm shook her. She arched her head back, opened her mouth in a soundless cry, felt the waves roll through her, over and over. She felt her muscles twitch, felt juices flow, felt the vibrator slide out and lie buzzing and shaking on the floor.

'Nice one,' Annie's thoughts entered her head. She snapped back:

'Get out! This is my time!'

All she heard was a laugh, a ghost of a laugh, trailing on her thoughts.

Mother and father were out again, an interminable golf club dinner dance or something. They were left alone so much lately they were almost abandoned, neglected children. One way of getting back at them would be to report them to the Social Service, thought Tammy, but they'd say they were old enough to take care of ourselves.

'They would, but it's a good thought, kiddo.'

'Keep out!' snapped Tammy, and felt Annie giggle. It was unusual for her to want to invade her thoughts to this extent, normally Annie kept to herself. She must be bored this evening.

Time to go. Twilight was darkening the edges of the sky. Tammy hadn't realised time was slipping away.

She was already wearing the briefest of clothes, a tiny black skirt and an equally tiny white top. She had her hair loose, cascading down her back, a shimmering cloak of blonde hair brushed until it shone.

'Go get them, kiddo!'

'Get lost!'

The roads were deserted. A cat slinked past and ran for safety. Nothing else disturbed the evening.

'You there, sis?'

'Sure am, kiddo.'

'Stay with me.'

'All the way.'

Remembering: "I wonder who you fantasized about, or was it a faceless stranger, someone passing through Salldown, a businessman on his way to a conference, stopping overnight at the Coach and Horses, wandering around to walk off a late dinner and too many drinks. What would he think if he saw a girl looking as young as you do, kiddo? All the long blonde hair shining in the streetlight, that short short skirt, you know, the one we made together, the black one, with the slit up the side, the one that makes your behind stick out, would he think twice at your offer to give you a good tanning? In the back of his company car, a big one, upholstered seats, plenty of room, skirt up, pants down, hand coming down again and again, you wriggling and writhing and wanting to be free, knowing he won't let you free, knowing he'll give you a good fucking afterwards, and knowing I'll want to inspect you when you come in - is that what kept you and the vibrator busy all night?"

Annie would have the vibrator now, clutched in her hand, sliding it around gently, gently, teasing herself, waiting, watching the street through Tammy's eyes - the empty lonely streets.

Tammy walked, her heels clicking, breaking the silence. A sound, a car, fast, slower, slowing right down, squeal of brakes, worn discs? Hiss of window rolling down.

"Hey, kid, looking for a ride?"

She took her courage in both hands. A rep, coat swinging from the hook in the back, damp under both armpits from the heat of the day, tired world-weary look about the eyes, but a genuine smile, a real smile.

"Yes."

"Good, hop in."

Tammy walked round the bright red car with shaking legs. It was going to happen this time, after two false starts, it would really happen.

The car started off immediately she slammed the door. She scarcely had time to fumble for the seat-belt and slip it on.

"What are you looking for in particular?" he asked, hardly taking his eyes off the wheel, shaking a cigarette out of a packet and lighting it.

"A good spanking," said in a firm voice which belied her shaking and trembling stomach and legs. And the wetness that threatened to make her come before he even touched her.

"Oh, like that, is it? Well, I don't mind doing that either, if it means looking at a bit of behind for a while. Anywhere in particular?"

"There are woods along here," Tammy gestured to the right.

He smiled round the cigarette. "Done this before, haven't you," and it wasn't a question.

"I have," she was cautiously bold.

Deep in the twilight of the woods, leaves whispering their secrets to one another, night creatures scuttling away, the car was switched off. The engine ticked and cooled. The man turned to Tammy, smiled in the darkness, said:

"Want to get in the back?"

She nodded, and climbed out of the car, her heels sinking into leaf mould and soft mosses. The back of the car smelled of upholstery and papers, musty yet new. He got in the other side, and without another word pulled her over his knees. Left handed, thought Tammy inconsequentially as her tiny skirt was ripped away roughly. Without preliminaries he began to spank her hard, his hand looked white and smooth but it stung and stung. She began to wriggle after the first few smacks and he held her still.

"A good spanking, you said, and that's what you'll get," and he slapped her again, harder.

It seemed to last forever, the relentless smacks falling again and again on her cheeks, her thighs, occasionally the backs of her legs if she kicked too hard. He knew how to spank. Tammy briefly wondered, between feeling nothing but pain, whether he was really into the s/m scene or just exceptionally good at it.

Then he sat her up roughly, and pulled a condom packet from his pocket.

"You got what you wanted, now it's for me," and he opened his trousers. Tammy stared at the thick cock which protruded, felt herself go even wetter at the sight of it encased in rubber, shining in the pale light which filtered through the leaves and into the car. Her bottom burned as she sat, feeling the heat spread through her stomach and into every part of her, feeling the wetness creeping out, knew she would take him, no matter how thick, no matter how long.

With a little manoeuvring they were on the back seat, she had her legs wrapped around his waist, he pumping hard and long, raining kisses round her face, into her ear, into her neck, until they exploded together in a shuddering climax.

Back in the front seats, clothing adjusted, he turned on the engine.

"I don't suppose you want money, do you?"

"No."

"It was for the experience of the stranger?"

"Right." She smiled at him, shaking all over, wondering if Annie had felt it.

"Someone told you to do it." Again it wasn't a question. "You submissives are all the same." The car swung round and back out on the street.

237

The man dropped Tammy off where he had picked her up, and she made her way home, slowly, dragging her feet, her legs wanting to give way. She longed for her bed, for peace, for a chance to go over the memories, to stand and admire the redness in the mirror. She wanted a hundred things at once.

Her pace increased just a little.

Whatever else, Annie was waiting.

CHAPTER THIRTY SEVEN

Q. How did you feel after that walk?

A. Exhilarated. I rode the adrenalin high for at least two weeks, thinking about him, how hard he was, how severely he spanked, whether it was his scene or not! And the screwing afterwards, well, beats Niall and Mark any day of the week!

Q. And Annie?

A. That was the odd thing. She got insanely jealous of me. It was all her idea, she wanted me to go out, me to take the risk, the pain, the terror of finding someone so she could view it through my thoughts and my eyes, then when I did it and it worked out as she wanted, she got jealous! I think because it worked out better than she thought; I actually enjoyed the whole think. At the time I was simply terrified. But later I walked around wearing a smug grin and feeling very satisfied, and she hated it.

Q. And your parents never found out?

A. If they did they never said a word. Actually we were getting more and more distant from each other, a coolness had crept in. I'm sure they still loved us, but they were puzzled by us, or something. Anyway, they spent more and more time away from home, and from each other. Separation was definitely looming, I could see it a mile off. Annie could too, and she gloated; another punishment, another paying back for what she visualised they had done to us.

Q. There was a holiday, wasn't there?

A. We're getting close to the end now, aren't we? You're getting closer to what you want to know, and I'm about to tell you anyway. Yes, there was a holiday planned. Florida. Brochures everywhere, suitcases arriving, new ones! And Mother flapping around like - well, I don't quite know what she was like. You see, Annie and I refused to go with them. We gave the excuse that they were in need of 'quality time together' so they could rediscover one another. It's as close as Annie dared go to saying she knew they were on the verge of separating. Now, a holiday can do one of two things; bring people closer together, or drive them further apart. She was sure it would drive them further apart. So, because we weren't going, Mother had to get loads of food in the freezer and arrange for someone to call round, all that kind of thing. Panic panic.

Q. And did it drive them further apart?

A. You'll have to answer that. In the light of what happened, there's no way we could know, is there?

Q. You girls stayed home.

A. We were almost 19 by then, grown up adult people capable of taking care of the house and ourselves - or should have been.

Q. And Annie planned -

A. You're guessing, but you're right. Annie planned a party. With me as the centre of attraction. We talked about it far into the night, both of us busy with vibrators and visions. Oh what a time we had planning it!

Q. And a time you had during the party. It did take place, didn't it?

A. Sure did! Actually we had two parties. One for our real friends, Mark, Niall and a few girls and boys we knew from College and discos. That was a good one, just an enjoyable party, plenty of music and food. We had a 'bring a bottle or food' policy, and it worked very well. No one got drunk, everyone danced and had a good time, and we

239

cleaned up the next day better than the house had been cleaned before. We got behind the furniture and did the skirting board and everywhere.

Q. But the other party?

A. The other party was a week later, and was when it all happened. And I mean *all*.

CHAPTER THIRTY EIGHT

"Who's coming?" asked Tammy for the hundredth time. She laid back on the sun-chair, felt the heat penetrate her skin, wondered about skin cancer and dismissed it. The feeling was too good to worry about, and after all, this was England where it rarely stopped raining for longer than seven days at a time. Or so it seemed.

Annie stamped her foot on the patio stones.

"I'm sick and tired of telling you! People who wrote to us, that's all you need to know!"

"No, I mean who in particular? I mean, there were some right weirdos -"

"Kiddo, I'd not ask weirdos, I have too much affection for you to do that!"

The garden drowsed in summer heat, drone of lawn-mowers, distant sound of cars, birds busy staking out territory, insects working on the flowers. The pool glistened, beckoned, but Tammy had no energy with which to go swimming.

Annie grinned suddenly over her iced Coke.

"I know what you're at, you want some details so you can go imagining before they get here!"

Tammy smiled back.

"Right, I need to get my kicks when I can, sister!"

"You'll get kicks enough, when you're helpless in a room full of dominants all with one intention in mind, to hurt you as much as they can!"

Tammy went cold and hot, felt a surge of adrenalin course through her, felt the sexual high hit her, and orgasmed right there in her bikini. Annie smiled.

"Enjoy that one, did you, kiddo?"

"I wish you'd get out of my head sometimes," Tammy blushed, not wanting to give too much away, but knowing there was nothing but nothing she could hide from her twin.

Annie looked at her watch.

"Come on, we've a meal to cook." She stirred out of the sun-chair, set her glass down and headed for the house, her cheeks jiggling in her black bikini. Tammy followed, feeling oddly inferior to her twin, and wondered why. Her figure was as good, her hair as long, her face as pretty, and yet, Annie's sparkle, Annie's zest for life had added inches everywhere, she was altogether bigger, almost larger then Life itself.

Which might not last.

Tammy stopped, sweating on the hot stones, unaware of the wasp circling her, trying to land on her Coke glass. Normally she would have dropped the glass and run, screaming.

Where had that thought come from?

And why?

Annie was fine, nothing wrong with her. If there was, Tammy would have known it. Cancer, heart disease, anything troubling her twin physically always hurt her too.

Yet the thought had come and refused to go away.

It might not last.

Annie's overwhelming love of life - bigger than everything - larger than Life itself - might not last.

Cold swept Tammy. Unlike the sexual cold which she had experienced earlier, this was a dread, a loneliness so chronic it seized her throat and brought startling, unexpected tears to her eyes.

Annie stood inside the house, staring back at her.

"What's the matter, kiddo? Been stung or something?"

Tammy moved at last, the spell broken by her twin's voice.

"Oh, I had a couple of wasps round me, too scared to move."

"You and the wasps, you're a million times bigger than they are, scare them off, don't let them scare you!"

"Right." But the sadness lingered, a cloak that settled over her bare tanned shoulders, along with the cloak of blonde hair.

Her twin. Gone.

Following the empty feeling came another one.

Freedom.

And that was one thought that needed a lot of consideration. A lot.

Annie brought out half a dozen of her mother's cookbooks and set them out on the worktop. Tammy sat on a bar stool and looked at her.

"A proper dinner party, kiddo, this is no 'bring a bottle' game we're playing here. These are men, not kids."

It might not last.

Freedom. What would that feel like?

"So we could have a cold soup to start, something we can prepare earlier. Come on, Tams, we only have five days!"

Five days.

What would it feel like to be free? No orders, no probing mind, no touch of her thoughts when trying to sleep, no spiders in the room, no snakes, no mice, no - Annie.

Make an effort.

"Fine, cold soup, that Spanish one with tomatoes and stuff, that would be nice. Main dish, why don't we go for a roast? It's safe, and we can stretch it if more come than we thought - how many are coming, Annie?"

"Five at the last count. The others long to come but business/life/whatever is stopping them. Those we can have later. When we see how this one goes."

Roast is safe, thought Tammy, I won't be.

"Roast. Nice idea, kiddo, like it. And we can choose some fancy ice cream for dessert, they won't want too much."

Five days.

Annie paused, her head tilted, her eyes shining.

"Kiddo, I just realised something! These guys don't know

242

we're twins! What a shock they'll get when they arrive and find two of us! They think they were writing to one sub!"

Tammy smiled. It was going to be fun, wasn't it?

Five days. They passed in a blur of activity. Annie bought coloured paper napkins, polished candlesticks, agonised over vegetables, washed the dessert dishes over and over. She stood in front of her wardrobe trying on dress after dress, hair up, hair down, high heels, low heels, smart hostess or casual -

"Why don't we do what we did the night of the dinner party?" suggested Tammy with a sudden spurt of inventiveness. "Matching dresses and shoes, nail varnish and hair, that kind of thing? Give them something to feast their eyes on! I mean, you said they don't know we're twins, it would look like we've cloned or something!"

Annie giggled. "It might distract their attention from the food!" She paused, considered the idea, and then nodded. "I wanted you to be the centre of attention, but what the hell, we'll share it, after all, you'll get to display for them later, won't you?"

The red dresses were found, hung up to rid them of creases, the shoes cleaned, the curling tongs ready. Everything was prepared ... except Tammy's peace of mind.

Without consciously deciding to do it, every time a car rolled into the drive, Tammy and Annie went to the front door together, smiling identical smiles, the late summer breeze ruffling their identical curls. Each time the look on the face of the man who had arrived would be something to giggle over in the dark recesses of their minds, shared humour behind welcoming faces that showed nothing but pleasure at the latest arrival.

Each man also said the same thing.

"I didn't know -" and trailed off as he looked from one to the other, trying to work out the differences.

"Come in." Annie took the lead, escorting them to the lounge where casual conversation drifted across the thick pile carpet, over the sweet smelling sherries and the sound of glass on glass as another drink was poured.

Tammy stood by the patio doors, open to the afternoon breeze, watching the men as they talked to one another, or eyed Annie and herself speculatively, probably wondering which twin was the submissive, or whether they both were, or just what they had gotten themselves into.

And as she watched, Tammy felt herself going through paroxysm of apprehension and anticipation, eyeing their hands, wondering what they would do, what they wanted to do, who would be the hardest, what she would do when they hurt her. How many orgasms would she have during the course of this particular party? She asked herself, aware for the first time of the smell of roast beef from the kitchen, wondering whether the soup would be cold enough, and whether anyone would notice anyway.

And just how did Annie plan this? She hadn't said! Before dinner? After dinner? How could she handle five men?

"Stop worrying, kiddo, you can have two before and three after, if that suits you."

Annie suddenly struck the side of her glass with a red nail, making a sharp pinging sound. Everyone turned to look at her.

"Introductions," she smiled brilliantly at them and at Tammy. "And explanations, which we owe you, of course!" She moved round the room, pointing at each man in turn.

"This is Don, you'll remember him, he has the crew-cut and is blond as we are. Don comes from Camberley in Surrey, he's a Master, or so he says." Don blushed a little, looked down at his glass, fingered his collar in embarrassment as the others laughed, a little self-consciously.

"Moving right along, folks," Annie pointed to a dark haired man with a mass of tight black curls. "This is Jerry, a dom. from London. We - sister and I, were taken with his letter. So he's here for the games." Jerry smiled, nodded and looked at Tammy with a confident air.

244

"This is Gerald, not to be confused with Jerry. Gerald is a dom. from Shropshire. He's driven a long way to be with us today." Gerald, a small man with brown beard and moustache, acknowledged everyone's smiles with an arrogant air that Annie found attractive.

"David, also from London but a different part entirely, is a Master with a lot of experience." David, partially bald, a strong hard looking man, rose and bowed ironically to the others.

"And finally but not last - if you see what I mean, William, from Essex. William's letter also intrigued us." He stood, looked around him, afternoon sun glinting on his grey hair.

"OK, that's you introduced. Now -"

Tammy walked across to stand beside Annie, looping an arm around her waist.

"Anastasia and Tamasine. I'm Anastasia, this is Tamasine. We didn't mean to deceive you all, but it was easier to let you think you were writing to just one woman, wasn't it? We are in effect one person. What we think and feel we share, as all identical twins do. Before you get any ideas, I'm a dominant and Tamasine is a submissive. She is very experienced, in that she has been disciplined by a number of people, including friends of ours. This is the first time we have invited a bunch of dominants into our home, and it's only because our parents are in Florida right now that we decided to do it. We are over 18, nearly 19 in fact, so it's all legal, and you were invited here by us."

She paused, smiled at Tammy, and looked round the room again. "However, we have a problem, and that is - there are five of you, and you'll all want to participate. But only one can get the unmarked Tammy, of course! So we thought (did we? wondered Tammy, it's the first I've heard about it - and again wondered what it would be like to be living a full life separate and apart from her twin) we'd let you draw lots for the privilege, Tam."

Tammy walked over to the coffee table where dishes of tiny cheese biscuits rested. She picked out four square biscuits and one round one, concealing them in her hand.

The one who picks the round biscuit gets me first," she said in a soft, almost frightened voice. She began the rounds of the men, thighs quivering as she watched them take one biscuit, watched as they looked at it, trying to divine which one was to go first, how she felt being close to them, came to the conclusion she was shaking with sexual excitement. It was the most exciting, the most exhilarating thing Annie could ever devise, for man after man would put his hands on her, man after man would hurt her to a degree she had not felt before - even when Annie had had her whipped for disobeying orders. Her late night walk had been dangerous - this was less concerned with danger and more with sheer domination.

Each man stared at her, trying to impose his will. And she wanted to fall to her knees in front of each one and say:

"Take me, I'm yours," but Annie's strength held her back, made them wait, held her power over these men who professed to be dominants but who obeyed the whims of an eighteen year old girl in a tight red dress with long flowing hair - a girl who was offering half her soul, half her mind, and her own blood sister for disciplining by strangers.

"I have it," Gerald spoke slowly, wonderingly. "How do you handle this, Anastasia?"

Tammy noticed she wasn't referred to in any way.

"The garage is out the side, Gerald. Take Tammy out there and do what you will, but remember there are four others to come after you. I'd rather you didn't draw blood, but all else goes."

"God," someone murmured, but Tammy didn't know who it was.

Gerald smiled through his soft brown beard.

"Come," and it was an order not to be disobeyed. Tammy left the security of the wall and went with Gerald to the cold dark garage. Even in the September heat it held a chill of old grease and oil, of old dust and aching rust -

"Not very inviting out here, is it?" He looked round, disapproval writ clear on his face.

Tammy tried to smile.

"It's soundproof. If I make a fuss no one can hear."

"Oh, I see. Actually I like spanking best of all, is that all right with you, Tammy?"

"That will leave me relatively fit for the others, Gerald, thank you." Tammy wriggled her tight red dress up round her hips, revealing tiny filmy black briefs. Gerald all but groaned at the sight of her.

"It's been a while, so -" he broke off as she walked over to him, confident on her high heels, sure of her beauty and her body, and equally sure of the urge of emotion coursing through her; knew it lit up her eyes and her smile.

"So it's been a while, make it worth your drive here, Gerald."

"Oh, I will." He sat down on the stool conveniently left in the garage, swung her over his knee, and brought his hand down hard on her left cheek. Tammy clenched her teeth, felt the other cheek spanked equally hard, settled down, knowing this was indeed a dominant with experience, and sighed. What would she be like at the end of the session? Did it matter? Just enjoy!

And the spanking took over, filling her with pain, hard resounding smacks covering her small cheeks, feeling them bounce under his hand, feeling the briefs begin to strain as the flesh swelled, felt herself go red and burn, felt the surging of emotion through her as she anticipated his hardness, his firmness, his confident spanking.

It seemed to last forever, yet when she finally stood up, burning and hurting, clutching both cheeks in both hands, it seemed no time at all.

Indeed, when they went back into the lounge everyone was in exactly the same place as before, except Annie had gone to the kitchen to get dinner under way.

Tammy stood a little shakily in the doorway.

"Who wants to go next?" and then: "If you don't mind, I'd rather wait until after dinner for the next session."

She wondered if anyone had noticed her small scared voice had gone away, to be replaced by a stronger, more assertive one.

David pushed forward, putting his sherry glass down.

"We decided while you were gone it would be me - now." His voice was thick with lust, and Tammy took a moment to wonder why Gerald hadn't wanted to fuck her as well. The spanking appeared to be enough for him; he was glowing with satisfaction.

"Good, was it?" someone asked as she left with David close behind her, feeling his eyes on her bottom, as if he could see through the red to the red.

David too screwed up his nose at the garage. Tammy again reiterated its soundproof qualities, and then smiled.

David looked at her. "Fine by me. What do you like then, young lady?"

"I like you to tell me what to do, and what you want to do, and then to do it," she answered, supremely confident, wondering just how much of a dominant he was that he had to ask.

"Well, my decision might be different." He pulled a small plaited whip from his pocket. "Seen or had one of these before?"

"Sure." Tammy pretended indifference, trying to control the sharp intake of breath, plaited whips hurt like hell. Maybe he wouldn't do too much.

David spied the hook in the overhead beam, smiled and then laughed. "Now I see why we came out here. Strip off!"

Tammy obediently took off her red dress and hung it carefully on a hook away from the oil and grease. David picked up a rope from the bench, wound it round her wrists and hung her from the hook. As Tammy spun slowly on the hook he slapped at her already reddened buttocks.

"Did a good job, didn't he? I'm going for another part of you," and he lashed out with the whip, catching her diagonally across her back, shoulder to waist. Tammy screeched and screwed up her eyes, hoping she wouldn't cry and destroy her make-up. The whip landed again, across her back this time, another line of fire that shrieked through her body.

"Twelve, is that all right?" But he didn't wait for an answer, his arm was strong, his aim perfect, another ten times the whip lashed out, catching Tammy clear across her back, never touching her hips, never coming near her breasts, a true master of the whip.

He let her hang there, admiring the red lines scored across her white skin, admiring the redness still evident from her spanking. He undid the rope and let her down.

"Suck me off," he ordered, and Tammy knelt at his feet, willingly. She opened his straining trousers, and swallowed his eager erection deep into her mouth. He came quickly, taking his pleasure without thought for her.

Dinner was an elegant affair. Annie had done miracles with a few choice vegetables, with the roast so finely cooked it was near perfect, and a gravy which poured rich from the jug. Mother's teaching had not been wasted. Everyone praised her cooking. Everyone watched Tammy, whose eyes glittered with pent emotions in the rich glow of the candlelight. She sat very still, despite her aches, despite the twelve neat lines of pain writhing their way across her back. Annie had been with her during every single lash, she had experienced every one, every bite of leather on skin, and she knew it. The men didn't; it was a secret they shared, one never to be shared with others.

Dinner was her breathing space, her chance to recover from their ministrations before three more men took her one at the time, to the lonely garage where rust waited, where oil waited, where pain waited, and -

Satisfaction waited.

Jerry took her first after dinner, pulling a flexible tawse from his pocket, a thick band of pain that repeated itself over and over, like a copying machine, laid on harder than anyone had tawsed her before, and it delighted her while she screamed her agony.

Don used a cane, taken from the boot of his car. He caned

her hard and slow, bent over the stool on which others had sat, wrists bound to the metal legs. Twelve deliberate cuts with the cane over the spanking and tawsing she had taken. Pain indescribable. He dropped the cane and thrust into her wetness until he came.

William wanted her to parade herself around the garage. She did, displaying her wounds, her bruised flesh, her rope-burned wrists. She stood before him, waiting for his verdict, saw the tiny strap which he pulled out, knew this would be different and more painful - and it was.

William bent her backwards over the stool and used the strap between her legs. Then he used it on her thighs, both front and back until she screamed in agony ...

The last car left the drive. Annie closed the front door, locked and bolted it, and came back to the lounge where Tammy was lying full length on the settee, exhausted and almost asleep.

"Brilliant stuff, kiddo. How may times did you come?"

"Lost count." Tammy spoke through the thick surges of sleep threatening to overtake her.

Annie sat on the arm of the settee and touched her twin's face.

"You were just brilliant, you know that? I had a wonderful time, but those men! Wimps the lot of them! A real disappointment. I thought we picked some good ones, but not one was stronger than me!"

"How strong are you, Annie?"

"Strong enough to say - go out in the garden, find a worm and eat it!"

"Annie, not again!" Tammy was totally dismayed, feeling sick at the very thought.

Annie stared at her. "Disobeying me, are you?"

"No, I -"

"Then go."

Tammy got up on weary, shaking legs, stumbled across the lounge carpet, put on her high heeled shoes and went out onto the patio, feeling the dark reach out to caress her arms and aching body. Annie was close behind her, smiling so brightly, so viciously - the moon could not outdo her.

Then she began to sing in a low but strong voice.

"Nobody loves me,
Everyone hates me,
Think I'll go and eat worms!"

Tammy swung round, anger fuelling through her, touching every nerve which had been excited and hurt by the men.

"I hate you!" She snatched off a shoe and threw it.

CHAPTER THIRTY NINE

Q. What happened then, Tammy?

A. Well, believe it or not, the doorbell rang. I walked barefoot over the patio, over Annie lying there with the shoe sticking out of her face, and went to open the front door. It was poor Phil, he looked terrible.

Q. What did he want?

A. Well, me actually! But after the evening I was in no shape to see him or anyone. So to stop him going on about how much he needed me and could he please spank me just once, I led him, protesting his love for me and arguing about his need, into the lounge and out onto the patio. And he saw Annie and began to shriek like a woman. God, what did Phyl see in that man?!

Q. And he called the police?

A. Yes, when he got himself together. I just sort of collapsed on the settee and stayed there.

Q. You do realise it was death by misadventure, don't you?

A. I know - I couldn't have known the shoe would go into her eye like that, could I? I mean, I knew they were sharp high heels but not *that* sharp. It was one of those things; she was closer than I realised, and I threw it with more strength

251

than I realised, and -

Q. What really happened, Tammy?

A. What really happened was I thought she was some distance away from me, so I threw the damn thing, but she was right behind me, so what I thought was a throw was a direct hit into her face. The stiletto heel went right into her eye. You have to understand this, Annie was always with me, her voice in my head, her singing her direct words, whatever. I never really knew if she was away from me or close to me because she was always there. Sometimes we spoke without words - I had left her inside the patio doors. I was sick to my stomach at the thought of another worm; the dirt, the slimy body, the sensation of it going down. I was about to be sick before I even ate the thing, and there she was singing to me about eating worms - I snapped, that's all. But I honestly didn't hear her walk toward me, come up behind me, I never realised she was that close. Trouble is, I believe I've only done what so many would have liked to have done. Mrs Gibling for one, Alfred Wrayland for another, Danny had he lived, Mark, Niall, Phil even - they all knew one way or another that Annie had destroyed their lives, changed them forever. Just as she did me.

Q. This might seem silly, but was there a - a last thought from Annie?

A. Yes. How did you know that? She thought: 'You really did it, kiddo, the biggest punishment they could have!' and then it all went black.

Q. How do you feel now, Tammy?

A. Free.

Q. And?

A. Lonely. I miss her. She's gone, there's no voices, no thoughts, no songs, no sensations, no nothing. I feel empty. And - guilty as hell. Because I did hate her so much in that moment, every part of me hated her. I was hurting all over, dying for sleep, satiated with emotion, and she had to go

252

and spoil it with that damn silly worm song! If she'd not done that I think I'd have found the damn worm and eaten it, just as I did before! But no, Annie had to go and spoil it, didn't she? As always!

Q. You still hate her that much?

A. I hated her then, I miss her now.

Q. Where do we go from here?

A. Well, as you're here, and we're alone, could you, I mean would you - discipline me? Punish me? Hard? I mean, I've been such a naughty girl.